IT DIDN'T TAKE LONG FOR THE SIOUX TO SPOT US.

With the moonlight pouring down from a cloudless sky, the only shape in sight was Snow's white flank. A chorus of howls resounded through the night as the Sioux set out after us.

Sioux ponies were the best animals on earth for a short chase. Snow could run with any horse over a quarter of mile or so, but in the short run he was losing ground. Soon I could feel the buzz of arrows behind us, and the taunts of the warriors grew terrifyingly close. I swallowed hard, then grabbed my pistol and unloaded three hurried shots at our pursuers. Snow responded with renewed effort.

"Just a little more," I whispered as I felt Snow fight for breath. "Not far now. . . ."

POWELL'S ARMY
BY TERENCE DUNCAN

#1: UNCHAINED LIGHTNING (1994, $2.50)

Thundering out of the past, a trio of deadly enforcers dispenses its own brand of frontier justice throughout the untamed American West! Two men and one woman, they are the U.S. Army's most lethal secret weapon—they are POWELL'S ARMY!

#2: APACHE RAIDERS (2073, $2.50)

The disappearance of seventeen Apache maidens brings tribal unrest to the violent breaking point. To prevent an explosion of bloodshed, Powell's Army races through a nightmare world south of the border—and into the deadly clutches of a vicious band of Mexican flesh merchants!

#3: MUSTANG WARRIORS (2171, $2.50)

Someone is selling cavalry guns and horses to the Comanche—and that spells trouble for the bluecoats' campaign against Chief Quanah Parker's bloodthirsty Kwahadi warriors. But Powell's Army are no strangers to trouble. When the showdown comes, they'll be ready—and someone is going to die!

#4: ROBBERS ROOST (2285, $2.50)

After hijacking an army payroll wagon and killing the troopers riding guard, Three-Fingered Jack and his gang high-tail it into Virginia City to spend their ill-gotten gains. But Powell's Army plans to apprehend the murderous hardcases before the local vigilantes do—to make sure that Jack and his slimy band stretch hemp the legal way!

PRESCOTT'S LAW

G. CLIFTON WISLER

ZEBRA BOOKS
KENSINGTON PUBLISHING CORP.

ZEBRA BOOKS

are published by

Kensington Publishing Corp.
475 Park Avenue South
New York, NY 10016

First printing: April, 1990

Printed in the United States of America

for my Godson, Mark O'Connell
who knows about journeys

Chapter 1

Some say life is a journey — a long, difficult trek from the wooded hollows and shallow streams of childhood across the high mountains and wide gorges of youth. And at the end lies a fertile valley where hopes flower fragrantly and cool streams ease the troubles of the weary pilgrim. Those are a poet's words, meant perhaps for candlelit parlors or wide verandas. If life is a journey at all, it is an endless wandering from place to place. Rare moments of peace or belonging are all too soon swept away by the winds of change.

So it seemed to me anyway. My own life often resembled a strange dream, haunted by yesterday's bright hopes and threatened by tomorrow's disappointments. And occasionally there came vivid nightmares from which I prayed to awake.

"Better not to dream," old Tom Shea often warned. "It's enough to know there's a sound horse beneath you, dry powder in your rifle, and those nearby who'll bury you if it comes to the worst."

Shea was a man to cut away the fat and leave the meat of the matter. He'd have you live for the moment and trust tomorrow to the clouds. Or to him. For better than a year I'd ridden at his side, and before that he'd led the way west. Now the two of us were guiding a hundred and fifty emigrants down that same dusty trail — to Oregon.

Oregon! My, what wondrous adventures that word could inspire in a pilgrim's heart. He might envision great mountains crowned with snow towering above raging rivers. Or perhaps he would see fields of golden wheat stretching toward a far horizon. Meandering streams might etch their way between orchards bearing peaches and apples enough to fill the horn of plenty a dozen times. It all lay waiting in Oregon—lumber to build houses and barns . . . churches and courthouses . . . towns, and even a fresh future.

Oregon was a dream to be fulfilled, a paradise worth risking the transcontinental migration. If treacherous rivers and great hulking mountains lay in the way, well, they were but obstacles to be conquered. Marauding Indians, nightmare epidemics, searing heat, and freezing cold were the trials expected by a pilgrim.

My father had certainly thought so when we headed west from Pike County, Illinois, back in '48. Recalling the sandy-haired boy of fourteen who had set his feet on the rutted trail, I found it difficult to believe that four years later I should again be riding westward, bound for Oregon on that same rocky path. Who among the Prescott party of '48 would have imagined that others would look to feather-brained Darby as a guide?

Shea might have, I thought as I swallowed the final trace of muddy black trail coffee. "Four years can change a man," he was fond of saying. But I don't suppose even he could have imagined that skinny tenderfoot would amount to much.

"Well, I guess I've shown 'em all," I muttered as I emptied the contents of the coffee pot onto our small morning fire, then kicked sand over the remaining embers. Wouldn't do to mark our passage by leaving the grass scorched black from carelessness. The prairie wind could convert a bit of spark into a sea of fire come summer, and it was May already.

"You figure them pilgrims'll ever get 'emselves into a line,

Darby?" Shea called as he led our horses over from the grassy hillside where we'd left them to graze. "You'd think it August and us camped in the Cascades. Fools! Like as not gatherin' 'round for a prayer meetin' or havin' a ladies sewin' circle!"

Shea added a few other comments less suitable for polite company, and I laughed.

"Want me to go hurry 'em along?" I asked.

"Well, it's for certain sure somebody ought to!" he barked.

I buttoned my muslin shirt, pulled a leather suspender atop each shoulder, and grabbed my weatherbeaten leather hat while Shea threw a blanket onto the broad back of the pure white Indian pony I'd appropriately named Snow. I added saddle and bridle myself, and moments later I was riding through the rock-studded hills above the Platte to where the Martinson company had located its camp.

Streaks of yellow dawn slashed the cloudy eastern horizon. The golden sky seemed in harmony with the harsh burnt brown tint of the landscape. The white canvas covers of the emigrant wagons, on the other hand, stood out as the intruders they were. Yellow-scarlet pinpricks of light marked the cook fires I could smell long before seeing.

"Pilgrims," I grumbled in the same fashion Shea used. "Sun's already over the horizon, and they're still frying bacon!"

When I reached Captain Martinson's wagon, I said as much.

"After all," I reminded him, "you've been on the trail long enough to know the best miles are made early, before the sun bakes us all to death."

"Just listen to him," sixteen-year-old Marietta cried to her father. "We're only bound for Scott's Bluff today, remember? And nobody's gone and made you a general, Darby Prescott!"

I couldn't help laughing at myself. Scarcely eighteen and

9

yet to get my full growth, how could I take on such airs? And still, gazing into Captain Martinson's solemn eyes, I saw he both respected and expected such a tone from me. Young or not, I was a scout. I might lack Tom Shea's bushy beard or gnarled face, but I was expected to speak my mind and share my knowledge.

"We'll hurry it along, son," Captain Martinson promised, tossing me a biscuit as he waved his boy, Martin, out toward the oxen. "It takes a bit of time to get thirty wagons formed in line, you know."

"Yes, I do know," I reminded him. Shea and I'd been with the train two days now. And while the company's sluggishness could be excused as due to the sickness that had plagued their passage west along the Platte, those who continued to lag often wound up stuck in Rocky Mountain snowdrifts. Soon we'd have to coax extra miles out of stock and company both.

I wondered how, though. It was a struggle just to get the wagons ready. The Alstons, whose wagon should have been fifth in line, were nowhere to be found, and the Grays had managed to locate only two of their oxen. The last five wagons had set off on an old Indian trail toward the Platte, and the Howell boys had wandered off while looking after the saddle ponies.

"Was there ever such a helpless bunch!" I cried when Shea joined me beside the Martinson wagon.

"Just pilgrims," Shea grumbled, spitting a sour taste out of his mouth. "Green as grass! I seen worse, though. Seem to recall a bunch back in '48 wasn't so much better."

"We were rolling west by first light," I argued. "Maybe not in Kansas, but for sure by the time we reached the Platte."

"Well, you had ole Three Fingers Shea to break you in right. These ones been on their own. Too many kids along, too. Snakes'll thin 'em out some, I'll wager."

"Could be," I said, frowning. "They've already had a bit

10

of fever."

"Trail's that way, you know," he remarked rather solemnly, and I nodded my agreement. We both had dug graves alongside the rutted trail. I think it's why we agreed to set aside our wandering ways and guide the Martinson company. Their St. Louis scout had already led them to hard times, and the sight of so many suffering had touched our hearts.

Shea would never admit that, of course. He could put on that cast iron scowl of his and act hard as granite.

"Miz Martinson knows her way 'round a kettle," he said instead. "Pay's right. Care to sign on, son?"

As for me, I'd known enough quiet hillsides. I hungered for the sound of English words and an evening's singing. I missed the pranks and games and dances that accompanied the trail. Most of all I missed that sense of family.

"Wayfarers get accustomed to the lonelies," Shea had told me more than once. But that was the problem. I never could.

"Fools!" Shea shouted then, and all other thoughts vanished from my mind. "They won't ever get this mess sorted out."

I stared at the jumble of confusion behind us. The Alstons had finally arrived, but their wagon led them by a good fifty feet. The oxen rumbled along on their own while young Wyatt, who was maybe fourteen, hung onto the water barrel and pleaded for the team to halt.

The five rear wagons continued to stray, and half the company raced about trying to catch horses or collect children.

"Figure to lend a hand or just sit there cackling like a couple of dumb crows?" Marietta suddenly shouted up at us. "Well?"

"See 'bout headin' off that fifth wagon, Darby," Shea said, laughing as he turned his horse about. "I'll gather the strays."

Without waiting for a response, he bellowed out a chilling cry and charged down the uneven line of wagons, scattering children and animals to either side. I grinned at Marietta and nudged Snow toward the runaway Alston wagon.

I believe mine was the simpler chore, for the errant oxen responded to Snow's sudden white blur instantly. As they slowed, I managed to hop down, dash to the wagon, and climb atop. Once a firm hand collected the lines, the oxen revolt came to a quick end. Wyatt Alston sheepishly accepted control of the wagon, but from the look on his father's approaching face, I knew Wyatt's days as wagonmaster were numbered.

While Shea brought the rear wagons back to the main body, I busied myself running down reluctant horses and wandering children. The Howell boys, it turned out, had fallen victim to a prank. Someone had made off with their shoes and trousers during the night, and when Marty Martinson located the boys in a thicket, their faces were red as a ripe tomato.

"Must've been Indians," Richard, the elder, declared when they rejoined the company.

"Not too wise to doze off on night guard," I told them. Indians, of course, would likely borrow more than boots and britches. I suspected another culprit, a seedy oldtimer with a long beard and a talent for teaching boys the tricks of the trail.

Shea enjoyed a good prank, all right, but he wasn't responsible for the three saddle horses missing from the stock. I was loathe to tell him, as we were already late setting out, and we could ill afford an encounter with the Sioux or Cheyenne horse raiders who frequented the Platte Valley in springtime.

"Could they have wandered off?" Captain Martinson asked when I announced the news.

"Maybe," I admitted. "More likely they had help."

When Shea returned with the tail of the train, I shared the ill tidings.

"Three, eh?" he mused. "Well, let's get the pilgrims headed along. Then we'll have a look."

"You know the Howell boys had a visitor last night."

"Well, boys need some lookin' after, don't they?" he asked with a grin that was as good as a confession.

"Well, they'll be glad to get their trousers back," I said, laughing at the thought. "See any signs of other company?"

"No, but I saw some when I brought the strays in. We'll have a look."

"Cheyenne?" I asked a bit nervously.

"Shod horses, two of 'em. More likely light-complexioned raiders."

I wasn't one bit more relieved to learn that.

Not so long ago, Shea frequently reminded me, a man heading for Oregon had only the intemperate weather, the rough terrain, and the melancholy that accompanied any journey to contend with. Now there were warring Indians, overgrazing, and renegade whites as well.

"And we've got too many fool wagons!" Shea added. "Twice the people, too, and most of 'em too little to be much help."

I myself was glad of our thirty wagons, but it did seem a small army of children marched alongside. A small canvas city exploded into being each evening, and it never got altogether silent.

I found some comfort to that. I was raised in a big family, and I missed the noise of brothers and sisters. It was something Shea couldn't understand. I warmed in the admiring glow of the young ones' eyes, and I welcomed the attentions of the older girls.

"If you ask me, you welcome them a bit much," Marietta Martinson had scolded me the night before. "Just look at you, Darby. You're thin as a wagon tongue, rough as cowhide, nearly as big as I am, and you smell like a horse's

13

behind!"

"I'll get my growth," I promised her. "And when there's less to do, I might even wash."

"Look there, boy!" Shea called out, and I cleared my mind instantly. On a nearby hill a slight-shouldered boy stood guard over four horses. Three belonged to our train.

"Can't be by himself," I warned.

"I only saw one set o' tracks," Shea said as he turned toward the horses. "Best we have a look."

I followed cautiously. One hand rested on the cold butt of my Colt pistol. But by the time we reached the bandit, I had begun to agree with Shea's view. The boy was alone.

"Mornin'," the smallish figure said, balancing an antique flintlock in his strong hands. His voice was deep and somewhat hoarse.

"Mornin', Jed," Shea replied, pushing his hat back from his forehead. "Stealin' horses now, are you?"

"Stealin'?" the young man asked, shaking his head. Now that I could get a good look at him, I saw our bandit was close to my own age, if a bit of a dwarf sizewise. His dark hair and bronze-colored skin hinted of some relation to the plains tribes. His eyes, though, were bright blue.

"Darby, this is Jed Caswell," Shea finally explained. "His papa carts goods for old Robidoux."

"No more," young Caswell said, spitting in Shea's direction. "He scouts for the army sometimes. And we trade horses."

"Back to their owners, I suppose?" I asked.

"If it suits us," Jed declared. "Trail's full o' strays, you know."

"And when it's not, you help things along," I grumbled. "That how it is?"

"Sometimes," Jed admitted. "Now, you want 'em back, Shea?"

"How much?" Shea asked.

"You're not going to pay him, are you?" I complained.

"Don't you figure he's entitled to a finder's fee?" Shea asked. "I'd say ten dollars's fair."

"I'd say twenty," Jed argued.

Shea had already pulled out a ten dollar greenback, though. This he handed Jed as he waved for me to collect the horses.

"Twenty!" Jed barked.

"No, ten's fair, isn't it, Pete?"

"Take it, son!" a voice boomed out from a tangle of brush fifty yards to the right. "A man doesn't argue with Three Fingers Shea, Jed."

I led the three horses off, and Shea followed, taking care to see our retreat covered.

"I thought you said . . ." I began.

"That he was alone?" Shea asked. "He was. But I can smell a Caswell trap a dozen miles comin'."

"We going back to settle with him?"

"For ten dollars?" Shea exclaimed. "We got miles to cover, Darby. We'll leave those two to the next company. These hills never took to renegades nor horse thieves. Man takes that path's bound to come to a bad end."

I nodded. As we returned to the wagon train, I couldn't help wondering what set a man to thieving. And the same answer always came to me. There was nothing else. The fur trade had gone sour, and there were only so many freighters needed. If a man gets desperate enough, he's apt to do anything.

Once back with the train, I had little time to worry over such things. Shea returned the purloined horses, taking care to collect five dollars for each animal's return.

"Got to recover my expense," Shea explained. " 'Sides, they'll tend their stock better."

"And the extra five dollars?" I asked.

"A scout's entitled to a profit now and again."

I thought it more likely that he couldn't split ten dollars three ways. Shea was a wonder finding a trail or leading a fight, but he wasn't well-acquainted with figures.

Soon there were other matters for my attention. Shea and I took our accustomed place at the head of the train, and our eyes scanned the well-traveled route for signs of trouble. Sometimes a section of trail would give way to flood or be blocked by a rockslide, and a detour would be necessary. There were always the possibilities of prowling renegades or parties of Indians. Sometimes the train would actually benefit from a bit of trade with the natives, especially if the Indians happened to be Crows or Arapahos. Shea was well-acquainted with both. We had less truck with other bands.

Around midday we sighted the next landmark on the trail, Scott's Bluff. In other years emigrant trains had labored up the dry gullies alongside the Platte, but now trains took a shortcut through the Mitchell Pass. Shea and I had come east that way, delivering supplies to Jonah Redding's new trading post.

"Best ride back and hurry 'em along, Darby," Shea told me. "Cap'n Martinson spoke of a need of supplies. I'll go on ahead and get Redding in a tradin' mood."

I nodded and turned back toward the train, knowing Tom Shea meant to devote his afternoon to emptying jugs of corn liquor. It was only an occasional vice, and I dismissed it as harmless enough. In fact, Redding would be apt to agree to more generous terms for the train after a sip or two.

We were a long way yet from the bluff or the trading post, though, and I devoted the remainder of the day to nudging the plodding wagons along. Oxen are, by nature, rather prone to be sluggish, and an untried teamster will often get less effort from them than is desired. Captain Martinson entrusted his own team to Marietta, and between her jabbing prods and sharp words, the lead wagon was constantly rolling onward. Among the twenty-nine wagons completing the company, several were notable laggards, though. The Dardens, a pair of newlyweds, followed the Martinson wagon, and the captain spent half his time hurrying them along. Farther back, I judged the McIntoshes and Grays the worst. Sometimes I thought they must engage in a personal duel as to which could be the slowest. To make matters worse, the McIntosh boys, Ray and Randy, had their eyes on Cecilia Gray. What they saw in the spindle-legged girl I could not imagine, but Mr. Gray would abandon his team to chase after those McIntosh boys, and the rear half of the wagon train would slow to a crawl.

"Yes, it's a vexation, Darby," Captain Martinson agreed when I mentioned the problem. "We'll have need to move the McIntoshes up or the Grays back. I'll have a word with the boys, too."

"I'd say it's due," I told him.

"Of course, I may need to speak to a certain scout as well. It seems he's paid a fair amount of attention to the young ladies of this train as well."

"Mostly it's the other way around," I claimed. "The Nez Perce near had me married last year, you know."

"Marietta's not Nez Perce," he said, giving me a serious gaze. "And you've not been so long in the wilds you don't recall what civilized folk judge proper behavior, have you, Darby?"

"No, sir," I answered.

As I rode among the wagons, I couldn't help laughing to myself about the captain's warning. I suppose he expected me to ride off with Marietta in the night, maybe build a cabin on the Platte. Back in that Nez Perce camp the notion of taking a wife had turned my insides to cold mush. Put me on a fast horse, and I could give the wind a fair race. I'd hunted buffalo and grizzlies. But as to women, well . . .

Scott's Bluff was a great tall tower of sandstone striped by shades of purple and dull green in the afternoon sunlight.

Along the trail knifelike blades of Spanish yucca, which the Plains tribes called soapbrush, sprouted tall spire-like buds. Children occupied themselves picking berries. As the company neared the bluff itself, the trail opened onto grand vistas. Pines stared down at us from the heights. In the distance the North Platte cut deeper into its banks as melting snows upstream lent their swift waters to the river.

We reached Redding's Trading Post an hour short of dusk. Captain Martinson got the wagons formed in a circle, then detailed men and boys to guard the stock while others secured such supplies as were needed by all. Wood and buffalo chips were gathered, and cook fires were started. I made a camp of sorts on a small rise near Redding's storehouse. After tending Snow and the rest of our horses, I set off to assure myself Shea hadn't altogether lost his senses.

Actually Tom Shea was sitting with Jonah Redding on the storehouse steps. They were halfway through a second jug, and Shea was spinning a fresh tale about how he'd come to lose two fingers off his left hand. A wolf gnawed them this time, so he explained to the wonderment of the trader and numerous emigrant boys and girls who gathered nearby.

He paused but once in his tale—to nod in my direction—and I judged him good for another jug at least. So satisfied, I headed back toward the main camp and lent a hand with the animals.

Marietta and Marty were especially grateful of the help.

"Mama's busy with supper, and Papa's got the whole company to bother with," Marty explained. "And, well, a sister's not much help with oxen."

"Just who is it gets these fool beasts up the trail every day, Martin Martinson?" Marietta countered. "If you'd work half as much as talk, we'd finish in half the time!"

Marty barked back, and the two of them hollered insults while I placed hobbles on the horses and released the oxen

18

from their yokes. Afterward Marietta extended an invitation to supper.

"Best I tend Shea," I explained.

"He'll be half the night at his drinking," she insisted. "Now, you know Mama's the best cook in the territory. Come."

I never was any good at arguing, even when it made sense to do so. So I agreed.

I didn't take dinner invitations lightly. I also took to heart certain comments about my appearance. I managed to scrub off a pound of trail grit from my body, shave the stubble off my chin, and put on my best outfit before arriving at the Martinson cook fire.

I was something to see. There I was, five feet ten inches of Westerner. I wore buckskin boots and trousers, a beaded Crow shirt, with a bear claw choker adorning my neck.

"My word, who's this?" Mrs. Martinson asked, grinning.

"A mountain man, eh, Darby?" Marty asked. "Are those real claws? Did you make the boots yourself?"

"I can't believe it," Marietta added. "He's actually clean. And he shaved his whiskers. Our first miracle on the trail."

"Well, this is fine treatment!" I complained. "I only cleaned myself up some. You'd think I grew horns."

The captain appeared then. He instantly put an end to the jests and announced it time to eat. Mrs. Martinson filled plates with pork pie, and I devoted my efforts to emptying one of them.

I was a fair cook in my own right, and Shea and I ate well. We were forever scaring up fresh game, and Shea knew where to dig up tubers and which herbs added a taste of this or that. Even so, Mrs. Martinson put us to shame. Not since Mama died had I filled myself so completely. Afterward, as I sat beside the fire, I half imagined I was part of their family, the elder brother perhaps. It was a warming illusion, one which quickly faded as Marietta and her mother began cleaning the dishes, and Marty went to check on the stock.

I had a habit of chasing off the lonelies with a tune now and then, and I carried a mouth organ in my hip pocket for just such a purpose. As I blew a somber tune, the wind grew still, and my notes seemed to echo tauntingly back at me from the far bluff.

"Do you know something a trifle more cheerful?" Mrs. Martinson asked. I did, and the lively notes soon brightened the mood. Others wandered over until two thirds of the company were assembled. I played another tune, and another.

"Mr. Shea's been tellin' tales," Richard Howell told me. "Have you got one to share?"

"Tell us about the bear claws," Marty pleaded.

I glanced around at the many small faces.

"No, that's for another time," I said, not wishing to fill their dreams with phantom grizzlies. "But I'll share a story. It's a strange one, and you may not half believe it. I'm not certain I do myself, and I was there."

"Yes, tell us," a smallish boy cried, and the smaller ones huddled close.

"It's been a year now, I guess," I began. "I was high up in the Tetons, mountains well west and north of here. Winter was still gripping the land, and snow was everywhere. Tom Shea and I rode with the Shoshonis, mountain Indians, and we set out to hunt buffalo. The night was dark, and a heavy mist was upon the land. You could scarcely see your feet, for there was little moonlight and few stars.

"Among the Indians, all life is held sacred. There are prayers to be said before setting upon the hunt. The Shoshonis asked the buffalo spirit to give up his children to end the winter hunger, to keep away the cold, to fend off the rain. There is dancing and singing. Then the hunt begins. I set off with others, but as I said, it was dark, and I became separated. As I made my way across the land, I heard sounds. I smelled something dark and heavy. Then I saw it."

"What?" Marty cried.

The eyes of the others echoed his question.

"The white buffalo," I whispered. "The rarest of all creatures."

"They're usually brown, aren't they?" one of the men asked.

"Or red or black. But the white buffalo . . . is especially sacred. Some say it is the buffalo spirit itself. I don't know. I only can tell what I saw . . . and heard."

"Heard?" a smallish boy whispered.

"Yes," I explained. "You see, there I was, in the dark, suddenly faced with the white buffalo. I held a gun in my hand, but the buffalo seemed to be singing. It bid me have patience, and faith. For if the people needed meat for their bellies and clothes to keep out the cold, the buffalo would provide. And if I had courage and used wisdom, I would become whatever I chose to be."

"It said all that?" Marty asked.

"Not in words exactly," I explained. "In its song. Or maybe it was a dream. I don't know. I do know that when morning came, I led the way to a great herd of buffalo, and we had a great feast. And I found this," I added, taking a small tangle of coarse white hair from a pouch at my waist.

The company gazed in wonder at the hair that could only have come from the white buffalo.

"Did you ever see it again?" Richard Howell asked.

"Yes," I told the boy. "It visits me to warn of danger, or to urge courage. Maybe some of you will come to see the white buffalo in the days to come. It calls the brave of heart, or so the Shoshonis believe. And all who set out on this trail have need of courage."

"And need of rest," Captain Martinson added. "I think it's time some of us find our beds."

The company agreed. Already many a small head rested on a mother's lap. As the gathering dispersed, Marietta took my hand and led me off toward the fringe of the camp.

"You're a strange one, Darby Prescott," she declared. "Telling stories of spirits and ghosts. Dressing in beads and bear claws. Having us all believe you're half wild."

"Maybe I am half wild."

"Then why is it you can play Mozart on the mouth organ? Or maybe the white buffalo taught you that, too."

"No, my grandmother."

"And tell me, have you decided what it is that this buffalo spirit will grant you? What you want to be?"

"I knew once," I told her, gazing sadly at the sparkling stars overhead. "But I've taken so many turns in the trail since then that I don't know anymore what I want. I just try to get by day to day."

"Don't you ever plan to return to your family?"

"My mother and father are dead," I explained. "I've got brothers in Illinois, but they've little use for another hand on the farm. My sister's in Oregon with her husband and little girl Bessy. Maybe there's another one by now. I'll see them at trail's end maybe."

"You could write, you know. Your sister could answer."

"Oh? Where would she send a letter? I'm little more than a wisp of smoke out here."

"Well you're not altogether alone. There's Mr. Shea."

"Yes," I said, nodding.

"He's a kind of father, isn't he?"

"No, not a father," I told her. "But more than a friend."

"He's a loner, Darby."

"Not so much as he'd have folks believe. He leaves money with missionaries on the Columbia who take in trail orphans. Once he risked his life to rescue a wagon train trapped in a blizzard south of Ft. Hall. Oh, he plays the hard-crusted old hermit, but he feels things. He's brought me back from death's door plenty of times, and he's taught me more than I'll ever realize."

"So now you can lead people down this trail. Doesn't it seem strange to you, Darby? All the rest of us, thirty families, know where this trail will lead us. Do you?"

"Does it matter?"

"It would to me."

"Well, I guess that's how we're different," I told her. "I quit figuring things a long time back. When death reaches out and takes your mother, then your father, you don't expect much. These days I just greet the sun each morning and do my best. It's enough."

"Is it? Don't you want more?"

"Want?" I asked, trembling slightly. "What's want got to do with it?"

She reached out to grip my hand, but I stepped away. I could hear singing at Redding's, and I turned in that direction.

"Darby?" she called.

I should've answered, but I lacked the words to make her understand. When she returned to her father's wagon, perhaps he would explain. I hoped so.

I found Shea still sitting on the steps of the storehouse. Redding and a pair of freighters were sprawled nearby, snoring away. I got Shea to his feet, and we headed for our camp.

"Was good corn," he said as we stumbled along. "Good for forgettin'."

I knew what he meant. Drunk, Tom Shea could for a while forget the pain and torment that had visited his life. But it was a brief respite, and tomorrow a different kind of torment would surely plague him. As I feared it would me.

Chapter 2

I often thought how ill-suited a partner I was for Tom Shea. He was tall, gruff of manner, and hard as the mountains he loved. I was none of those things. And yet, as I set the coffee pot to boil on the morning cook fire, I recognized in his swollen, red-streaked eyes a kind of kinship he never shared with anyone else. If he rarely revealed the sadness that haunted his recollections, he at least didn't hide its effects from me. I guess he saw that same hurt in me, and he judged I understood.

"Darby, you figure you can get those pilgrims headed on up the trail?" he muttered as I began rolling up our blankets.

"Not much to it," I told him. "Figure to lay up a day?"

"No," he said, scowling. "Got the urge to put some miles behind me. Thought we might try to drop a pair of buffs, have ourselves a good eat before movin' on to Laramie."

"Sounds fine by me. Sure you don't want to rest a day, though? Those buffs won't run off, you know."

"That buffalo spirit tell you so? No, I'll be all right. Just can't abide all that pilgrim noise."

"Head hearing bells?"

"More like cannons," he said, laughing to himself. "Ole Redding's corn liquor leaves its reminders."

"I judged it so by the color of your eyes. I'll fry us up

some bacon, then head down to the wagons and tell Captain Martinson we'll meet them two days up the trail."

"You keep the bacon to yourself," Shea said, holding his belly. "Just coffee and a slice or two of bread for me."

"Sure," I said, trying not to grin too broadly at my suffering companion.

Captain Martinson was none too pleased with my news.

"I hired scouts to look after this company," he told me. "Not to ride off and leave us to ourselves."

"We'll be close enough to warn of trouble," I assured him. "It's how it's done. You won't have any trouble following the road to where the Laramie River meets the Platte. We'll meet you before you get there, and we'll have fresh meat for everyone. It'll prove more welcome than the face of a skinny sort like me or a crusty old cuss like Tom Shea."

"We're relying on you two, Darby," he reminded me.

"Know that," I said, scratching my ear. "Won't let you come to grief. Keep a good pace, and we'll have buffalo steaks waiting."

I gave him half a salute in parting, waved to Marietta and Marty, then urged Snow into a gallop. Soon I was back at my camp, helping Shea pack up the rest of our belongings.

"He's a little nervous about us going on ahead," I explained as I tied our supplies on the back of the pack horses.

"Can't blame him much," Shea said as he glanced at the rising cloud of dust to the east. "He's had one scout go sour and die on him. We'll stay close enough to keep watch."

"Likely it's best."

"You takin' 'em to heart already, are you?" he asked, a trace of laughter flirting with his face. "Well, she's pretty enough, I'll grant you. Only watch the civilizin' kind, Darby. They'll have you wearin' stiff collars and sittin' through sermonizin' every Sunday."

"That bad?"

"Ruins a man for the mountains. You take to such ways, you be sure she can cook real good, hear?"

"She'll have to do more'n cook, Tom."

He laughed, then slapped my back. We tied the last of our things on the horses and then set off westward.

The Platte Valley in 1852 was a wide swath of gray hills dotted with scrub brush and buffalo grass. There were no settlements between Scott's Bluff and the military post at Ft. Laramie. Occasionally an Indian village might nestle beside the river, but the large parties of emigrants sweeping westward had thinned the grass and depleted the hunting grounds. Most summer camps were north or south of the white man's road now.

The buffalo was slower to change his ways. From the beginning of time the great herds had roamed the Platte. Though their numbers had been thinned considerably, buffs were still to be found along the creeks that fed the river and even beside the North Platte itself before the summer onrush of wagons.

Shea led the way across the river, then northward a half dozen miles. From there we began a long sweep west. It was familiar ground. We'd hunted there before when I was but an Illinois farmboy too ignorant of Western ways to know it. I could tell by the hollow gaze of Shea's eyes that he, too, recalled that time.

"Not much sign hereabouts," I observed as he drew his horse to a halt.

"We'll make camp in the hills to the west. Tomorrow we'll hunt."

I nodded my agreement, and we led our animals into a line of low hills. Shea found a small spring-fed pond sheltered by a stand of cottonwoods, and we made camp there. Once the animals were tended, I built a small fire and began readying an early supper. All I'd eaten since breakfast were strips of jerked venison and a stale biscuit, and I could feel the hunger welling up inside me.

"Been a while since we were up here the last time," Shea said as he cut slices of pork and set them in a skillet.

"Four years," I said as I began kneading dough for biscuits. "Lot's happened since then."

"Mostly sad times for you, eh?"

"Some," I admitted, closing my eyes and recalling Mama's cold hands, Papa's solitary grave.

"Trail's like that, you know. Hard and cold, with mostly graves to mark the way."

"Mostly," I echoed. "But there've been good friends, too. And adventures aplenty."

"Enough to balance off the loss?" he asked.

"Can't balance your folks, Tom," I muttered. "Anymore'n you can balance your wife and boy."

He stared a moment at the two missing fingers on his left hand, then turned away a moment. It was the Crow way to cut a digit to mark the loss of a loved one. I'd learned that elsewhere. Shea never would have told me. It was the direst hurt of all, and he buried it deep. More than once I thought he'd open up, but it had yet to happen. It wouldn't now.

"Ever wish you were back with your sister on the farm?" he whispered.

"Oh, there've been times in the winter when my toes have near frozen when I wished I was back somewhere," I confessed. "But never come spring when it'd be time for planting. I don't have the patience for farming nor the disposition for hard work."

"Now that's a truth."

"I'm a fair cook, though, which is more than I can say for some."

"Fair hand with that mouth organ, too. I heard you last night three miles away. Care to blow a tune?"

"Once I get the biscuits to baking," I answered, showing him my flour-coated fingers.

He laughed, and I noticed a bit of the pain seemed to

flow from his face. His eyes brightened, too, and he grabbed an ax and set to chopping firewood. I contented myself working the dough, rolling it out on a bread board and shaping the biscuits. Then it was merely a matter of greasing the dutch oven, setting it in the coals, and adding the biscuits once it heated properly.

It was a typical trail dinner, I suppose. Fried pork strips, a tin of beans, and biscuits, topped off by overcooked coffee. But it had an agreeable enough taste. Afterward, while Shea scrubbed up the plates, I blew a few trail tunes and even sang a chorus or two of "Sweet Betsy from Pike."

It was still early when the fire burned down to embers, but Shea declared tomorrow would start early. I nodded my agreement, saw the animals were secure, and returned to the fire. I didn't entirely believe in spirits and such, but I took the time to say a brief prayer to the buffalo spirit. Then I put out the fire and climbed between my blankets.

I fell asleep instantly, and I might never have awakened had not Shea's rough hand roused me an hour after dawn.

"Can't sleep the day away, boy," he grumbled. "Horses are waitin'. Let's go."

I blinked my eyes open, then gazed in disbelief. Shea's old gray and Snow paced anxiously. The two pack horses stood ready to take on loads of buffalo meat. I noted with amusement that the only missing things were a pair of riders.

"You figure to leave camp as it is?" I asked, pointing out the supplies and belongings spread out around the pond.

"Buffs aren't far," Shea declared. "I can smell 'em. Tomorrow we'll have time to ride down to the Platte."

Another man might have doubted his words. I admit that I did sniff the air, and I found not a hint of buffalo scent. But I knew what Shea meant. He'd ridden that trail often, and he knew where the buffalo would be. I pulled on my trousers and headed for Snow. Soon we were riding westward.

I kept my eyes and nose alert for buffalo sign, but Shea merely rode confidently toward the northwest. And sure enough, it wasn't long before we spotted prairie torn by hooves and spattered with fresh dung. Just before midday we located the first dark shapes on the horizon.

I pointed first, but Shea was already drawing out his rifle. He waved me along, and we approached cautiously. There were three or four of them prowling along the fringe of the herd, with another forty or fifty beyond. We rode silently through the high grass to a knobby rise crowned by boulders. There we dismounted, picketed the horses, and prepared our first shots.

"Take the cow on the right," Shea whispered as he aimed at a second animal to the left. I nodded, then waited for his shot. Even as the discharge echoed across the valley, I fired my own rifle. Both buffalo dropped instantly, and we fought to reload.

Nothing was as unpredictable as a herd of buffalo. Sometimes they'd just stand there and let hunters shoot for half an hour at a time. Another time they'd stampede at the sound of a shuddering horse. I was never really at ease with thousands of pounds of pure thunder before my eyes, and when that herd turned in our direction, I was tempted to race Snow to the Mississippi. Shea confidently fired again, dropping a third beast, and I swallowed my fear. I took aim and shot the lead bull through the heart. Leaderless and confused, the herd took to circling. We could have killed a dozen more, but four would feed the company past contentment, and a wise man knew to leave the herd strong for future need. We watched a new lead bull emerge and lead the buffs off to the north.

Hunting was a job, true enough, but there was a touch of adventure to it. First a man stalked his game. Then he set up the shot. Finally, if he made no mistakes, he completed the kill. Somehow it brought a man back to his beginnings. I always fired my rifle reluctantly, feeling a kinship of sorts for the quarry. I needed a strong reason to take a life. Shea once remarked he'd never make a living as a hider, and I judged I'd fare as poorly. But when there was purpose at hand, I had the hunter's heart.

Once the buffalo had left, the real work always began, though. From the time Papa first handed me a chicken to pluck back on the farm in Illinois, I'd taken a dislike to butchering. As if the smell wasn't bad enough, the blood and gore were sure to drive a man to distraction!

Nevertheless I followed Tom Shea down the hill toward the fallen buffalo. He drew out his knife and walked from one to the other, making the throat cuts so the blood would drain. When he came to the final beast, he halted.

"Best you do this one your own self, son," he called.

I hesitated, and he frowned.

"Darby, you been saddlin' your own horse a long time now. There's other things to do, too," he told me.

There was no arguing about such things with a man who'd helped work the baby soft off you. I drew my own knife from its sheath inside my boot. He helped me place the blade, then stepped back. Making the cut was as hard a thing as I ever did. I had to fight to keep from retching when the blood spattered my hands.

"Time we got on with the skinnin'," Shea declared. "Do that one, then fetch the horses."

I understood. He had decided it was time for me to learn, but he accepted I wouldn't take to it straight away. Shea stripped off his shirt and kicked his boots aside before starting to work, and I did likewise. It was the only way. It was work sure to paint the world red, and shirts were hard to come by.

As I carved away the tough buffalo's hide, a strange sensation crept over me. I felt eyes on my back. Instinctively I turned around. Sure enough, five figures on horseback gazed out from behind a slight rise.

"Tom," I called.

"I seen 'em," he grumbled. "Go ahead with your work, Darby. They're Cheyenne, and if they take it into their heads to ride down here, ain't a thing we can do to stop 'em. Best thing is to show 'em we know what we're about, and that we're not ridin' 'round slaughterin' their winter food for the hang of it."

I did as he suggested, but I couldn't help feeling uneasy. I hadn't just shed my clothes. I'd left my pistol and rifle a dozen yards away, too, and my skinning knife wouldn't put much fear in a Cheyenne horseman. On the other hand, a shaggy brown scalp might do his lodgepole proud.

The riders finally did approach us, but they never did speak. Wasn't much need, I guess. Their eyes said it all. We were unwelcome intruders who had slain their buffalo. Like as not they'd killed us if the sight of a pair of half-naked white men didn't seem a touch crazed.

Shea judged it so, too, for he hopped up and down and shouted to them like a lunatic. I aped him, and the Cheyennes fled.

"Can't say I'm pleased to see those fellows," Shea said as he resumed work.

"I'm pleased to see 'em leave," I added. "Wish 'em godspeed as far as they can go."

"Won't go far," Shea said, frowning. "They'll be watchin'."

The thought was about as welcome as sunshine in August.

We had no more visitors the balance of the day, though. We got the meat packed in buffalo hide on the backs of our pack horses and tied our belongings atop the saddle horses. We then led the four horses southward toward the North Platte. By nightfall we sighted the river.

"Look yonder," Shea bade me, pointing westward. From a horizon painted deep purple flashed tiny yellow stars.

"We're almost to Ft. Laramie," I observed.

"Give us tomorrow to cook up that meat. Train should be along by then."

31

"We'll cook for them tomorrow," I declared as I collected chips for a fire. "Tonight I'm eating buffalo steak myself. No more burnt coffee and beans. No, sir!"

Shea laughed, then helped me build up the fire. We did indeed stuff ourselves that night.

Cooking a few buffalo steaks on a chip fire was nothing to the task awaiting us on the morrow, though. Just slicing the meat into strips took us most of the morning, and I devoted two hours to collecting every dead scrap of cotton-wood or willow for five miles around. We started smoking meat to last us in the days ahead. We wouldn't begin the feasting meat until the train itself appeared.

That happened in the middle of the afternoon. Captain Martinson was the first to appear. He rode up, applauded our efforts, and promised to hurry the others along. Word of fresh meat must have had an effect, for the company moved at a brisker pace than I imagined possible.

We were soon set upon by a party of women who shooed us from the fires and took over the cooking. Shea and I retreated to our nearby camp and began working the hides. Soon half the children in the company collected nearby, and Shea quickly found himself explaining our every move. Finally he stepped aside, cut a strip from one of the hides, stuffed it with buffalo grass, and made a ball of it by binding it with strips of hide.

"Enough questions," he declared. "Time you pilgrims started your education."

I knew what he had in mind. He located a stick and gave the ball a sound slap. Then another. He tossed the stick to young Ev Gray and motioned for the boy to do likewise. In short order the children rushed around gathering sticks. Then Shea split them up into two more or less equal sides, and the game was on.

It had a name, some convoluted Pawnee phrase I couldn't begin to pronounce. I called it stick and ball, though in truth the ball wasn't the only thing to receive a whack. Shins and foreheads were especially popular, and more than one player howled in pain as a companion thrashed him. Little Wil Alston, who was scarcely eleven, had the dual displeasure of having his rump rapped by Becky Bragg and then sliding belly first into a tangle of cactus. Shea and I spent close to an hour digging spines out of his hide.

"To tell you the truth, Wil, we all thought you a goner sure," Mal Anderson said after we plucked the last needle from Wil's shoulder.

"Might've been better dead," Wil grumbled when Shea began dabbing brown paste on the red bumps that dotted the boy's front.

"Truth is, you smell dead," Ray McIntosh observed. His brother Randy pinched his nose, and several of the others laughed loudly.

"I'll admit the smell isn't much," Shea said, "but it does feel considerable better, eh, boy?"

Wil nodded reluctantly, then gathered his clothes. But even with Wil more or less mended, the youngsters didn't leave. In fact, others arrived. They encircled Shea, then engulfed me as well.

"Tell us about the hunt," Mal begged, and the others echoed the plea.

I gazed at Shea, but he started to work on a hide. He looked up but once as if to say, "Well, Darby, you're doin' nothin' else." And so I spoke of the buffalo, of their charge, and finally of the Cheyennes.

"They might've killed you," little Wil spoke nervously.

"Indians need a reason to kill a man," Shea said, grinning at the boy. "Mostly."

"They could come back," Ev Gray whispered.

"Most likely will," Shea admitted. "Not somethin' to worry you. Rattlesnakes, now you look out for them. And cactus," he added, winking at Wil.

"Lots of things kill you out here," Marty said, sliding past the others and sitting beside me. "Swamp fever got Victor Gaines."

There was a nervous shudder among the youngsters, and more than one head nodded agreement. It was as if a veil of sadness suddenly descended upon one and all. Not a smile survived it. All eyes seemed to fix on me, and I was without words to answer.

"I didn't know him," I finally spoke. "But when I first came West, I had a friend. Jamie McNamara was his name. He was red-haired, like you, Ev. Into every manner of mischief. Why, he had the both of us near hung from pranking this family or that. And when we got caught spying on the young ladies down at the river, well . . . that's another tale. He caught the fever, and the laughing stopped. One day he was chasing me through the buffalo grass, and the next one we were digging him a hole in the ground."

"It's hard, losing friends," Mal Anderson muttered. "Mark and I had two baby sisters born dead."

"Sometimes I wonder who'll be next," Marty said, and a terrible silence seemed to freeze us all. I waited for Shea to speak, but his eyes fixed on me again. I swallowed hard, then coughed.

"I lost my best friend, then my mama and papa," I told them. "Hated near everything for a while. But a real smart man told me it's the way of life to be short sometimes. The trick's to treasure each day, to spend it well. Then, well, even if you've only got a few years, you've left something behind."

"Guess so," Marty said.

I took out my mouth organ and tried to bring forth a tune to cheer us. Instead I found myself playing a mournful ballad. Mrs. Martinson then cried out that dinner was waiting, and our gathering disintegrated in a charge of hungry mouths.

"I don't have your way of explaining things, Tom," I said

as I helped Shea set aside his work.

"Seems to me you did just fine, Darby. Isn't the words that matter, after all. It's the feelin'."

I nodded my agreement. And afterward, when we sat among the others chewing buffalo steak and chomping such greens as the ladies had collected, I knew he was right. I recognized the admiring gaze of the youngsters. After all, I'd been them not so long before.

Lord, don't let me fail them, I prayed as I huddled in my blankets that night. For admiration breeds weighty responsibility. And I worried I might prove unequal to the task.

Chapter 3

I was up with the sun that next morning. There was a murmur of excitement in the air. For once the cook fires in the main camp burned brightly, and already boys were leading oxen and mules toward waiting wagons. Families were packing belongings or eating breakfast.

"Laramie fever," Shea declared with a grin.

I knew what he meant. For many of those folks the thought of camping outside the fort held out the promise of at least a hint of civilization.

"Jerked buffalo meat and cold biscuits this morning, eh?" I asked.

"Happens," Shea muttered. "Especially when the cook sleeps in."

Sleeps in? I thought. It was barely light. I yawned, scrambled into my clothes, and set about getting ready for the trail.

I confess that as Shea and I led the way westward, I began to feel a tinge of Laramie fever myself. The fort marked a change of sorts in the trail, with greener valleys and high mountains on the horizon. There were friends there, too. Music and laughter.

Snow seemed to sense my eagerness, and he bounded forth with rare zest. I drew out my mouth organ and blew up a storm of notes. Shea even bellowed out a bit of "My

Carolina Gal." I guess Laramie fever was catching. I judged it a good kind of sickness. For the first time we acted like a real emigrant train, a company eager to see the Willamette.

Actually, train was a poor name for it. Any train worth the name was a series of cars neatly bound together, a sort of rolling chain. A wagon train was nothing of the sort. Even the best of them more nearly resembled a snake without a backbone. And on either side of the wagons spread clusters of walkers and occasional riders.

"Somethin' akin to a movin' city . . . gone mad," Shea once told me. "Or an ant hill somebody stomped good."

There was truth to it. Cradles rocked back and forth in the back of wagons. Children chased each other down the trail, and wagons were often decked out with lines of drying clothing or bedding catching a bit of fresh air. Mr. Payne, who had been a schoolmaster in Indiana, ran a sort of walking school beside his wagon, ninth in line. And on any particular day somebody was getting a boil lanced or a fever tonicked by Mrs. Faith Brown, who was as close to a doctor as our company possessed.

She wasn't needed that particular day, though. The road to Ft. Laramie proved wide and dry, and we were within sight of the post by early afternoon. A party of soldiers escorted us the last few miles, and the colonel had a bugler trumpet our arrival. While Shea introduced Captain Martinson to the officers, I helped get the wagons formed up into a camp across the Laramie River.

I wasn't long about the task when I heard my name called. It wasn't all that unusual, as I'd come to be in high demand for tales or a helping hand. But this voice, though oddly familiar, belonged neither to Tom Shea nor a member of the Martinson company. Instead I turned to gaze out at Laveda Borden, daughter of the post trader at Laramie.

"Finally put your hand to honest work, eh?" she called.

"More honest than trading pilgrims out of their cash," I answered.

"Well, they haven't worn the edge off your tongue," she said, laughing. "If they don't keep you too busy, maybe you'll come by for some supper this evening."

"That an invitation?" I asked.

"When you were here last time, you weren't altogether bad company, Darby Prescott. I suppose that warrants an invite."

"Then I'd best accept. Provided you can offer me something better than salt pork and cold biscuit."

"Fried trout, stewed carrots, and fresh melon?"

"Enough to tempt the colonel's lady, I'll wager."

"Well, you can't bring her," Laveda grumbled. "Nor anyone else. And maybe later we can take a walk down along the river."

"A short one," I warned. "My days have a way of starting early these days."

"And mine go on forever when there's a wagon train in," she said with a frown. "Best I get along to the store now. Pa's bound to be at a loss."

I waved farewell and went back to my responsibilities. Soon, though, the wagons were formed in a square, the stock left to graze, and the company set out to replenish goods not available at Redding's or have a look about the fort.

Ft. Laramie was an odd assembly of buildings spread out around a parade ground. It was more of a small town than my idea of a fort, for there was no stockade, and except for a pair of parked cannons and a row of tents, there was nothing very military about the place. Moreover, I didn't count enough soldiers to put much fear in the Sioux or Cheyenne.

"Mostly we just help the folks movin' West and keep out of the way of the Indians," Sergeant Finch, who doubled as the blacksmith, told me when I lent a hand at the forge. "Soldiers all know that. Every odd once in a while we get a young lieutenant out to make himself a name, and then we can have a bad time of it. He'll ride us into the ground before he figures out the Indians don't want trouble, and neither does the army. Me, I hammer rims back into shape or shoe horses just like I did back in Missouri, and before that in Ohio."

"Yeah," I said, nodding as I worked the bellows. "Simple folk like us don't much bother ourselves about things."

"You, simple folk?" the sergeant asked. "Why, I wish I had the gumption to ride this country alone like you and Shea. How old'd you be, son? Sixteen?"

"Eighteen," I barked.

"Well, no wonder Laveda's set her cap for you. Watch that one, Darby. She has her way most times."

"Well, she'll have a high time roping me," I argued. "I've been out on the plains too long. It's easier trapping an Indian pony than a fellow who's wintered in the high country."

The sergeant laughed, then gave me a slap on the back with his bearlike hand.

I devoted another hour to the forge. By then all the rims were repaired, and we even had a pair of spare wheels thrown in against mishap on down the line. I dashed out to make myself presentable for dinner and ran right into Mrs. Ernestine Randolph, the commanding colonel's wife.

"Hello there!" she gasped in surprise as I bounced off her shoulder and collapsed in a pile at her feet.

"Sorry, ma'am," I said, grabbing my hat from the dust and shyly wiping the embarrassment from my face.

"Why, you're the piano boy, aren't you?" she asked. "Donald, isn't it?"

"Darby," I said, surprised she would remember the bit of playing I'd done for her during our brief stay at the fort.

"The piano's still here, Darby. Won't you play a tune or two for the colonel before supper tonight? We've invited Captain Martinson's family and Mr. Shea."

"I, uh, already accepted an invite elsewhere," I explained.

"Laveda?" she asked, grinning. I nodded. "Well, you'll still have to play a song or two. Only then will I excuse you."

"Yes, ma'am," I said somewhat reluctantly.

It wasn't that I minded the music. In truth, my fingers hungered for piano keys, and Mrs. Randolph's pianoforte was a fine, delicate instrument. It's just that I might have managed to pass Laveda's muster with a fresh shirt. Going to the colonel's house meant taking a bath at least. More probably I'd get my hair clipped as well.

It was even worse. I was sent upriver with Marty and a cake of lye soap and ordered to undergo a thorough scrubbing under the watchful eye of Captain Martinson. Then the post barber gave me a scalping sure to last till midwinter. I found myself squeezed into a starched shirt borrowed off some poor unfortunate and a pair of trousers so stiff I was afraid to take regular steps lest I embarrass myself before the whole fort. It might well have been Easter Sunday back in Pike County!

Laveda had a good laugh at my expense, but I think she was rather pleased about the chance to visit the Randolphs' quarters before retiring to the store for supper. I played a pair of lively tunes, then concluded with a military march.

"Your talents are sorely missed at Ft. Laramie, son," Colonel Randolph proclaimed afterward. "Any interest in a military career? I hope to have a regimental band here one day."

"Just now we seem to have difficulty managing a regiment," Miz Ernestine quipped. "Now, off with you, Darby and Laveda. You're certain to have a better time elsewhere than saddled with such tame company as we could offer."

"Thanks, ma'am," I said, making a half bow as Laveda tugged at my arm. I caught a gleeful glance from Marty, and a matching one from Shea. Only Marietta seemed displeased. We'd barely spoken in three days, but the abandoned look in her eyes was unmistakable. Just then, though, Laveda was plenty of worry for anybody.

"Who's the girl?" she asked as we walked to the store.

"Captain Martinson's daughter. Marietta by name."

"You haven't been much more than a week out of Laramie, and already you've struck up acquaintance with another girl. The heart is fleeting indeed."

"I don't remember you sewing me any promised shirt, Laveda Borden," I objected. "Nor has she, either. Now there was that little Crow gal back in February . . ."

"You really are a vexation, Darby!"

"Try my best," I said, grinning.

Laveda didn't exactly answer that with words, but her handbag left an impression on the back of my head.

Dinner was a lot more pleasant. Her father sat at the head of the table, looking a bit distracted. I judged the long day's labor filling needs and haggling over prices had left him more than weary. Laveda sat at his right hand, and I was across the table next to her brother Laurence—safely out of range of her handbag. In truth, she was the perfect hostess, and the trout close to melted on my tongue. As for carrots, well, vegetables were gold on the trail, and the melons proved to be both juicy and delicious.

As for conversation, Laveda spoke some about me playing the colonel's piano, and I told of the buffalo hunt and our encounter with Jed Caswell.

"Ah, yes, his father's gone renegade," Mr. Borden declared. "He's stolen Army supplies. The Sioux are at odds with him over some horses, too. He'll come to a bad end."

"Shea says so, too," I explained. "Shame his boy's sure to suffer the same fate."

"Bad blood spells a bad fate," Mr. Borden argued. "What ever became of your folks, Darby? They set you loose on the world awful early, didn't they?"

"Well, I'm the youngest lived, sir," I told him. "We came out West in '48, just before the big rush. It's when I met Shea. Mama, she died just short of Ft. Hall. We buried

Papa two years ago this harvest. So I guess it was God's will set me loose so to speak. Early maybe, but I've seasoned up well enough."

"And now he's signed on with the Martinson party," Laveda added. "Not bad work for a man."

"I suppose a company always needs extra drivers," Mr. Borden grumbled.

"I'm a scout," I said, frowning. "Maybe not of the mark Tom Shea is, but I'm on my way."

"Are you?" Mr. Borden asked. "You look a bit short of that mark to me. Make better parlor music than you read trail sign, I'll bet."

"I spent all afternoon helping at the forge," I declared, rising from my seat. "And I've seen more of this particular trail than I figure you have. If my company troubles you, just say so. I've got other places I can be."

"Pa!" Laveda complained.

"Never you mind me, girlie," he said, rubbing his head. "I've been havin' my headaches again. You know where my medicine is."

"Yes, Pa," she said, rising and fetching a whiskey bottle from a nearby cabinet.

"Let me help clear the table," I offered as Mr. Borden poured himself a liberal dose.

"No, that's Laurence's job," she insisted. "We have a walk by the river promised, remember?"

"Maybe you'd rather put that off to another time," I suggested, nodding toward her father as he downed the whiskey and poured a second glass.

"He'll drink a bit and then find his rest," she explained. "You're apt to go West and get scalped by some Indian or else eaten by a bear. I may not have another chance at you."

"Then come on," I said, offering my arm. She gripped it firmly, and we escaped out the side door as Mr. Borden called out a protest.

"He used to be the best man west of the Mississippi," she

told me as we headed past the barracks and on toward the Laramie River. "He took Ma's passing hard, and he drinks too much."

"Must be a heavy burden to bear," I observed.

"Well, it won't be for long, I'm told. He takes fever easy, and the pains in his head are real. Laurence and I'll need help running the store, Darby. It makes a fine living, and . . ."

"I'm no storekeeper," I told her. "You don't even know me. We just met a bit ago, and this is really only the second time we've spent so much as an hour together."

"I make up my mind, I go right after a thing."

"Laveda, I'm not much more than a boy, and I've not worn half the wild off my edges. There are lots of mountains I want to see, and even more horses to ride."

"You think about that come winter."

"If I'm lucky, that'll be in Oregon. Tom and I'll pass the season with my sister on her farm. That next spring we'll come through maybe, or the one after that. If that Indian misses his chance and the bears don't care for the taste of my hide."

"You'll never know what you're missing," she said, gripping my fingers so hard they ached.

"Maybe not," I told her. "I'll be hoping you come across something better, though."

She grinned, and we stared at the stars lighting up the late spring sky. Then we walked alongside the river half an hour before she excused herself and returned to the store. I then walked to the camp.

It wasn't hard to find our place. Even in the faint moonlight, Snow's ivory flanks drew my attention. I sat on my blankets and loosened the stiff shirt collar. To my surprise, Marty and Marietta then stepped out of the shadows.

"What's brought you two out here?" I asked, scratching my ears. "I figured you'd be up at the fort, listening to tall tales and war stories."

"Oh, they had stories to tell," Marty assured me. "Then they started on politics. We escaped."

"And besides," Marietta added, "we had something to do." She then presented a thin crust pie, and I stared in surprise.

"She spent all afternoon baking it," Marty said, grinning. "I picked most of the berries myself. She bakes fair for a sister. So, want to eat some of it?"

"I don't understand," I told them. "It should be for your family. I . . ."

"It's meant as a thank you," Marietta explained. "For coming with us. For curing the swamp fever. I planned it for dinner, but then I found out you, well . . ."

"Yeah," I said, glancing nervously toward the lights illuminating the fort. "I met Laveda a while back, and she invited me this afternoon."

"You're not at all what you seem, are you?" Marietta asked. "First you play Mozart on Mrs. Randolph's piano. Next you excuse yourself and escort the prettiest girl on the fort off into the night. I can almost believe some of those stories you tell the boys about killing bears and seeing white buffalos."

"Never killed a bear from choice," I explained, laughing. "As for white buffalos, I might've been a bit tired."

"We going to talk all night or eat pie?" Marty cried. I nodded, and Marietta set the pie on the ground and began cutting slices. It was still warm to the touch, and the three of us devoured it totally, handful at a time. It was even better than Laveda's melons!

"Ever look really hard at the stars, Darby?" Marietta asked as the three of us collapsed in the soft grass above the river.

"Sometimes," I confessed. "I draw pictures and make shapes of them."

"What do you see tonight?" Marty asked.

"I see wagons pulling out . . . early," I answered. "And I think we're apt to need our sleep."

"He's right, Sis," Marty confessed, and Marietta reluctantly agreed. I saw them safely to their camp, then returned to my blankets, shed my clothes, and found a peaceful sleep.

Chapter 4

We moved westward but a short distance from Ft. Laramie that next day. The company seemed reluctant to leave the security of the post, and when Shea located a cluster of hot springs not far from the trail, a halt was ordered. The women especially celebrated the bubbling springs as it afforded a chance to do a thorough scrubbing of linens, clothes, and children. Some of the younger members of our party objected to the rough handling they received—and I believe between lye soap and coarse scrubbrushes a few boys might have lost a pound of hide. But in the end the warm water soothed many an ache, and toward nightfall I even coaxed Shea into the waters.

"It's a fool's labor, of course," he argued. "Trail's just bound to dust us all over again tomorrow."

"Maybe," I admitted, "but it's a fine thing to be clean for once. A bath in the North Platte or the Laramie's one thing, but a real soak makes you feel almost civilized."

"Never knew you to take to civilized ways," Shea said, grinning as he tossed the soap at my head. "Maybe we ought to take you back to Laveda Borden after all."

"A man doesn't have to smell like a skunk to live in the high country," I argued. "A bath now and then might just get you a taste of berry pie, too."

Toward nightfall we had our first visit from Cheyennes.

There were seven of them in all, but you'd guessed it was a small army by the commotion that followed their arrival. People ran around screaming and hollering, searching for rifles, hiding women and children, and preparing for the massacre certain to follow.

"They've only come to trade," Shea announced. I fetched Captain Martinson and a few others, and we joined Tom at the edge of the main camp. We smoked a pipe, and a few odds and ends were swapped. Shea assured the Cheyennes we would stay to the white man's road, and we exchanged a few tales.

After the captain and the others returned to their camp, Shea and I spoke with the Indians a bit more. Their leader, Spotted Horse, complained bitterly about the emigrant trains.

"Too many whites come," Shea translated for us. "They destroy the game, and their animals eat the grass to its roots. The buffalo herds grow smaller. Sickness empties our camps. Why do you bring them here?"

"Yes, it's hard times comin', all right," Shea told them. "Change'll come, though, with or without us."

Shea then produced a flask and exchanged a gulp of spirits with the Cheyennes. Finally he passed it to me, and I took a swig. I thought my throat would catch fire, and my ears felt like bursting. Afterward, I felt oddly lightheaded.

Shea found a jug, and the Cheyennes joined him in emptying it. Me, I contented myself with sitting on a blanket and watching the crazed dancing and singing. When the Indians left, Shea and I gathered our belongings and stumbled to our beds.

"Guess you don't have the taste for spirits, eh, Darby?" he asked when I collapsed in my blankets.

"Likely a good thing," I answered. "There wouldn't be enough corn liquor between here and Oregon for the both of us."

He laughed, slapped me on the back, and took to

singing. I made a point of finding my rest right away. Tom Shea wasn't apt to be at his best come sunrise.

He wasn't. I barely managed to get him in a saddle before the first wagon rolled onto the trail, and I ended up tying his horse to the back of the Martinson wagon while I kept an eye on the trail ahead. Ole Tom passed most of the day slumped over his mount, snoring away to the amusement of Marty and some of the other boys. Around noon, though, I spied a pair of young Cheyennes skirting the left flank of the train, and I roused Shea so he could investigate.

"Cheyennes can be as curious as Illinois-born wagon train scouts," he grumbled.

"Sure, but there's something going on out that way I don't like."

He read the uneasiness in my eyes and rubbed the red from his eyes. We rode out to have a look.

"There," I said, pointing toward a stand of stunted cottonwoods twenty yards from the trail. "See?"

There was a movement in the trees that didn't fit with the wind, and a pair of shadowy figures appeared and vanished in the same instant.

"Likely a pair of pilgrims gone to nature's call," Shea suggested. "Sure's no place for an ambush."

"Somebody's there," I argued. "And they've been there better than an hour now."

Shea shook his head and muttered to himself, but he followed me toward the trees. I circled around one way, and he took the other. As we closed the distance between us and the trees, I half expected a pair of riders to dash out. It didn't happen. Instead we soon found ourselves staring down at a trio of emigrant boys, hobbled like ponies left to graze on the plain, and naked as the day they came into the world.

"Well, I'll be," Shea said, laughing at the squirming youngsters. Their mouths were gagged as well, and they stared up at us in helpless embarrassment.

I recognized the oldest one as the Hazlett's elder son, but I didn't know the others. I climbed down, took my knife, and cut their bonds. Immediately the three plucked pilgrims babbled away about how they'd followed a Cheyenne boy into the trees to do a bit of trading and wound up peeled naked and tied up to boot.

"An old trail game," Shea said, grinning wildly. "Lucky they didn't throw you over a saddle and take you along to their womenfolk. You youngsters'd made a fine supper boiled just right."

The younger boys, who proved to be Bassetts from the rear of the train, took Shea's words for the truth and gazed up in horror. Elliott Hazlett just pleaded for the use of a blanket and a ride back to his wagon.

"Here," I said, loosening the leather straps holding my bedding in place behind the saddle. I tossed him a blanket, then bid him climb up behind me. Shea, on the other hand, reached down, grabbed a Bassett in each arm, and bore them back to the train with less ceremony than he would have taken a pair of skinned rabbits to a cook fire.

The whole train had a fine laugh at their expense, though I guessed they'd soon spin a yarn out of it that would spread their fame far and wide. For my part, I put together a few lines with a tune. That night, around a campfire, I sang the "Ballad of the Platte River Raid" for the enjoyment of all, and ever afterward Elliott and the Bassett boys were remembered for the "bare attack" suffered at the hands of the Cheyennes.

Actually another such occurrence would have been welcomed in the days to come. Life on the trail soon settled into a dull routine. It was rise before the sun, cook breakfast, ready the teams, and set out along the dust-choked trail. Around midday, without pausing, bits of dried buffalo meat and a cold biscuit sufficed for lunch. Finally, as the sun set or the animals wore down, we would make camp. Animals wanted tending, and dinner would be cooked. If it wasn't too late, the company might enjoy a bit of singing or a few tales. Then it was to bed, only to rise again on the morrow and start all over again.

We did manage a few diversions. Among the trail landmarks were a line of chalk cliffs favored by emigrants as a camping place. The cliffs themselves provided a sort of register, and travelers were prone to etch their names into the rock to mark their passing.

"It's just one of the places," I told Marty and his friends when they questioned me about the custom. "Chimney Rock's a favorite spot, as is Independence Rock on the Sweetwater farther west. Shea doesn't think much of the custom, but others plainly do."

"And you?" Marty asked.

"I've left my mark here and there," I confessed. "In the end, it matters more what you hold in your heart. Up there," I added, pointing to the bluff, "the wind'll erase the names, given time."

Time didn't mean much when you were thirteen, I guess. I'd given Marty and the others all the encouragement they needed. They gathered, once camp was made, and snaked their way up the cliff to where the names stopped.

"Best have a look to 'em," Shea suggested, and I went along. I was, after all, sure to get the blame if one of them fell or stepped in a hole.

As it turned out, that wasn't the danger encountered. I followed Marty up the crumbling trail a quarter mile before detecting that most feared of trail sounds. It resembled a clicking or snapping, often joined by a second and third like noise.

"Hold up!" I yelled as Marty's hand reached toward a narrow crevice in the rock. Something shot out toward that hand, only to explode as I fired my Colt.

"Lord, what'd you do that for?" Marty cried, jumping a foot in the air and falling back against my side. "You crazed?"

"No, and I'm not stupid enough to stick my hand into a rattlesnake's mouth, either," I declared, kicking the headless body of a five foot diamondback with my toe. "Don't you know to heed a warning?"

Marty froze in silence, then gazed up nervously.

"I never knew what a rattlesnake sounded like," he explained.

The others nodded as if to echo Marty's words, and I led them aside while I took a long stick and cleared the path of three or four other snakes.

"Aren't you going to kill them, too?" Wyatt Alston asked as I nudged the snakes hither and thither.

"Why?" I asked. "Snakes do a fine job of eating rats and such. You like rats, Wyatt? Me, I never had much trouble with snakes. 'Course, you do need to keep your hands out of their jaws."

I then waved them along up the cliff, but none of them would take a step before I did. Those rattlers had pure taken the exploring spirit out of my companions.

"You never can take your eyes off the trail, can you, Darby?" Marty asked when we reached a smooth, unmarked section of cliff.

"Oh, you can," I told him. "May not live long, though. Lots of things can kill you out this way, and it'll get worse."

"You saved my life," he whispered as Wyatt took a chisel and began etching his name.

"Well, you're certain to return the favor if you have the chance, now aren't you?" I replied.

"Certain," Marty declared, wiping his forehead.

I noticed when we set off again the next day, the children kept a steady watch out for snakes. Two were sighted. Mal Anderson shot the first one, and the Howell boys chopped the second up considerable.

"Wasn't even a rattler," I complained when I saw the dismembered reptile. "Rat snake. We lose a horse to a gopher hole, we'll think about you boys."

Aside from finding spots for our camps and keeping children from getting snakebit, Shea and I devoted ourselves to watching out for trouble and scaring up a bit of fresh meat. The night we camped near Natural Bridge, I shot an antelope, and we had a fair feast. Our camp in that cool, sheltered spot provided a chance to catch our breath. The beauty of the place lent force to the evening prayer meeting, and the water was clear and cool. We filled barrels, and later on the women and men separated and took the opportunity to bathe.

The boys in particular delighted in the bridge. It was really a great hunk of rock that the river had cut the middle out of. The older ones jumped from the top and splashed into the water below. The younger ones swung on ropes. Marietta told me later the girls enjoyed it near as much, but I was kept a considerable distance from the water while they had their chance. Sully Payne and the McIntosh boys were caught peeking, and afterward the fathers in the company kept a wary watch over anybody thought to have a spy's inclination.

Early the next morning Marty appeared with news he'd found an unearthly sight while gathering firewood. He held up an old bow of carved ash which he said he'd found amid a pile of human bones.

"Bones?" I asked nervously. "Were they atop a platform of sorts, maybe covered by a blanket."

"Wasn't any blanket. Just a square of deerskin," he answered. "Ev Gray took that."

Shea, who had overheard it all, turned as pale as I did.

"Get the youngsters together, Darby," Shea said, snatching the bow. "Now!"

I led Marty toward the main camp, and we hurried to assemble the boys and girls. Shea then swallowed deeply and gazed into their puzzled eyes.

"Any of you ever dig up a graveyard?" Shea asked.

They all shook their heads and mumbled to each other.

"Well, somebody's done close to the same thing this mornin'," he explained. "Yonder's a place of the dead. Arapaho or Cheyenne, I'd judge. It's the way they place their dead, high, so the spirit's got a shorter journey to heaven. Now you've gone and robbed the dead, bringin' down on you the worst kind o' bad luck."

"Not me," they quickly pleaded.

"Somebody," Shea said. "I'll put this bow back if I can, but if anybody else's taken anythin', you'd best tell me now. We got to put the place right straight away and pray the spirits'll be satisfied."

"Spirits?" Mr. Gray asked, gripping Ev's shuddering shoulders. "You don't believe in such surely, Shea."

"I believe," Shea replied. "More important, they believe."

Shea pointed toward the hillside where a pair of scowling Indians sat atop ponies. If Gray had doubts, the sullen glares of the riders silenced them. Ev produced a faded breechclout, and other children brought forth bits of this and that. Shea slowly, solemnly led a procession back to the graveyard, and each item was replaced as best was possible.

"Best not disturb a place of the spirits," Shea said when all was returned. "You wouldn't want to bring down a whole tribe on our train, would you? It's the worst kind o' ill fortune, too."

I'm not certain even then they all believed, but Shea's wide eyes were enough to argue against pilfering from scaffolds. So I judged anyway. When we rolled out onto the trail that morning, though, our shadowy riders trailed along.

"Most likely just seein' us clear o' the place," Shea declared.

I thought so, too, but they followed us fifteen miles and were still there when we made camp that night.

"Something's wrong," I declared. "I can feel it. We'd best go talk to them, don't you think?"

"Good enough notion, son," Shea agreed. "Only look to their faces."

I did. Both riders wore black paint now, and the slightest move in their direction sent them riding away.

Captain Martinson had watched those riders, too. He announced his uneasiness when he brought us half a pork pie for our supper.

"What do they want?" the captain asked. "Could they be part of a raiding bunch?"

"No, it's somethin' else," Shea said. "They've got a kind of death mask on their faces. Could be mournin' somebody. Could be to show they're not afraid."

"And it could mean they've sworn to kill," I added, recalling a Sioux who'd worn similar paint in the Big Horn country.

"He's right," Shea admitted.

"But why?" Martinson asked.

"Don't know," Shea answered. "Puzzles me, too. We took the bow and the other things back. Least I think we did."

"I'll muster the company," Martinson declared. "We best have a hard talk with everybody. Could be somebody's hidden away a necklace or maybe a hatchet."

"When we traded with those Cheyennes, the women took a real shine to beaded moccasins," I reminded the captain. "Might be a temptation."

Martinson nodded, then hurried to summon the company.

It surprised no one. The riders had done little to conceal themselves. They were a sort of haunting conscience. But no one seemed to know of any stolen articles.

"You're certain?" the captain cried. "Not even an arrowhead or perhaps a buckskin pouch?"

All shook their heads, and Shea repeated the call.

"If it's somethin' important, and I can't see why they'd followed us for somethin' that wasn't, we could find ourselves crosswise to a whole tribe. Means a lot o' people dyin', folks. Well?"

"It was me, Papa," Marty finally cried out.

"Marty?" I gasped. "Was you I told about the bow."

"It's nothin' so big as a bow, though," he declared as he unrolled a blanket and revealed a wonderfully carved pipe. Its red bowl and intricate stem spoke of great power, and Shea paled instantly.

"It's Arapaho, all right," he said more to me than anybody else. "It's why they're followin'. Boy, you pray they'll take it back and let things lie."

Marty nodded nervously, and Captain Martinson scowled heavily.

"That's all," the captain announced. "We'll settle it if we can."

The company disassembled then, and the captain grabbed Marty by the neck and prepared to lead him back to their wagon. Shea blocked their departure.

"I'll talk to the Arapahos," Shea said, "but the boy's got to come along. It's for him to return the pipe."

"They could kill him," Martinson objected. "Or worse. I'll do it. We'll say I took it."

"Can't," Shea said, handing Marty the pipe. "Best chance we got is they believe the boy didn't know better. And even if they believed your lie, and I don't think you're good enough at it that they would. I'd never save you from 'em."

"He's my son," Martinson complained.

"We'll do our best," I added. "Trust Tom, Cap'n. When you have trade with Indians, you fare better telling the truth. They got a way of seeing through a lie."

"Papa?" Marty asked, trembling as he stared at the pipe.

"No," Martinson insisted. Shea frowned, then turned angrily away. I didn't. Instead, I grabbed Marty by the shirt collar and sat him down.

"I saved your hide once, remember?" I asked him. "Well, what do you figure'll happen when two hundred Arapahos encircle us tomorrow or the next day? Won't be enough to

55

give up the pipe then. We'll need a graveyard of our own."

"Darby, that's uncalled for," the captain barked.

"No, it's just being honest," I argued. "Marty, you got us in a fix, and it's you'll have to work out of it. Coming along?"

The boy got to his feet, stiffened his back, and nodded his head.

"Darby?" Martinson called.

"We'll be close by," I assured the captain. "Do our best, too."

I never was as proud of anybody as I was Marty when we walked behind Shea out to where the two black-faced Arapahos waited. Marty had held up the pipe, and they hadn't turned away as before.

"You look 'em square in the eye and own up to it," Shea advised the thirteen-year-old. "Whatever you do, don't cry. Stand your ground. Act ready for whatever they decide. They'll honor that, maybe even let you go free."

Marty didn't show much confidence, and he kept glancing back over his shoulder as if to see his father. I judged it the worst kind of hardship, the captain keeping his distance.

Shea began speaking to the Indians when they were still a dozen feet away. He gestured to Marty, to the wagon train, then bowed his head.

"Now, boy, tell 'em," Shea said, and Marty explained about taking the pipe, about hiding the truth, then held out the purloined item.

The Indians showed no sign of comprehending, and Shea translated.

"I told 'em you came here without understanding," Shea told Marty. "Nod, showing you agree."

Marty did so, then gazed solemnly at the grim-faced riders. Clearly they were angry. The taller of the two launched a tirade of words at us, then snatched a knife from his waist and waved it at Marty. The boy flinched, but

56

he was too frightened to cry out.

The second Indian intervened.

"Those without understanding must not come here," he spoke in better English than I would have imagined. "You," he added, pointing at Marty, "steal no more from the dead!"

"I won't!" Marty answered.

There was an unspoken promise that another theft would be met with death. The three of us each read it in the wild eyes of the Arapahos. They then turned and rode away. Marty fell against my side, and I helped him regain his senses.

"You've got the Lord's own good fortune," Shea muttered as Captain Martinson raced out to greet his son. "I wouldn't make a practice out o' temptin' death, though."

"No, sir," Marty agreed.

Chapter 5

After Marty's encounter with the Arapahos, most of the company kept respectfully close to camp. Oh, a boy might wander a bit from the trail now and then, and wagons did stray sometimes, but there was a growing respect for the perils of the trail.

Tom Shea and I, on the other hand, passed more and more of our time riding out in advance of the train. Our eyes kept watch for trouble, but except for parties of Indians scouring the plain for game, we rarely saw anyone at all.

The trail itself bid farewell to the Medicine Bow Mountains and dipped south before leaving the southerly-curling North Platte and sweeping westward along the Sweetwater. I welcomed the sight of that rolling river. It was familiar country, a land of gentle grade leading toward the South Pass and the Rocky Mountains. It cut its way through a sea of green and yellow grasses. A company could sometimes make twenty miles a day without wearing out its stock or breaking down its wagons. There was good water in the river, and plenty of good grass in May.

It was that section of the Oregon crossing where a company caught its breath and found its pace. Antelope and buffalo flirted with our path. That proved a fatal mistake, as Shea and I put our rifles to good use. We kept the supper pots full, and the fresh meat lent us strength and raised our spirits.

Most nights Shea and I sat down to dinner with one family or another. It was, I suppose, the company's way of welcoming us at last into their midst. Whether I ate with the Martinsons or not, Marietta usually found some excuse to draw me aside afterward. One time a wheel might need a spot of grease while her father was off on guard. Another time she'd beg a tune from my mouth organ.

"You don't always have to have a reason to ask me to your camp," I told her finally. "You're not so ugly that I object to a bit of conversation or a look at the stars."

"I'm not, eh?" she asked, planting a hand on each hip.

"Some might even say you had a pretty face, though you're a little thin, and your nose's long."

"And you think yourself perfect, I guess!" she responded. "Why, Darby Prescott, you've got a pointed chin, you can scarcely boast a moustache after eighteen years on this earth, and you're impossibly proud!"

"Last time you told me I smell too much like a horse," I reminded her with a grin.

"Yes, there's that, too," she readily agreed.

"So, maybe you should cast your eyes on Mal Anderson," I suggested. "He's tamer, too."

"He swears, and he chases Agnes Payne most shamefully."

"She chases back, I hear."

"Makes it not a bit better," Marietta argued. "Besides, I'm not looking to raise a second brother."

"What are you looking for?" I asked, stopping long enough to search her eyes. "Somebody to help pass the time? An extra buffalo shoulder now and then?"

"A friend."

"You got that easy enough," I told her. "But don't look for a whole lot more'n that."

"And if I do, Darby?"

"You're apt to be disappointed," I warned. "I know this

trail well enough, and I'm a fair hand with horses and rifles. But I never have been much good staying in one place for long."

"Maybe you haven't found the right place," she suggested. "Or the right company."

"Maybe," I confessed. "But I've got a wayfaring soul like Tom Shea, and that makes it unlikely."

Even so we did manage to sing a few songs and read the stars. Some nights the older boys and girls would do a bit of dancing, and twice I paraded Marietta around the floor. My contribution to the entertainment was generally a description of the trail ahead or the recounting of my own journey west. But to be honest, I was more at home with the young ones, teaching them to work hides or salve a horse's sore tendon.

In the middle of May we came at last to that great mound of purple-black stone known as Independence Rock. A long time ago a westbound party had celebrated the Fourth of July there, and they'd christened the place accordingly. Shea and I'd carved our names there, as had countless others, and even Captain Martinson considered the place deserved a scratch of a few letters. We made camp in the rock's shadow and declared a day of rest. After all, Independence Rock also marked the halfway point between Missouri and Oregon. Before you could count to ten, people set off to climb the rock and leave their names.

We weren't the only visitors to Independence Rock. A small Sioux hunting party appeared on the northern bank of the river. They seemed less interested in us than in a small herd of buffalo we'd passed a day and a half before, but Shea ordered the guard to keep a sharp eye out nevertheless.

It wasn't the easiest thing to do, though. A day without hitching teams to wagons or saddling horses brought out the devil in everyone, and while boys swam in the river or played stick and ball in the high grass, they couldn't watch stock. Their fathers gave more care to mending harness or getting in a bit of hunting.

"It's needed, this rest," Captain Martinson declared when Shea and I returned a dozen straying saddle horses. "We're weary of the trail, all of us."

"Some'll be more weary if they're afoot," Shea warned.

"I'll speak to the men," Martinson promised.

In the end, though, I don't think it did much good. Most of the boys ran bare the whole day, and the sun baked them as pink and purple as one of my grandma's plum puddings. Shea and I rode half the evening finding the right berries to make a proper ointment.

"Be a lot o' boys sleepin' on their bellies this night," Shea said as we started dabbing the pasty mixture on youngsters.

"Belly's just as bad," little Silas Payne declared. And so it was! The seven-year-old was burned as red as any Indian.

If sunburnt boys had been the only problem to haunt our stay at Independence Rock, I would have deemed the holiday worthwhile. It wasn't. Sometime during the night, while five of those assigned picket duty slept off their celebrating, our Sioux neighbors paid the pony herd a call. I was sleeping soundly when a rifle discharged, bringing me instantly to my feet. Even as my eyes blinked into focus, a terrible scream split the night, followed by a wave of confused shouting. Horses whined while others splashed across the river.

"Darby, let's ride!" Shea called, and I paused only long enough to pull on some trousers before climbing atop Snow bareback and charging off into the darkness.

The rifle shot had upset the raid, and the culprits, four or five boys scarcely as old as Marty, had fled empty-handed when they spotted Snow's phantom white flanks dancing through the shallows of the Sweetwater. Shea and I chased them a good five miles before satisfying ourselves they were unlikely to return. We then collected those horses that had run across the river and herded them back to the wagon train.

Something about the night told me all was not well, and even before reading the grief etched in the faces of our companions, I knew sad tidings awaited us. Captain Martinson welcomed our appearance, and those who'd lost horses expressed gratitude. But the captain quickly conducted us beyond the horses to where Faith Brown tended Richard Howell.

"If there's something you can do, Mr. Shea, I'd welcome it," she said, motioning to the stricken fifteen-year-old. Richard had managed to raise the alarm by firing his rifle, and he'd sent his brother Robert to collect the other guards. He'd then faced the raiders single-handedly and a knife had opened a great gash in his forehead.

"You got it bandaged," Shea observed, "and he seems quiet enough. Nothin' to do 'cept wait it out."

I think the captain had hoped for some mysterious Indian cure. Mr. and Mrs. Howell soon appeared with Robert and their girl, Jane. Shea told them much the same, and the family gathered to keep vigil over Richard.

"Won't matter much," Shea whispered when we walked back to our own camp. "Boy's eyes are empty. Skull's laid open. He'll be lucky to last past mornin'."

"He was fifteen," I muttered. "Younger'n me."

"Older than the little ones taken by the fever," he reminded me. "Older'n your friend Jamie."

"It's strange, Tom. While we were rounding up the horses, I was thinking how horse raiding's an old game with the Sioux. They ride down and throw a rope over a pony and ride for all they're worth. Somebody else turns around and steals it back, like as not. I was wrong, though. It's no game. Robert's lying there dying."

"Part o' life, Darby. Truth is we've had a fool lucky crossin' up to now. Back in '48 and '50 both, I saw kids snakebit on the North Platte. We lost a girl fallen from a wagon, too, and a man thrown from his horse. By and by it catches up with you."

"I guess so," I mumbled.

We made no miles that next day, either. Seven horses were still missing, and half the men scoured the Sweetwater banks looking for them. All but two were located, and those returned on their own.

As for Richard Howell, he lasted till almost midday. The whole company joined in prayer and awaited word. Captain Martinson announced the bitter news just after supper.

"Well, when do we go after those bloodthirsty savages?" Uriah Anderson cried. "My boy Mallie's just a year older'n Richard. Might've been him!"

"Might've been you," Shea answered. "You were supposed to be there, weren't you, Anderson? Left a boy to stand the night watch by himself. Those Sioux been raidin' horses in this country since the Spaniards let the first o' the four-legged critters run north from Mexico. Can't hold it against 'em for bein' 'emselves."

"Besides," I added, "they've ridden halfway to next week by now."

"He merits justice," Anderson argued. "We've got laws."

"This country's got laws, too," Shea countered. "It tells a company to keep watch, and when they don't, well, we've seen what comes to pass. Best save your comfortin' for the boy's mama and put your energy into diggin' a grave. We lost a day collectin' stock, and we'll have to be off early tomorrow."

Captain Martinson nodded his agreement, and Mal Anderson grabbed a shovel and started toward Independence Rock.

"Darby, show him where," Shea instructed, and I frowned. I knew what needed doing, but it pained me to be the one to explain it to Malcolm or to the Howells.

"He's best buried in the trail," I told them soberly. "That way our ruts can cover the sign, and he'll be safe from animals, or anything else."

"Who'd trouble a grave way out here?" Mrs. Howell asked. "In this lonely, desolate place."

"I've seen it," I told her. "Scavengers dig up bodies for their clothes, especially for boots or rings. I put my best friend in the ground this way, and my mother, too. There's nothing else to do."

"Ought to be a marker," Robert argued.

"We'll carve it there," I said, pointing to Independence Rock. "No one's about to use that for firewood. And we'll remember, won't we?"

"Yes," Mrs. Howell agreed, weeping openly. Robert grabbed the shovel and started digging. Jane sobbed on her father's shoulder, and Mr. Howell himself was unable to hide his feelings. I left them to do what was needed and set off to find Shea.

Instead I came upon Marty and Marietta.

"Hard news," Marietta declared.

"Yes," I agreed.

"Death sure has a way of coming quick on this trail," Marty added. "Makes you wonder who's next."

"You can't afford to think like that," I objected. "It happens. You read over 'em, pray they're at peace, and bury 'em. Trail's too long to take it all to heart."

"How can you be so cold about it?" Marietta complained. "Don't you understand how we feel? I went to school with Richie back home."

"We did our numbers together," Marty explained.

"Yesterday morning we were laughing about how Modesty Zachary ever came by her name," Marietta said, sobbing. "Now he's gone."

"And tomorrow it'll be somebody else," I told her. "You got to go on, though. Can't let it tear at you."

"You're heartless!" she screamed.

"No, it's just that death and me, we're rather well-acquainted. Known each other a fair time now."

I sighed and sat down on a flour barrel. Waves of

memories were threatening to overwhelm me, but I shook them off. Taking a deep breath, I shared Mama's last day, the cold touch of her hand when I said my good-bye, the sharp edge of the pain that tried to cut all the feeling from me.

"And now you're hard as Independence Rock, aren't you?" she asked, shaking from head to toe. "You don't need anybody or anything. I'm not like that," she said, resting her head on my shoulder. "I hurt."

Marty took her hands and tried to lead her aside, but I stopped their retreat.

"I do my best to look after myself," I told them. "There's nobody else to do it, you know. It's not a job I crave, though. To tell the truth, it's not a bad thing, having a shoulder to lean on from time to time."

"You're a fraud, Darby Prescott," she said, rubbing her eyes. "And a better friend than you'll know."

"No, just a wayfarer crossing the Rockies," I argued.

"I don't believe a bit of it," she told me. "And I'm going looking for berries tomorrow. What we need is another pie."

"I'll help," Marty said, tossing his hat in the air.

That's it, I thought. Let the sadness go. And when they turned and headed off to pay their respects to the Howells, I continued on toward my camp.

I was repairing a moccasin lace when Shea appeared.

"Robert Howell's waitin' on you, son," he told me. "Says you promised to help him carve a memorial."

"I did," I confessed. "I was hoping he might find somebody else to take him up there, though. I haven't got much heart for it."

"Best not break promises, Darby."

"Yeah, I know," I said, tying off the lace and rising to my feet. "You think I'm getting to be too much of a loner, Tom?"

"You?" he asked, laughing. "I scarce see you anymore. You've got that little Martinson gal hangin' on your every word, and half the little ones in this company'd take you in for a brother, I'll wager."

"I worry about it some."

"Bein' a loner?"

"Yes," I told him. "Keeping everybody at a distance."

"Isn't altogether a bad way to be," he argued. "If you don't take folks to heart, you don't spend a lot o' hours cryin' over the things that happen to 'em. Got nobody 'cept yourself to please. Eat what you choose, live where you care to, and do what strikes your fancy. A man alone knows peace."

"Does he?" I asked. "Doesn't he just know quiet and loneliness? I don't know I care for either, Tom. I'm more comfortable in a duststorm or a muddle of boys down at the river. Solitude gnaws at me like a winter chill."

"I've noticed," he told me. "It's why I was a bit shy 'bout takin' you with me into the high country. You had your sister and her husband on that farm, and a pretty little baby to spoil."

"But what I needed was a father," I told him. "I know you say you can't be one to me, but you were. You taught me to stand tall, to know who I am, and you've saved my hide from my own mistakes. That's what a father does, isn't it?"

"Not as I've seen."

"I've never thanked you for it. I guess it's time. Thanks, Tom Shea."

"So what are you lookin' for from me now, a nose wipe?" he asked, turning nervously away. "I told you that boy Robert's waitin'."

"Guess I'd best get along then," I said, turning back toward the main camp.

I helped Robert Howell etch his brother's name in the rock and mark the year of his passing. I added a testament to his courage, then sat on the slope while Robert told how the other guards were all gone, and he could find no help until it was too late.

"I hate 'em, you know," Robert said as tears rolled down his cheeks. "Those men should've helped."

"They bear a heavy burden, knowing that," I said. "But it's done, and you can't hate everyone."

"You don't understand," the boy complained.

"Don't I?" I asked. "I hated my own father for bringing my mama West when he knew the journey would prove too much for her. I was too stupid to realize he missed her more than I did, and he didn't mean her to die. Best to leave things to sort themselves out. You got enough to worry about growing tall and helping your folks. No point adding a lot of hate to that."

"You ever have a brother, Darby?" he asked.

"Several," I answered. "Haven't seen the older ones in four, five years now."

"Any younger ones?"

"One," I whispered. "He died a long time ago now."

"Ever miss him?"

"Only when I think about it," I confessed. "Now let's get along back to camp. There are chores likely waiting for both of us."

Chapter 6

After praying over Richard Howell's grave that next morning, we formed a circle beside the lead wagon. Captain Martinson then spoke rather eloquently to us of the trail, both that behind us and that still ahead.

"These scouts of ours say we've come halfway," the captain announced. "Well, it hasn't been without cost. Today we mourn, but tomorrow we must set aside our grief. We can no longer look back on the homes left behind. Now our eyes must gaze ahead, to the future."

It was a good speech, and the words were boldly spoken. It was a tonic to our despair, and I thought more of the captain for his having spoken.

The company soon dispersed, and each of us set about the varying tasks necessary for our company to resume its westward march. Shea and I led the way, and as Independence Rock faded from view, I tried, as Captain Martinson had urged, to sweep the death encountered there from my memory.

"Saw you with the younger Howell boy," Shea remarked as we rode. "For a loner, you sure seem to be takin' a lot o' folks to heart."

"Yeah," I admitted. "Gone soft in the head I guess."

"Well, it's been known to happen on the trail."

"Sure. I even heard the tale of how Three Fingers Shea

took in an Illinois orphan once upon a time."

"Made him into a fair horseman, I understand. Little thin on horse sense sometimes, though."

I grinned, and he kicked his horse into a trot. We were lagging a bit, and he soon galloped back among the company, hollering that they'd winter on the Snake at that pace. Drivers and oxen responded with fresh energy, and we regained our vigor.

The trail along the Sweetwater, called by some the Sweetwater road, followed a line of hills to the north and distant ranges of mountains to the south. The Sweetwater Rocks often resembled hard crumbs of bread scattered north of the river. The range of hard granite slopes sometimes afforded welcome wood and shelter, as the Sweetwater road crossed a treeless plain that occasionally turned into deep sand that trapped wagons. More and more we found ourselves lightening wagons by carrying belongings or tying them atop saddle horses.

Four days out of Independence Rock we came upon the next major landmark of the trail. Devil's Gate, it was called, because the Shoshonis and Arapahos told of a legendary devil who had caused the great gap in the ridge while fleeing a band of spirited warriors. It was a haunted place, for ancient burial scaffolds clung to the heights on each side of the opening. Below, alongside the trail, lay the graves of emigrants. Among them was a stone cairn that held the remains of a small girl taken by fever years before—Tom Shea's sister.

We'd visited the place before, in '48 and again coming east. Most times Shea's chin was like stone, and his eyes rarely betrayed his feelings. Not so at Devil's Gate. He was prone to leaving flowers there, or perhaps a bit of bright ribbon. I knew the moment I first spied Devil's Gate, far in the distance, that we would ride there again.

"It's a fine place to make camp," Shea told Captain Martinson. "After half a week of buffalo chip fires, we ought to relish a few cottonwood branches. There's shelter from the wind, good grazing, and fresh springs."

"Yes," I readily agreed. "But it's bewitched as well. There are burial places," I said, nervously eyeing Shea. "Best have a serious talk with the young ones. It's treacherous climbing, and there's the danger of trifling with the scaffolds, too."

Captain Martinson frowned at the words. Marty was close enough by to receive his father's scowl, and the captain soon busied himself riding throughout the train, speaking firmly to the others of the need to respect the burial grounds. Shea and I, meanwhile, vanished in a storm of traildust as we headed alone to Devil's Gate.

It was, as I'd said, a bewitched place. Loose pieces of cloth flapped from the burial scaffolds above, producing an eerie impression that somebody up there was watching. The wind whined through the gap, singing a chill, haunting refrain. To make matters worse, Shea sat stonefaced atop his horse, then slowly dismounted.

"Want me to come along?" I asked as he began plucking yellow flowers from the prairie.

"Suit yourself," he mumbled. "You been before."

Yes, I thought, but before you made me feel a particle welcome. Now, well, maybe death was heavy on his mind as well.

If it was, he didn't confess it to me. He spread the flowers out atop the rocks, then stroked the ground tenderly. Whatever words he shared with the spirit of his sister were imparted silently, and he shared them neither then nor later. I sat nearby, offering what comfort my presence might provide. But it did nothing to chase the redness from his eyes or lift his spirits.

That night, when the others made camp nearby, I recounted the Shoshoni version of the tale, complete with a horrific tusked monster who stomped the life out of more than a few of the warriors. The children listened with wide eyes, and I noticed more than a few kept their blankets a bit closer to their wagons than usual.

"Been better to play 'em a tune or two," Shea said when we warmed our hands over a twilight fire. "Soon enough they'll have hard times on their hands."

"Didn't keep you from telling me," I reminded him.

"Oh, you had ears for it all, Darby," he said, nodding in a far-off manner. "You pestered me with questions night and day, and you wouldn't have a tale postponed."

"They're not so different," I assured him.

"Sure, they are," he grumbled. "They don't have the hardness. They see things, but they don't remember 'em. Fool pilgrims could've eaten a week on the greens they've seen today. There's a solid mile o' wild onions growin' here, and they didn't dig up a single one."

"Likely feared of disturbing the spirits," I suggested. "Or just tired."

"Be hungry later. Soon the chokecherries'll be out. Like as not the fools won't notice."

"You're being awful hard on 'em just now."

"It's a hard trail we're comin' on," he grumbled. "Saw some Sioux tonight a few miles off. Was near here we had our tangle with 'em last summer."

"Yeah," I said, sighing. "Maybe we should take a turn at the guard."

"We got enough to do, boy," he remarked. "But you keep your eyes open."

"I always do," I assured him. "I'm not the one takes a nip at the jug, am I?"

"No, guess you aren't," he admitted, cracking half a smile. "I could use a nip tonight."

I reasoned he was entitled, too, what with the memories at that place. I confess I was glad no spirits were at hand.

Our next landmark on the trail was Split Rock. There was a notch cut in the distant ridge visible a full day's traveling away. I often thought it resembled a gunsight, and

I told those who'd listen an improbable tale of how it sighted in on the Big Horn Mountains, telling those with the eyes to see that bountiful game lay in that direction. The Big Horns were far to the north, of course, and nowhere close to our path. But when I described the great elk I'd shot there and told of the buffalo hunt when I'd ridden with Shea's Crow friends, the youngsters supposed truly the notch must have been put there to point the way north.

At Split Rock we encountered our first visitors since the unwelcome raiders at Independence Rock. When I first saw the dust they raised, I feared the Sioux Shea had spotted. It turned out they were Shoshonis come to trade, and I think we all breathed easier after that discovery.

Among the Indians were Beaver and Snake Boy, nephews of the feared chief Two Knives. I'd hunted with both, and I found myself greeted with grins, then wrestled off my horse and set upon by both. Startled members of our party prepared to come to the rescue, but I threw Snake Boy over my hip, then wriggled free of Beaver and proclaimed my triumph.

"You are stronger," Beaver remarked as he brushed the dust from his chest.

"Buffalo meat," I told them. "Remember, the buffalo spirit looks after me."

Snake Boy frowned. We'd been hunting together when the white buffalo confronted me. Snake Boy had never quite forgiven me for seeing the beast while they were elsewhere. Soon, though, a smile returned as they told me of spring hunts and new rifles traded off a Mormon train the week before.

"Hope they didn't trade with the Sioux, too," Shea said, gazing back up the trail. "Could have some trouble if they did."

"Sioux, here?" Beaver asked. "I must tell the others."

But even the presence of Sioux on the Sweetwater didn't

deter the Shoshoni traders from having a go at the company. I led a party of boys and girls into the hills to collect firewood, and we also gathered wild onions and turnips, not to mention some sweet grass to flavor the flames. The Shoshonis were especially happy to sniff the burning sweet grass as they believed it invoked the attentions of benevolent spirits. And after dinner the Indians danced and sang for our amusement. We then returned the favor.

Early that next morning as we broke camp, Beaver appeared with a sleek black stallion to challenge Snow and myself to a race around the camp.

"Pure foolishness that," Shea complained. "We've got miles to ride this day."

I could see past his words to the sparkle in his eye, though.

"Can't ride my horse into the ground with so far to go," I told Beaver. "Of course, if there was a wager involved . . ."

"Yes, yes," he readily agreed. "The winner will take both horses."

I gazed hard at the black. I wasn't about to lose Snow. He was more than a horse, after all. He was part of me, and a tie to the past besides.

"I don't know," I said, scratching my ear.

"Ever know anything without wings to catch you on that animal?" Shea whispered. "The black's a beauty. Worth a hundred dollars in Oregon."

I considered that. It was true enough. So was the fact that Beaver could ride with the best of them. It would be a close race, all right. Already the Shoshonis were engaging in a healthy amount of wagering with members of our company, and I found myself boxed in. It was as though I were upholding the honor of the train. I reluctantly agreed, then stripped Snow of the considerable weight normally carried. I even chose to ride bareback.

Beaver did likewise. As we gazed into the intensity of each other's eyes, Shea and Snake Boy marked off the course. A pair of kerchiefs were tied to a cottonwood two hundred yards up the trail, and the first to retrieve one and return would be the winner.

Snow stomped the ground in anticipation, and I readied myself for the start. Captain Martinson tossed a third kerchief in the air, and when it touched the ground, I urged Snow into a gallop. Beaver likewise kicked the big black into motion, and the contest began.

Indian boys cut their teeth racing horses, and to most it might have seemed an unequal match. Snow was Nez Perce, though, bred to run through the clouds of the Wallowa Valley, and I knew horses better than I knew people. Snow and I melted into each other as we rode, and that big black, for all its grace and power, lacked the heart to surge past us. I cut ahead, reached out to snatch the kerchief on the left, then turned Snow back toward the wildly gesturing crowd and prayed we could hold on.

It wasn't easy. Beaver had a heart, too, and he kept the big black thundering after us. I could feel the hot breath of the horse on my elbow. But try as it might, the Shoshoni stallion could not nose ahead of Snow. The ivory horse blazed across the line first, and I rolled off Snow's side into the arms of three dozen cheering pilgrims.

"It was him!" I told them as I hugged Snow's lathered neck. "Lord, did ever a horse run like that?"

Everyone agreed it was, indeed, a ride to remember. And even in losing, I knew Beaver would be remembered as well. He sadly handed over the big black, which I was loathe to take.

"Don't shame him before his people," Shea whispered. "Take the horse and say something."

I did take the stallion, but words wouldn't come. Exhaustion had finally devoured them. Instead I gripped Beaver's arms, and he did likewise. We grinned, and the Shoshonis cheered.

"Next time I will win," Beaver boasted.

"I'll be able to afford the loss then," I said, nodding toward the black. "I trust you won't be walking."

"Beaver?" he asked with wide eyes. "I have stolen more horses than you have ridden. Watch yourself, Buffalo Dreamer. The Sioux are still near, and they, too, know how to rob a man's horses."

I nodded to him. Buffalo Dreamer, he'd called me. It was the dream I'd carried in his uncle's camp, and I recalled the weeks we'd passed together chasing winter from the Rockies. Beaver, too, seemed to recall, for he lifted me off my feet and gave me a hug like a grizzly, nearly squeezing the life from me. I fell earthward, wheezing as I fought for air. He laughed, declared it was soft living with the white men, and promised me a hunt when next we met.

"Perhaps that will be soon," I told him.

"Not soon," he said, frowning. "You have your road to ride, and I have trading to do."

I nodded my understanding. And yet I also knew life was a circle, and paths hadn't a way of crossing each other again.

Maybe if the Shoshonis had come, or perhaps if we hadn't held the horse race, someone might have noticed that not everyone was in line, ready for the day's journey. As it was, we were four, maybe five miles past Split Rock when Captain Martinson and Joseph Howell rode out to relay the dire news.

"It's my boy Robert," Howell told us. "He's taken my spare saddle horse and gone off hunting."

"By himself?" I cried. "Little fool. He knows better!"

"Not by himself," Captain Martinson explained. "The elder Foster boy, Henry, and Ollie Zachary are missing as well."

"The younger Fosters say they went off hunting," Howell added. "Seems they got a headful of stories from the Shoshonis, wild talk about how a boy proves himself by shooting buffalo. Robert saw some grazing south of the river this morning. I'm sure they went that way."

"Hope you're wrong," Shea said, frowning. "That's where the Sioux were, too."

"Lord, no," Howell lamented. "I lost one boy to those heathens. Not Robert, too."

"What's to be done?" Captain Martinson asked. "We can't stop. Should we send somebody back to look?"

"Well, I'm for sure going," Howell declared. "My boy's back there."

"And your wife and daughter are with the train," the captain pointed out. "You don't know the country, Joseph. It's better to hope they'll come to their senses and return of their own accord."

"And if the Sioux . . ." Howell began.

"Then they're dead already," Shea declared somberly. "Too old to be taken in."

"You know Indians," Howell argued. "Shea, lead me to them. We'll offer them a trade. Maybe they'll . . ."

"And if those Sioux are up ahead, you'll leave the train to roll right along into the middle of 'em?" Shea asked. "No, can't go, Cap'n."

"I can," I volunteered. "I know this country well enough."

"We'll organize a party," Captain Martinson declared.

"No," I said, glancing at Shea. "Best for one man to go, eh, Tom? One's not likely to be seen. Or noticed."

"No, Darby," the captain argued. "I won't have another boy out there lost."

"Been a long time since I was a boy," I countered. "I like Robert. Maybe if I'd looked after him a bit more, like Richard would have, he'd be walking along beside your wagon, Mr. Howell. Tell 'em, Tom. I'll be all right."

"Give him a couple of spare horses so he can swap off," Shea advised. "That white's had a day of it already. And if he finds 'em afoot, they'll need a way back."

"Rudy Foster's got a pair of gray mares," Howell pointed out. "I'm sure he can spare them for the purpose at hand.

I'd like this better if I went along."

"Only make it harder," I assured him. "I'm used to hard riding, and if there's need, Snow can get me out of harm's way."

The white horse dipped his head and snorted. Captain Martinson nodded his agreement, and Howell set off to coax the grays from the Fosters.

I set out half an hour later, armed with an extra pistol and my rifle. I didn't think much of fighting Sioux, though. I'd had a tangle with them once, and I didn't have fond memories of it. They were ferocious in battle, seemed to fear nothing, and had a way of chasing the nerve out of the most stout-hearted of enemies. I shuddered to think Robert or the others had fallen into their hands.

I didn't exactly have a plan as I rode east and south. I hunted by instinct, and my intuition told me that if those three were in trouble, they'd likely found the buffalo . . . and maybe the Sioux. If they were still on horseback, they'd stand out on the treeless plain. If not, there were just so many places to hide.

I did, in fact, locate a band of riders about three miles south of Split Rock. They were bare-chested, though, and far too brown for my liking. We eyed each other for a while, and I could tell they were pondering whether or not Snow and the grays were worth the risk I posed. I rested my rifle on my knee to help them decide, and they galloped off to the east.

Not long thereafter I spotted a curious sight. In the midst of a mound of boulders, I saw what appeared to be a flash of yellow. I stopped and concentrated on the rocks, but I now spotted nothing. I might have ridden on had I not recollected Robert's straw-blond hair.

"Best have a look," I whispered to Snow as I turned toward the rocks. Ahead a pair of Sioux swept across the horizon, and I again readied the rifle. They did not approach, though. And when I reached the rocks, I heard a loud cry of welcome.

"Lord, Darby, we thought ourselves stewed proper for sure!" Henry Foster exclaimed as he climbed out from the rocks.

"We went after the buffalo," Oliver Zachary added. "Then the Indians came."

I gazed at the two of them. I think they were both fourteen, but standing there, shaking like elms in a high wind, you wouldn't have thought it.

"So where's Robert?" I asked.

"Didn't he send you?" Ollie asked, sweeping his sweat-soaked blond hair back from a wrinkled forehead. "We lost two of the horses, and he took the other one and rode for help."

"He's the youngest of the bunch, and half an inch short of your chin, Henry Foster!" I shouted. "How'd you let him go like that?"

"Let him?" Ollie asked, swallowing hard. "He had the horse. Wouldn't let us consider elsewise."

"He's a good rider," Henry argued. "He's sure to be all right."

"He's sure to've been run down by the Sioux," I muttered. "All right. Get atop those horses. We're going back."

"Without Robert?" Henry asked.

"Figure we can take on a Sioux hunting party, the three of us?" I asked, shaking my head. "Come on."

They mounted the grays and followed me westward in sober silence. My heart was heavy, too. I couldn't stomach the notion of little Robert lying on the plain stuffed with arrows, but I had the others to consider.

Beaver solved that problem. I'd scarce ridden a mile from the rocks when he appeared with a dozen companions.

"So, you hunt white men now," he said, grinning. "Wisdom has found you at last, my friend."

"Taking 'em back to the train," I explained. "One's still missing."

"The Sioux have him," Beaver said, leading me toward a nearby ravine. There was a muddle of tracks, and the sign of a struggle. More telling, a pair of trousers and a yellow shirt were flung into some chokecherry bushes.

"Robert's," Ollie declared.

"How far is their camp?" I asked.

"Not far," Beaver said. "There are twenty lodges. Too many," he said with a frown.

It was true. There might be a hundred Indians in a camp that large, far more than we'd seen signs of. But if they'd taken him there, he was likely still alive. Perhaps, leaning toward the small side as he did, Robert might be adopted into the tribe.

"I need your help," I told Beaver.

"My friend, there are too many," Beaver said, clasping my arms. "And they would come after us. My own camp is too near, and we have few warriors."

"I know," I said, nodding my understanding. "A raiding party stands a poor chance at best. What I want you to do is get these two back to the train. You'll do that, won't you?"

"Yes," Beaver said, his eyes betraying alarm. "And you?"

"Will see if I'm as good a thief as you are," I explained.

"No, my friend," Beaver argued. "Even the buffalo spirit won't hide a white man on a pale horse from the eyes of the Sioux."

"Night won't be so long in coming," I replied. "And Snow runs fair, remember?"

He gazed grimly at my pistols as if to say they would be more help. But he objected no more. Instead, he and his companions escorted Henry Foster and Ollie Zachary westward. I returned to the rocks and awaited the cover of night.

Once darkness settled in, I had little trouble tracking the Sioux camp. Fires blazed brightly, and the voices of the singers carried miles across the empty plain. Robert was even easier to spot, for his pale skin and yellow hair were a stark contrast to the bronze complexions of the Indians.

White boys, as a rule, make poor captives. They whine a bit too much, and they lean toward laziness. As for Robert, he was too thin and pale to survive much want. On the other hand, he was a fit subject for the attentions of the Sioux children, who busied themselves poking and flaying their captive as was the custom. Robert, stripped down to his drawers, spit and screamed and kicked out at his attackers in a way that had them unsettled.

It tore at my heart. And when the drum finally died, and the children stumbled off to find their beds, I tied Snow securely to a small cottonwood and crept toward the encampment.

Shea would have called it a fool's play, and likely it was. But the Sioux weren't expecting visitors, and with a pair of loaded revolvers, I could do a fair share of damage to any who happened along. Snow had rested a bit and was ready for hard riding. Robert wasn't apt to raise many complaints. I did, in fact, have but a single close call. An old woman left her lodge as I approached it, and she might have seen me if her eyes had been sharper. Instead she hurried past unawares and vanished into the tall grass beyond the camp.

Robert was securely bound to a cottonwood by buckskin straps about the chest and just below both knees. My knife sliced neatly through the straps, but the touch of cold steel brought a whimper from his dozing mouth, and it was all I could do to cover his mouth before he sounded out an alarm.

"Hush," I whispered. "Want to get us both killed? I'm taking you home."

For an instant he seemed not to understand. Then recognition flooded his eyes, and he collapsed against my side. I threw him over my shoulder as I might have carried a sack of flour and hurried toward Snow. Seconds after I got Robert onto the horse, someone discovered he was gone. A chorus of howls resounded through the night, and I hurried up into the saddle and nudged Snow into a trot.

It didn't take long for the Sioux to set out after us. In daylight I could have taken an evasive path through the hills to the north, maybe hidden for a time in a cave. But with the moonlight pouring down from a cloudless sky, the only shape in sight was Snow's white flank. The Sioux spotted us straight away and hurried their pursuit.

Sioux ponies were bred for the buffalo hunt. They had within them a burst of speed that could carry a warrior into a herd and back out before the jagged point of a horn could rip flesh off horse or rider. They were the best animals on earth for a short chase.

Snow could run with any horse on earth over a quarter mile or more, but in the short run he lost ground to the Sioux. Soon I could feel the buzz of arrows behind us, and the taunts of the warriors grew terrifyingly close. A rifle boomed out, but its ball fell wide of the mark. I swallowed hard, forced Robert's head down, then grabbed my pistol and unloaded three hurried shots at our pursuers. I heard a yell, but whether the result of wounds or a reaction to my shots, I couldn't be certain. Snow responded with renewed effort, and the onrushing Sioux finally began to fall behind.

"Just a little while more," I whispered as I felt Snow fight for breath. "Not far now."

The shouts were mere whispers on a distant wind now, and I began to sense we'd escaped.

"Easy, boy," I said as I began to slacken the pace. "Whoa."

Snow had already begun to lose his pace, though, and when I located a ravine in the dim light, I slipped within its natural concealment and rolled off Snow's back. Robert jumped down as well, and we both stroked my weary horse's warm nose. Snow heaved and shuddered, then suddenly dropped to his knees and collapsed altogether.

"No, boy," I pleaded, tugging at his great lathered head.

"Don't go down, Snow. We'll find the river. A good drink's all you need."

It wasn't true, though. Snow thrashed around violently, and I saw for the first time the splash of red that leaked from beneath my saddle. One arrow had found the mark after all. My gallant horse had run himself to death so that I could again escape from my own recklessness.

"He's dying?" Robert asked, touching the bloody spot.

"Don't see how he managed it," I said, staring bitterly at the arrow. Its point was clearly slicing into Snow's left lung, robbing him of life even as I watched. It would have been generous to hurry death, but a bullet would have brought the Sioux, and I lacked the heart to use my knife on the horse I had both loved and relied upon.

"It's my fault," Robert muttered. "Guess it was awful stupid, us going off like that."

"I'd say so," I told him.

"You lost a good horse."

"Yes," I agreed as Snow thrashed about a final time, then grew quiet. "Help me get the saddle," I told Robert. "They're hard to come by out here."

He trotted over and began working loose the cinch. I removed the blanket and gazed a long last time at Snow's prone figure.

"Here I leave behind the last beloved creature I shall know," I whispered as I threw the saddle over my shoulder and turned away. "Come on," I bade Robert. "It's a fair way."

"I'd be better off if that arrow'd hit me instead," he said as I passed him the bloody blanket. "Pa's sure to kill me."

"He's worried sick about you," I said. "And the company may have a laugh at you, coming into camp plucked near as clean as a chicken ready for the pot. But I figure anybody's spent a night as a Sioux captive can get through it."

"Guess I should make a story of it, eh?"

"No question to that. You put Snow's part in, hear?"

"I will," he promised. "I owe you, Darby."

"Yeah, you owe me a horse," I answered. "Someday, when you're a rich farmer in the Willamette Valley, I'll expect payment. A tall white one'd be best. Nez Perce maybe."

"Do my best."

"Sure," I said, feeling his hand on my shoulder. "Know you will."

Chapter 7

"Well, it's likely for the best," Shea said when I shared the news upon our return to the train an hour short of dawn. "A man who rides this country atop a white horse marks himself for an early end. Spirits may have known it. They sent you that black stallion, didn't they?"

"Guess so," I confessed.

But that next day, even as the Shoshoni horse ate up the miles, it did nothing to fill the hole left in my heart by Snow's passing.

From the sandy, sunscorched Sweetwater road we turned south into the South Pass of the Rocky Mountains. From the moment the first wheel of the Martinson wagon started up the long, grinding slope, we were beset by heavy rains. For once it was fog and mist that swallowed the train instead of dustclouds. Winds whined out of the mountains and drove daggers of sleet into wagon crevices. Children huddled together against the growing cold, and animals screamed their displeasure.

The big black seemed to enjoy the intemperate climate, for his feet were as sure as a goat's. Other horses found the slippery terrain less certain, though, and three different men were badly thrown while approaching the summit of South Pass. Mr. McIntosh landed badly and fractured his leg. Fortunately his boys, Randy and Ray, were able to take on their father's duties.

I worried about the little ones. It was awful easy for a child to slip and find a wagon wheel or an ox's feet rumbling down upon him. Ev Gray rescued his little brother Cameron from just such a fate, and Theola Dixon's father deftly avoided running her down when she stepped in a mudhole.

"Curse this rain!" Marietta exclaimed the night we camped on the far side of the pass.

"No, rain's a blessing," I told her. "It's the heat and the dry stretches that ought to worry you. You get so thirsty you'd gulp mud if you could find it. And besides, there's lots worse ahead."

Some of it wasted little time in arriving. Toward midnight the first snowflakes stung my nose. I blinked my eyes open and stared in surprise at the delicate white shawl nature had laid across our camp. Soon the cries of the children split the air, and fires crackled into being. Coughs and shivers haunted the night, and when the snow resumed, I felt its sharp teeth.

We wound up passing blankets and buffalo hides to those in need, and families were packed together under canvas overhangs. Others huddled beside their fires and prayed for a break in the weather.

Marietta was everywhere, helping with the young ones, offering corn fritters to the hungry, or rubbing the cold out of those who lacked the energy. She sang softly to the babies or read to their older brothers and sisters. I admired her for it all the more when she enlisted Marty and some of the older children to help.

"Can't do it all," she declared when I helped her to her wagon. She was nigh frozen herself. I managed to talk her into shedding gloves and shoes before Mrs. Martinson appeared and got things in hand.

"You'll bring my shoes back, Darby?" Marietta asked.

"Once they're dry," I promised. I then set her things near

a fire and dried myself at the same time. Snow continued to pepper the mountainside, but there were breaks in the clouds, and I knew that storm, like all others, would pass.

We found the trail frozen and treacherous come morning, so a holiday was declared while prayers were spoken for a thaw. Families filled their water barrels with melting snow, cooked food over fires plagued by wet wood, and then devoted their efforts to building snow creatures or engaging their neighbors in snowball skirmishes.

Mrs. Brown brewed up a powerful tonic of vinegar and molasses which she used to dose those with a cough, and I raided a hollow cottonwood of a considerable store of honey. Boiled and mixed with a sarsaparilla tea, it was a rather more welcome remedy.

The snows finally relented toward the middle of the afternoon, and the skies parted so that the company got its first good look at the peaks of the Rocky Mountains. Their snowy shoulders and gleaming spires stunned those viewing them the first time, and even old friends like myself and Tom Shea took time to marvel at their grandeur.

"Was there ever such beautiful country?" Marietta whispered as she gripped my arm.

"Up north a bit the Tetons tower above the Snake River," I told her. "Tom and I passed a time in a cabin there. It's as fine a place as I've known."

"Why'd you leave?" she asked.

"Same reason as always, I guess," I told her. "Your feet get the itch to move on. There are other places to see, buffalo to hunt . . ."

"Don't you ever tire of moving around?"

"Sometimes, but seeing new places, well, it brightens you some. Like right now. I can read it in your eyes."

"Yes, it's beautiful, Darby, but you wait till I'm home. That's when you'll truly see me smile."

I frowned. I hadn't known a place to call home since leaving Pike County, and now the farm there was just another place I'd left behind.

"So what's next?" she whispered as I started to leave.

"More of the same. Then there's a great sandy plain leading to the Green River. We'll ride a ferry, do some trading, and then head into the mountains themselves. Up the winding trail to Ft. Bridger, then on to Bear Lake, Ft. Hall, and the Snake River. Finally down the Columbia along to the Willamette."

"Rivers and mountains, huh?" she asked. "Tell me about Oregon."

"It's not just one place, of course," I said, closing my eyes and remembering. "To begin with, it's dry and sandy. Then there are mountains and great, towering forests."

"I don't care about the country," she told me. "I want to know about the people. The towns."

"I don't know much about towns. I'm not too fond of 'em, Marietta."

"And how do you feel about that mouthful of a name? Wouldn't Etta be easier?"

"Sure," I said, grinning. "But it won't help me describe what I never pay much attention to. Oh, I've been to Oregon City, The Dalles, even to Portland, but there's not much to say. They've got mercantiles and churches. Saloons, too. Don't know they're too different from Independence or St. Louis except by size."

"You lived on a farm with your father."

"And my sister Mary, her husband Mitch, and their baby. Till Papa died anyway."

"Was it a good farm?"

"As farms go, I suppose. We had an orchard there. I always did like fruit. But I never had the patience for farming. It was just work and more work. Papa, he loved to work the fields, and his face would light up come harvest."

"There's something magic about tasting the first ear of your corn crop," Captain Martinson declared as he joined us.

"Not to me," I said, frowning. "Just means the work's over for a bit."

"Darby, I think Shea'll be wanting your help," the captain explained. "He's got a small army of youngsters down at the Anderson's fire, and he's telling how he trapped a grizzly a few years back. I don't think he's got your talent with a yarn."

"He can spin tales that'd curl your hair," I argued. "And half'd be true."

I saw it was merely an excuse to shoo me from Marietta's side, though, so I shook my head and trotted off. Shea was, indeed, sitting beside the Anderson fire, describing grizzly claws and grizzly teeth, and the children alternately shrieked and shuddered. I appeared at the crucial moment when the bear was about to split him open, and he spotted me out of the corner of his eyes. His gaze then fell on the three Kruger girls, all curled into a blob near his feet. I made a low growl and pounced on all three. They screamed, leaped a foot in the air, and raced for their papa. The rest of the audience scattered a moment, too. Shea slapped my back and bellowed out a laugh.

Even after they calmed down and realized there was no grizzly in sight, a few of the littler ones insisted a bear had truly visited the fire that night. For my part, I sat beside Shea as he concluded his story with a fine narrative of escape.

"Tell us another," Marty then pleaded, and others begged as well.

"If you truly want a tale of bears, here's your man," Shea said, opening my shirt so that the jagged scars left by a grizzly's claws danced in the light. I then showed them the claws dangling from my bone choker, and a hush settled over the camp.

"It's how I won Snow, my white pony, from the Nez Perce," I explained. "Was years ago now, and we were riding ahead of the Prescott train, captained by my father. I was just fool enough to ride past a Nez Perce camp that was all torn up by a maddened grizzly, then get myself lost on the mountainside. Next thing I know, this mountain of a bear's thundering down on me, bellowing out so you'd think the world was coming to an end. He raised his paws up, blocking out the sun, and I aimed my rifle and fired. The ball tore through his heart, but there was enough life left to him so that he took a swat at me, ripping my shirt and leaving the reminder you see today."

"Must've been scary," little Silas Payne said as he walked over and touched the place where the knitting flesh had left the marks.

"I was close to witless," I confessed. "It's a wonder my hair didn't turn white."

"And the Indians gave you a horse?" Marty asked.

"That bear had killed some of their people," I explained. "It was sort of a reward, I guess you'd say. And Snow was as fine a horse as a man ever rode."

I caught sight of a sad-eyed Robert Howell, his pale, thin face made more so by guilt pangs. I wished I hadn't spoken, but a man's heart sometimes overpowers his senses.

"I can't help it," I told Shea as I turned away from the fire. "I miss that horse more'n ever."

"We'll find you another when we reach the Blue Mountains," he promised. "May cost us dear, but I'll wager the Nez Perce can part with another."

"Won't be Snow," I lamented. "But maybe he had brothers."

"I'd judge it likely," he told me.

And so that night I dreamed of graceful white colts dashing across mountain meadows. I myself sat atop a broad-backed stallion, my bare chest marked with Nez Perce paint. My hair was longer, and an eagle feather was tied in back.

Suddenly a soft voice cut through the scene.

"You lived on a farm with your father," Etta Martinson

89

spoke.

The dream changed. I sat in a rocking chair on the porch, bouncing little Bessy on my knee. The wondrous aroma of fresh-baked cornbread flooded my nostrils.

"Don't go," Mary pleaded.

But her words were swallowed by a larger dream of new adventures and fresh discoveries.

When I awoke, Shea already had a fire burning. I hurried into my clothes and joined in the work.

"Didn't sleep any too quiet, son," he observed.

"Too many dreams," I explained. "Memories."

"Well, it happens when you've time to think. We'll be back on the trail again come daybreak, and we'll be too tired to dream."

I thought it likely true, and it proved to be just so. The snow melted as rapidly as it had fallen, and a blazing late spring sun came to take its place. It was near eighty miles to the Green River ferry, and the last half of them were bone dry. The drastic change from freezing cold to blazing heat loosened harness and sprung barrel staves. It had the stock a bit jittery, and half the company was feeling the wearies.

Shea and I did a bit of hunting in the hills, but we had scant luck. Except for a pair of rabbits and one fat duck, we came back empty-handed. It was back to salt pork and biscuits for most of the company, though I did lead a third of the company off to pick onions and tubers, a considerable amount of greens and some herbs known to ease the discomforts a bit. Peeled and cooked proper, I found it all most welcome, but most of the children turned up their noses, and even the women eyed it mostly with suspicion. Oh, the onions and turnips were eagerly eaten, and the squash cooked up handsomely. I even talked a few into tasting biscuitroot, which is rather prized by the Shoshonis. As to other, less palatable-named greens and tubers, Shea and I ate ourselves bloated.

Down along the Big Sandy, where even a bit of prairie grass seemed a welcome relief from the deep sand and barren rock, there was neither game nor greens to be had. Our pace slowed to a crawl, for the water in the stream was seldom fit to drink, and exhaustion threatened to overcome the entire company.

Green River was a blessed sight indeed. Those afoot rushed ahead of the wagons and plunged like lunatics into the shallow water. I swear, people shed their clothes on the spot and washed a week's sweat and dust from themselves and their garments.

"Pilgrim's baptism," Shea called it. I thought the world had simply gone mad.

After the stock got a good drink, and some sense prevailed over the company, Shea and Captain Martinson set off to bargain with the ferrymen. Being a good-sized train early in the season, I thought us certain to get generous terms, but those ferry fellows had a way of holding up folks if they set their mind to it. As it turned out, the ferrymen wanted five dollars a wagon but settled for three. We chose to swim the animals across and wade the people.

"They're most of 'em already wet," Shea pointed out, and Captain Martinson grinned.

It was quite a spectacle, crossing the Green River. Each of the thirty wagons was lined up on the near bank, and as soon as one crossed, its owners and their animals would swim to the far bank as well. Sometimes Shea and I, together with some of the older boys, would help control the stock or swim the littler children over. I was most surprised to discover that so many of our people never learned to swim. Most lived along creeks or rivers, and Shea ordered lessons for any who would try to learn.

"Lots o' river crossin' ahead of us," he announced. "Too many likely places for a body to drown himself."

Nevertheless, most of the women refused, and of the whole outfit, I don't guess more than fifteen or twenty

91

learned to fend for themselves in the water. Those were mostly children, too.

I myself taught Etta and Marty to claw their way through the water, though I had less luck with their mama. Mrs. Martinson was a little too dignified to stick her face in a river, and she resented the habit her bottom had of sticking up out of the water. I judged some folks not designed for swimming and suggested she keep a board nearby when making a crossing as it was sure to keep her afloat.

I concluded the day waterlogged and tired past reckoning, but Shea bid me dress myself and hurry along to Burkett's store. We'd done some hunting for Burkett, and we were on fine terms with his whole company.

"Where you headed?" Marty asked when I rammed my feet into boots and headed for the store.

"Burkett's," I explained. "To see old friends."

"But Marietta's planning on you for supper," he called.

"Should've asked me," I answered. "Got some real celebrating to do this night."

When I arrived at the store, I found Shea had started his celebrating early. There he was, passing a jug around a table with a pair of our old friends, Ty Storm and Chet Eldridge. Across the way Nathan Burkett and several others waved. Ty and Chet weren't so much older than I was that they offered either invitation or hesitation. They raced over, lifted me off my feet, and carried me to the table.

"Well, you've grown some, Darby Prescott," Ty declared. "Not many pounds on you maybe, but you've added a whisker or two. No bear's gnawed your feet off, and you've still got all your fingers in spite of keepin' company with a renegade like Tom Shea."

Iris, the Shoshoni woman who looked after the both of them, appeared with buffalo steaks and corn cakes, and I set to eating mine. I confess to taking one pull on the jug, too, but it left my head floating a foot over my shoulders, and the food was more welcome to my empty belly than was the Green River corn. Besides, my companions drank enough for ten men.

When I left the store to return to the company, I learned we were not the only ones sampling the merits of Green River corn. Down along the river other members of the company had managed to acquire jugs, and together with idle trappers, hunters, and a party of soldiers, they were singing and dancing and making fools of themselves.

A short distance away the womenfolk bided their time. From the hard stares on their faces, I warranted retribution would soon be forthcoming. Then suddenly a pair of men began beating a call to arms on drums, and everyone grew quiet. A tall man dressed in a blue coat and wearing a wolfhide hat stepped out and called for attention.

"Friends, please, give me but a moment of your time," he pleaded. "Enjoy yourselves, but lend an ear. I know how dry the trail can get, and I've instructed my companions to provide you with sufficient spirits to bolster your resolve. My name is Lucien Reynaud, and I come to speak to you of the bounty of my home, Alta California."

"California," the people muttered. Instantly I turned back toward the store. Inside Shea and Ty were wrestling. I got between them and stared sourly at Shea.

"Tom, it's started all over again," I said, my face growing paler by the minute.

"What's started?" he asked.

"Talk of California," I explained. "There's a fellow down at the river passing out jugs of corn liquor and talking about heading there instead."

"Reynaud," Ty said. "Tried to buy us out. Says he has gold mines and such and is looking for settlers."

Shea's face lost its color as well, and he pulled me along as he started out the door and down to the river. Reynaud was a bit long-winded, and he was still talking when we arrived.

"Here, let me show you a sample of California's bounty," the speaker called, tossing small nuggets into the audience. The antic had the effect of sending the whole bunch grappling for the shiny yellow bits of gold. "More where they came from, all for the taking," he proclaimed. "Come with me. Turn your wagons toward the golden empire recently won from Mexico. Enjoy wealth and prosperity."

"Yes!" someone screamed, and another agreed. Soon three-fourths of them were ready to follow Reynaud to his promised land. The drummers struck up a tune, and others sang.

"Just who'd you plan on guidin' you to California?" Shea then bellowed.

Even the drummers quieted their banging at the sound of his forceful voice.

"Why, I'll guide them myself," Reynaud announced, drawing a small book from his pocket. "I've brought this guidebook along with me, and, as you can see, I have a small company of my own to protect us from hostiles."

Only now did I realize the soldiers were not part of the regular American army. Their stripes and shoulder bars were yellow with red trim, and their buttons were stamped with the prancing bear symbolic of California.

"Guidebook's not much use to get you west," Shea argued. "This fellow may've come east, with spring rains on the land and no wagons to work up and down the mountainsides. I've heard talk of California before, of gold and bounty, but I've lived long enough to know the value of talk. I know Oregon, and if it's fine farmland and good homes you hunger for, they're to be found on the Willamette."

"Listen to him," Captain Martinson urged. "We've had a fair crossing so far. Most of us are hale and hearty. Reynaud here promises well, and he hands out liquor to smooth the sound of his words. We followed a guide once before who could talk well, and it near got us all buried.

Trust in what you've learned, not in the temptations of words."

"But it's real gold!" Vernon Gaines said, holding up a nugget. "Gold!"

"We've paid a heavy price to get this far," Joseph Howell added, stepping over beside Gaines. "We've buried sons, the both of us. We want something better for what family we've got left. I'm for California, too."

Others, gazing at the nugget in Vernon Gaines's hand, seemed eager to join the splinter company.

"Please, friends, we've come too far to separate now!" Captain Martinson complained.

"Don't then," Reynaud answered. "I've work for all of you."

"You keep your gold-coated words and devil spirits," Mrs. Martinson said, pushing the Californian away. "You men ask your womenfolk what the Promised Land resembles. It's gold is in the yellow corn come harvest and the shine in your children's faces."

"Gold puts a shine to everything, Lilith," Gaines countered. "Wait and see."

"Jared?" Howell called.

"No need making decisions today," Reynaud declared. "My men will remain here another week, recruiting wagons. I myself will accompany you to Ft. Bridger, where the trails must part."

"What could be fairer than that?" Gaines asked. "Eh?"

Ty, who had joined us, watched the California group collect around Reynaud and cheer their would-be savior.

"Don't see how you can abide such folks, old friends," Ty grumbled. "You know the whole bunch of 'em's certain to be crowbait 'fore Christmas. I seen Reynaud before. He used to raid trap lines down on the Laramie."

"Then come with us and tell the others," I suggested.

"And get my throat slit?" Ty asked. "No, thanks. He's got a fair followin' hereabouts."

"I'll tell them myself," I declared.

"No," Shea objected.

"They're our friends," I argued. "We're supposed to guide them out of trouble's way."

"You can't argue against gold," Shea said, gripping my hand and pulling me back. "Let the spirits wear off. We'll talk again at Ft. Bridger."

"Be too late by then," I muttered.

"It's likely too late already," Ty said. "So come back to the store and let's get really drunk. Burkett's sure to have another jug waitin'."

"I've got some walking to do," I said, marching off toward the river.

"Best I go along," Shea said, hurrying after me. "I may be along later, though."

Chapter 8

Talk of California didn't go away. And though I'd been glad to learn half the train wasn't going to split off at Green River, I soon discovered what a poor bargain it was bringing Lucien Reynaud along.

I didn't, in truth, know quite what to make of the swaggering braggart. He was more French than Spanish, and I was sure Ty was right about his days on the Laramie River. I'd come across enough skunks to recognize one by the stripe of his tail. What's more, Reynaud's ignorance of the country gave me a sense of impending tragedy.

He spent the better part of his days sleeping in the back of the Gaines wagon, or else riding his chestnut mare from wagon to wagon, elaborating on the ease of striking it rich in California. He was generous with the dozen jugs of corn he brought along, but as to doing any work, I never saw a hint of it. I could tell Mrs. Gaines had soured on him already, but other folks took to him like a long lost uncle, feeding him supper or mending his clothes.

"Makes me sick to see good people led astray," Shea remarked.

"You could speak against him," I suggested. "They respect you. They're bound to heed your advice."

"No, son," Shea said, frowning. "Not when gold's promised at the end o' the other trail."

97

It was maybe sixty miles to Ft. Bridger, and not long ago we would have crossed that distance in four, maybe five days. The difficult terrain still awaited us to the northwest, after all, and there was better grass along the trail now. Our company seemed to lack energy, though. Our soul had left us. Captain Martinson urged us on, speaking of the sacrifices already made and the rewards awaiting us in Oregon.

"We're headed for California!" more and more replied.

"You ain't boss o' this outfit for much longer," Edna Alston complained.

"Ingrates!" Etta exclaimed to me one night. "Papa's heart is near broken over the way our company's coming apart. I've half a mind to find that Reynaud and stick a knife in him, Darby!"

"It's not Reynaud," I argued. "It's the trail. It wears at a man. The first month isn't so bad, but when summer finds you still months from your destination, and you've not had a bath or a stitch of clean clothes on for weeks, you get all crosswise with yourself and everybody else."

"Will it get better?" she asked.

"Well, after Bridger, there'll not be so many around. That ought to cut out some of the complaining at least."

I don't think that's what she wanted to hear, though.

"Maybe if we scared up some game, it would help," I suggested to Shea.

"Don't dare leave 'em to 'emselves now," he explained. "Ole Gaines and the cap'n like to come to blows this mornin'. That Reynaud worries me some, too. Don't trust him, Darby. He narrows those little eyes o' his, and I can't help feelin' he's turned into a snake out to bite my leg when I'm not lookin'."

"You remember what Ty said."

"Likely it's the truth, too. Still, he had those nuggets. Could be he's tellin' the truth."

"You're not getting the itch to try California, are you?"

"Not with a few sheets o' paper and that fellow to lead the

way."

I laughed at the notion. It wasn't humorous, though. When we finally arrived at Ft. Bridger, I watched in dismay as Vernon Gaines pulled his wagon out of line and started his own camp circle. Soon others joined him, five, six, seven in all. It broke my heart to see Robert Howell in that camp. I'd kept some distance from the boy of late, but when you save a fellow's hide, you get to feeling responsible for him.

The sight of Ft. Bridger seemed to sober everyone up some. It was little more than a long stockade, a warehouse, and the trading post. A few Indians of varying tribes camped on the far hillside, and trappers occupied a huddle of huts. It offered little security and scant hospitality.

I was especially disappointed not to find a company of soldiers. I thought maybe they might send Reynaud packing. Then I struck upon the notion that Jim Bridger himself might be some help. He'd been to California with Fremont and Kit Carson, but old Gabe, as folks called him, had settled down to the life of a trader and only nodded at my questions.

"Oh, California was Spanish, or Mexican. Can't recall just which, the two bein' much the same," Bridger recounted. "Gold? No, I didn't see much o' that. I've heard plenty o' talk since, but then those that ever find gold's just the lucky ones."

"And the trail?" Joseph Howell asked.

"Mostly sand and steep passes. The mountains can freeze you stiff if you get there late in the season. Not so many good rivers. Hard trail, as I remember."

"See?" I said, gazing hard at Reynaud.

"Ah, but the route's been refined and improved," Reynaud boasted, opening his guidebook. He began reading, and the people paid little heed to me or to Jim Bridger.

"Told you, Darby," Shea reminded me. "They want to believe there's gold there for the takin', so they will."

99

And even before night fell, two more wagons joined Gaines's camp. Captain Martinson issued the call for a camp meeting, and those who remained collected between our camp and the fort to consider the future.

"Our company's been rent in two," the captain announced. "Some of us are faced with the difficult choice of leaving friends or abandoning our dream of a new home in Oregon. I think it best for all to speak their mind here and now, in the open, for tomorrow many of us will take the path north, and those who choose to stay behind with Mr. Reynaud should know what hazards they risk. Mr. Shea?"

Tom strode out amidst the pilgrims. There weren't any so raw as when we'd first joined them, and each family had some cause to thank Tom Shea for his attentions and advice.

"I can't speak much of the California trail," Shea told them. "I don't know it. Oh, I've seen those who came to a sad end headin' that way, gettin' trapped in the passes or havin' their wagons break down. I've buried some. I've traded children off the Paiutes and sent 'em east to grandparents and such. I'm for Oregon. Leave that gold fever to some other fool pilgrims."

"Sure, what use does he have for gold?" Gaines asked. "He wouldn't know how to live among civilized folk. Look, friends. Gold!"

The nugget flashed in the afternoon sunlight, and there was a stir among the people.

"There's another thing, too," Martinson said, raising the charter of the company in the air. "You each of you pledged your lives to the success of this endeavor. Will you now break a promise solemnly sworn."

"Oh, there's enough left to get west," Gaines said, shaking his head disdainfully. "We could have a vote here and now as to whether all of us go to California or Oregon, and I'd likely win it. But we don't mean to force you upon a path you don't want to take, Jared. We choose for ourselves, though. We're free men and entitled to do so."

I could tell the captain was beaten when he dropped his chin. Gaines led a cheer, and the meeting disintegrated as Reynaud brought out the last of his jugs, and a spirit of celebration settled over the camps.

For my part, I set off into the woods alone. For a time I followed a deer's trail. But when I spied the whitetail, I had no rifle with me. Anyhow, I mused, I lacked the heart to kill that day, even if fresh meat would have been welcome.

I was sitting on a hillside listening to the singing in the camps when Marty located me.

"I've been looking for you everywhere, Darby," he declared. "That braggart Reynaud's boasted his mare can best any horse in the territory. We want you to race him with your black. You're sure to win, and we'll silence his boasting at least once."

"I've seen that chestnut," I answered. "She's fast."

"I've seen her, too," Marty insisted. "You'll win easy."

"I haven't got the heart for racing anymore," I explained. "Not since Snow died."

"There's money at stake, Darby. Tom Shea's even wagered on you."

"Tom sent you?"

"Well, not exactly. He did hint where you might be, though."

"I can't," I said, frowning. "A man has to have the will inside him."

"What about honor? Don't you think you should defend the honor of our company. Reynaud's said things that need answering. Ride him into the ground, Darby. Show everybody what kind of scout he is, what manner of liar."

Suddenly the notion appealed to me. I didn't know the big black, but Beaver had put him to good use at Split Rock, and we were well acquainted on the trail. I reluctantly agreed, and Marty dragged me along to the camp.

Reynaud seemed pleased to discover I was to be his

opponent, but he was less excited when he saw the big black. The horse snorted and stomped angrily, and Reynaud's calculating eyes seemed unable to find an advantage. The terms of the race had been already agreed upon, and the course was set by Jim Bridger himself. We were to race twice around the fort and return.

"Watch that Frenchy," Shea whispered as I mounted. "He wears spurs. I never trust a horseman who gouges his animal."

"Won't be anybody watching when you get on the far side of the stockade," Captain Martinson added. "Darby, you get out ahead and stay out of his reach. He's got a whip tucked in his belt. He won't need that to urge his mare along."

"No," I agreed. "It's for me."

Some might have been frightened at such prospects. Me, the thought of that whip stinging my back burned away my doubts and filled my insides with a burning hatred. It was almost as good as love to drive a man onward, and when old Gabe started the race, I kicked the black into a furious gallop and took the lead.

The chestnut mare lagged behind, and for a moment I thought it might be easy. I underestimated Lucien Reynaud. As I bounded along the back of the stockade, a trapper stepped out and tossed a loop toward my head. He meant to unhorse me at the least and more probably to break my neck. The big black wasn't fond of nooses, and he immediately dodged the rope. Then the horse reared high and sent the trapper to flight. The chestnut closed the gap, though, and when we returned to view, the race was as tight as I feared.

The second circuit I kept the black thundering onward, but Reynaud and the mare kept pace. Then we vanished behind the log wall, and the whip cracked across my shoulder, then crashed against my ribs, stealing the air from my lungs. I could barely breathe, and tears of pain stung my eyes. When the rope lashed out again, I slid halfway off the saddle, then reached out my bare hand and took the blow. My fingers felt moist as the rawhide strips cut the flesh of my wrist, but though numbed, they managed to gain a grip. I urged the black on, then tugged with all my might. Reynaud had come out of his stirrups in his efforts to reach me with the whip, and my sudden movement pulled him off his saddle and onto the rough ground. For a few moments I dragged him along. Then, when I was sure the company had seen everything, I released the whip and sped on across the finish line.

"Darby, you're hurt," Etta said, drawing out a handkerchief to dab the blood from my exposed arm.

"Yeah," I said, holding my ribs. "He had a few tricks."

Shea's face filled with rare fury, and if I hadn't reached out and turned him away, he might well have finished Mr. Lucien Reynaud then and there. Instead I turned the black over to Marty, left the captain to settle all wagers, and followed Shea and Marietta to a nearby spring where I could wash.

The spring fed a shallow pond, and several boys were availing themselves of it when we appeared.

"Hey, Marietta, go away!" Ollie Zachary pleaded as he dove beneath the surface. Ollie was about five feet tall, though, and the pond wasn't half that deep. Part of him was thus exposed no matter what he did.

"Better leave," I told her as I peeled off my shirt.

"Lord, no," she argued. "You're purple. I'll . . ."

"Go," the boys shouted, and Shea pointed the way.

"I've mended this boy's tears before," the scout said, grinning. "Will so long as he gets himself in these fixes."

"Oh, all right," she grumbled. "But you come along later, hear, Darby?"

"Sure," I said, wincing as Shea spattered a bit of whiskey on my bleeding back. "One o' those ribs may be cracked, son. Got to bind it."

"Then go ahead," I said, and he set to work doing just

103

that. Thereafter, I lay on the hillside, my midsection wrapped in cloth so tightly that I could scarcely breathe. I was, again, a celebrity, as the boys alternately congratulated me and poked my tender side.

"Leave him alone," little Robert Howell finally roared, and the younger ones lit out for home. The others headed back to the pond to do a bit of fishing. Robert stayed.

"I'm not much good for company just now," I told him.

"We'll be leaving for California tomorrow. Came to say good-bye."

"Guess I'll have to get down to California to get my horse now."

"I'll bring it up to Oregon. It's not my idea, us going south, you know. Nor Mama's. It's just, well, Papa sees the men as having let Richie die, and he's got the gold fever. Who knows? Maybe we'll get rich."

"You keep a watch on that Reynaud," I warned.

"I saw the whip. Mean trick, Darby. We'll watch him, all right."

"I meant to keep an eye on you, what with your big brother gone and my small one dying a while back. But I guess we'll have to look after ourselves."

"That's what Papa says."

I wanted to say something more, but I never was much good with words, and I felt a little uncomfortable. I wound up giving him a quick nod, then painfully getting to my feet.

"Watch yourself," I urged as I started for camp.

"You, too," he called.

I found my way to the Martinson wagon, where I was surprised to find an old Ute Indian woman clipping Marty's hair.

"Just in time," Mrs. Martinson declared, excusing a shorn Marty and forcing me painfully into the barber's chair, or rather bench. The Ute snapped her shears at my nose, then began chanting away as she untangled locks of my sandy brown hair and began cutting them back first from my forehead, then my ears.

"Who'd thought it?" I asked when Marietta appeared. "I escape the Sioux only to get scalped by a Ute."

The old woman seemed to understand, and she cackled and clipped a bit more. When she finished, she produced a razor, but I'd undergone enough hazards for one day. I slipped away to the safety of my blankets.

"Looks like they gentled you some," Shea observed when I joined him beside our small fire. The singing and dancing at the twin camps was still going strong, and he was emptying the remains of one of Reynaud's jugs.

"My winnings," he explained. "Got you a new knife, finest British steel. How do you feel?"

"Like a fat woman's sat on me," I told him. "And cut off all my hair."

"Oh, she left a fair bit. Grows like summer grass on you, Darby."

"Tom, how come you let the company be split. Last time, when some spoke for California, we stole all the guns and forced the others along."

"Was late then," he said, his face betraying his own mixed feelings. "Your papa's train couldn't afford the loss, either. We're early, and the train's a bit big for its own good. Best thing was to leave each man to make his own choice."

"How many are going?"

"Thirteen at first, but that's bad luck, isn't it? Gaines talked the Fosters into goin' along. Gaines'll lead, o' course. Then there's the Dardens, Alstons, Grays, Krugers, Browns, Schneiders, Hazletts, Howells, McWilliamses, DeVries, and the Bassett brothers."

"We'll miss Miz Brown's doctoring."

"Cap'n said so, too. But her man's determined to dig for gold."

"Will they all of them end up dead?" I asked.

"Most likely they'll fare fine," he said, laughing. "Maybe

105

make 'emselves a fortune."

"I hope so. I hate to think little Robert or the Kruger girls would come to harm."

"Best spend your worryin' on those left with us," Shea suggested. "We're considerably thinned so far as watches and such."

I nodded. It would work a hardship on those left, but the train was less likely to straggle.

I fell asleep immediately thereafter and dreamed of racing horses across golden fields alongside the Willamette. When I awoke, camp was already stirring. A particular urgency seemed to fill us that day, as if departing would be too painful to long delay it. Breakfast was cooked and eaten hurriedly, and teams were coupled to their wagons. Then, amid a fair stream of tears, we waved farewell to friends and continued northward toward Bear Lake and Ft. Hall.

I wish it had been our final glimpse of Lucien Reynaud, but such was not the case. That next night, camped ten miles north of Ft. Bridger along a meandering stream, I was restlessly wandering through camp when I heard the sound of someone rustling around in a nearby wagon. A shadow leaped at me, and I only just managed to dart away. There was little moonlight, and a nearby campfire didn't provide enough illumination to identify the intruder. I pulled my pistol and cried out.

Instantly the camp came to life. One shadowy form fled off into the nearby trees, climbed atop a horse, and escaped. Two others were less fortunate. One received the full impact of Ellen Warner's shotgun. The second, encircled by a considerable company, was merely subjected to a thorough battering.

"Lord, I'll be," Mrs. Martinson exclaimed when the captain dragged the culprits to the fire. "It's Reynaud."

So it was. The other thief was the very same trapper who had tried to lasso my head during the horse race.

"Wake up," Shea said, jabbing Reynaud with the toe of

his boot. "What are you doin' here? What do you want?"

"Come for horses," Reynaud claimed. "Cap'n Gaines said there was a company reserve of eight, and supplies as well. We're short on flour."

"Could've asked," Captain Martinson replied. "Truth is, the horses were parceled out a week ago, and the flour's been gone since South Pass. We would have shared, though, if any were wanting."

"They could buy flour at the fort," Shea argued. "Wasn't of need they come, but from greed. I'd check his pockets, cap'n."

We did, discovering some banknotes and Odell Zachary's watch together with a pendant belonging to Mrs. Zachary.

"Thief!" Zachary said, spitting in Reynaud's face as he retrieved his family's belongings.

"What's to be done with him?" Captain Martinson asked.

"Best be finished with him," Shea said. "Man who'll rob you once'll do so again."

"Summon a sheriff," Hiram Dixon urged.

"No jails or courthouses in these mountains," Shea explained. "Either let him go, or . . . "

"Or what?" the company demanded.

"Shoot him," Shea said, fingering his pistol. "You want me to, I'll take him off in the woods and do it myself. I've got a sour taste in my mouth, and this one's put it there."

"You can't," Reynaud argued. "I've come at the behest of my company, and I only came for what we felt was due us. What's more, there are fourteen families depending on me to get them safely through to California. Would you have them all on your conscience."

"No," Martinson said, stepping in front of Shea and motioning for Reynaud to leave. "But if you return, I'll see you dutifully hung."

"I won't," Reynaud assured everyone as he stumbled from camp. He had a bit of trouble locating his horse, but once he did, he climbed atop the chestnut mare and rode southward in a cold panic.

"I couldn't leave friends at the mercy of the elements without a guide," Captain Martinson declared.

"Those're good folks, and I wasn't feared for 'em till now," Shea said, more to me than anyone else. "That Reynaud seems the worst sort o' man, and I figure they'll come to hard times 'fore they see California."

I nodded my agreement and started toward my blankets. I tried to convince myself it wasn't our worry, but my dreams were full of recollections, especially of riding from the Sioux camp with little Robert Howell across my saddle.

The worst part of all, I realized that next morning, was that we would never know.

Chapter 9

The trail north toward Bear Lake was a narrow, treacherous path prone to rockslides and tangled overgrowth. Shea and I often had to cut trees or roll boulders out of the way. Sometimes half the company would labor clearing a strip for the wagons.

"It's not always an advantage being one of the early trains," Captain Martinson remarked after we spent half a day moving rocks from the trail.

"At least there's grass for the horses," I told him. "And sometimes after a few hundred wagons roll through, the road turns to mush or simply blows away."

Indeed, the going was truly treacherous during the frequent midday rain showers. Wagons and horses would slip and slide, and even the sure-footed oxen labored to scale the slopes. Such trials called for distraction, and I deemed it a fine moment for cherry gathering. Actually we began by picking wild plums. Later the chokecherries ripened, and we added them to our baskets. Sprinkled with sugar or baked in a pie, they provided a tasty treat. The mountain meadows also gave up treasures of wild strawberries, and some of the boys developed quite a talent for snatching honey from beehives.

By mid-June we reached Soda Springs. The springs lay in a high valley, and their bubbling waters were said to have the taste of lager beer. The youngsters certainly thought so, for after guzzling a fair quantity, they stumbled around, laughing and carrying on like a party of trappers just finished with a jug of Green River corn.

The drunken antics of the boys elicited laughter from their fathers. The mothers acted somewhat less tolerantly. Captain Martinson was forced to call a camp meeting where the evils of strong spirits were elaborated for the benefit of all. Mrs. Bragg, who surely earned her Christian name, Prudence, provided some special instruction to Shea and me.

"The devil uses drink to steal a man's senses," she warned. "Whiskey is a sure path to the fires of eternal damnation."

Shea nodded respectfully.

"Why not?" he asked later. "Last jug's been empty a week now."

North of Soda Springs the going grew even more difficult. Wagons had to be lightened, and those with stronger teams or fewer trunks began to take on goods from the overloaded vehicles. Shea and I helped by offering our spare horses to carry supplies. In the end, though, it wasn't enough.

We weren't the first company forced to part with treasures along the trail. The mountainside was littered with boxes of fine porcelain or chests of clothing. Some bore notes.

"Kindly take care of my Aunt Sylvia's tea service," one read.

"Make use of little Jonathan's coat. He's gone to glory and needs it no more."

Some of the families availed themselves of the opportunity to fit growing children with new shoes or a fresh coat. But soon we, too, were depositing belongings along the trail.

"Each chest means a bowl of tears," Etta told me as we

helped Mrs. Conway carry a box of prized dishes from her wagon.

"Yes," I told her. "But tin plates serve as good. Tears ought to be saved for more important times."

"Such as?" she asked.

"Graves," I muttered.

Mama was in my thoughts just then, and the next day I rode out alone to search out the marker I'd put up for her. The trail seemed so familiar, but ice and snow and wind erased the best efforts of man to leave something more permanent than rocks or trees. I couldn't find the spot.

I supposed it didn't matter. I felt Mama close then, and I dismounted. I walked a ways until I found myself in a grassy meadow overlooking a distant panorama of bluish tinted mountains edged by pine and spruce.

"Mama, I've grown taller," I whispered. "Got some growing yet to do, but I've done my best to put my hands to good purpose. You've got Papa there to comfort you now, too. Me, I'm all alone."

The wind seemed to whisper a comforting tune, but there was no soft shoulder on which to rest my head and no understanding voice to still my doubts.

I lay in the soft grass, and my mind drifted a thousand miles. I saw myself led along by the white buffalo, leading the hunt, showing my valor. I saw a dozen wagon trains following me west. But always I was alone, and I couldn't fend off that sense of being different, apart from all others. It was a chilling sensation, one I would gladly rid myself of, if that were possible.

I met the train late that afternoon, but though I rode at Shea's side the last five miles we covered, I said nothing. He remained as mute, for there was an understanding in his eyes of the solitude I needed.

"You two hermits are to eat with us tonight," Mrs. Martinson insisted when we made camp in a broad clearing at the base of a considerable climb. "Marietta's baked a pie, and I fear Marty's eager for a story."

"I thought to ride ahead a bit," I told her. "I've got strong feelings for this place."

"Nonsense," she announced. "You've been entirely too much on your own lately, Darby Prescott. Better to be around youngsters for a while. Eh, Mr. Shea?"

"Taste o' pie couldn't hurt, could it, Darby?" he asked.

I reluctantly agreed. But while helping Marty gather firewood, we came upon another ghost of the past. At the base of a steep embankment lay a shattered piano.

"Look there," Marty said, sadly shaking his head.

"It's a piano," Agnes Payne said, trotting over. "I wonder what could have brought them to leave it behind. It's a fine one, too. To toss it over the cliff like that, shattering it! What a horrid thing."

"You don't know anything!" I hollered. "Nobody tossed it there. It was tied in the back of a wagon, and the wheels began to slip. It belonged to a Mr. Hogan, a lumberman, and he brought it all the way from the East for his wife. It meant more than a hundred wagons, and we were determined to save it."

"We?" Marty asked.

"I was there," I explained. "I climbed up on the wagon and tried to push the piano forward. Then I tried to get the wheel back on the trail. The ground was loose, though, and soon the whole wagon seemed doomed to go. Me with it. That's when Mr. Hogan cut the ropes. He did it because I was in danger."

"And so it's smashed to pieces," Agnes said, sighing. "That's what this country does to precious things. We had to leave Mama's bedposts yesterday."

"Bedposts," I muttered. "Don't you understand anything? It wasn't just the piano! There's a dream down there. He brought that piano across half the country for his wife, only to have it smashed to pieces in these mountains. He's not the only one, either. Lots of people have their dreams stomped out like that. One minute they're bright and happy, so alive you grow warm just being nearby. Then the heart's crushed out of them, and you're colder'n winter snow."

Marty frowned, and Agnes solemnly nodded. Neither of them understood what I felt, though. They couldn't.

That night, as I picked at my dinner, Marietta sensed something was wrong, but she couldn't pry it out of me. I'd learned not to share sadness. It had a way of spreading over everyone and everything.

"You can tell me," she whispered over and over.

"I told your mother I'd be better off out on the mountainside," I answered finally. "Thanks for the pie, but I've got no taste for softness just now."

I turned to leave, and she tried to stop me. Shea led her aside, saying, "Sometimes, when the memories eat at a body, solitude's the only cure."

I didn't have much time to myself, though. We managed a difficult ten miles through the mountains the next day before finding our path blocked by a Shoshoni camp. I was a little nervous until I recognized the long, straight nose and powerful chin of Two Knives, our Shoshoni friend. His nephew, named Long Nose for the family's most pronounced feature, rode over and clasped me about the shoulders.

"Buffalo Dreamer," he said, "where is your white horse?"

"Dead," I said mournfully. "Shot by a Sioux arrow."

"Ah, that was a good horse," he said, frowning. "This black is known to me. I traded it to Beaver for three spotted ponies."

"And I won it from Beaver in a race," I explained.

"I would race you, too, but I know this horse, and I know its rider. The wind could not catch you."

"I miss Snow," I muttered.

"Yes, but it is safer to ride a dark horse, my brother."

I nodded, and he climbed down from his horse and bid

113

me do the same. Soon he produced a buffalo hide ball, and we took sticks and started up a game. Others joined, and the air quickly filled with taunts and shouts.

Later the Shoshonis provided other distractions. The men played a sort of dice game, and the children tossed balls, stalked each other through the woods, or splashed around in a small creek. Some traded clothes while others exchanged keepsakes. Women swapped mirrors and skillets for beaded moccasins or woven blankets.

I employed my time wrestling and riding. I wasn't much good grappling with the bigger and stronger Shoshonis, but I could sit atop any animal they offered. One particularly rebellious horse, Bonebreaker by name, near threw me, but I hung onto its mane until Long Nose bid me dismount.

The boys from the train fared worse. Marty, in particular, suffered misfortune at the hands of Bonebreaker. He was bounced half a dozen times before being rudely flung to the rocky earth.

"Lord," Marty cried, rubbing his abused backside.

I grinned for the first time in days, then led him to a secluded spot. As I rubbed salve into his battered skin, he muttered a few curses and complained bitterly of his plight.

"How could I be so stupid to climb onto that fire-breather?" he cried.

"Don't know," I confessed. "But if it's any comfort, I did the same thing myself once. Got bounced halfway to St. Louis. My brother Jeff slapped a bit of salve on my bottom and declared I'd mend."

"Lucky you happened by," Marty said. "I don't have a brother. 'Course, if you were to wed Marietta . . ."

"What?" I gasped. "Got my future all planned out, do you?"

"We're sure to need help with the farm, Darby. As for Etta, you say yourself she's fair to look at, and you know she can cook."

"How'd you like to get paired with Althea Dixon, Marty?

Without so much as asking her to walk the river."

"It's different. You like Etta, and she likes you."

"I like my horse, but I don't plan to marry it. Marty, you best set such plans aside. For one thing, your papa'd whip the both of us within an inch of our lives for thinking such. Even salve wouldn't do you a lot of good then!"

Any other argument might have fallen on deaf ears, but the mention of the captain paled Marty instantly.

"Pa's against it?" Marty asked.

"Spoke to me about it. Says I'm too wild to keep company with anybody, and he's right. Marietta'll be winter snug in her bed, and I'll be riding the Rockies, most likely."

Marty frowned and rubbed himself a bit. Content the salve was working, he pulled on his trousers and set off toward camp, leaving me to myself.

I passed the remainder of the day with Long Nose. We recounted our winter adventures, then set off into the wood to stalk deer. We each shot one, and his people cooked the meat. I slept in his lodge that night, away from the civilized ways of my own people. And when morning came, I was sorely tempted to remain with the Shoshonis in their mountain domain.

"Come on, Darby," Shea called, and I rode out with him, though.

As we grew closer to Ft. Hall, other reminders of past trials came into view. We rode past the skeleton remains of wagon boxes, arranged in squares of four. Horse and mule bones nearby spoke of disaster, and I told the story that evening around a campfire.

"Was two winters back," I explained. "As fierce a storm as any I recall. Snow blew across the hills, swallowing wagons and freezing children. There was no hope of continuing, so the people stopped and built shelters out of their wagons. They sent riders out for help, but the snow was so furious that it blinded the riders. Some rode right over a cliff to their deaths. One boy survived."

"You?" Ray McIntosh cried.

"Not me," I answered. "Shea and I were off to the west, riding the Snake River. I spotted something in the snow, and when I dug deep, I found a boy, maybe fourteen years old, choking with fever and cold. I hauled him to our fire, and we thawed him out. Then he told us about the wagon train."

"Did he die?" Marty asked.

"No, and he had a map to show us where the others were. Shea went in search of help, and I came here. It was a terrible place, full of frozen people, all half starved."

"A lot of them died," Marty observed. "There are a bunch of crosses in the trees."

"Crosses?" I asked, surprised. "They must've come back and buried the dead."

"Does that surprise you?" Mrs. Martinson asked. "I wouldn't like to think of a husband or child of mine lying here exposed to the animals."

"No, those were good people, though they were poorly led. I brought some food with me, and their captain ate near all of it when there were children hungry. I guess they even buried him, though I'd sure left him to the crows."

"I hope that won't happen to the Gaines family and all those others," Mercy Zachary prayed. "Maybe we should have stayed together."

"Were we right staying on the trail to Oregon?" Mal Anderson asked. "It seems a hard road, and if there was gold . . ."

"You only know what's behind you," I whispered sadly. "Up ahead's a wonderland. The Willamette Valley's as green and fertile a land as any in creation. We planted our farm in corn that grew taller'n my head. We grew apples so plump and juicy you swore they came from the forbidden tree. And the Cascade Mountains, with Mt. Hood crowning the whole horizon, make a man mindful of God.

"I think about gold, too, Mallie, but you know I guess

there's different kinds. For me, there's gold in a sunrise over your own land, in a sea of corn come harvest. And as for money, I never yet found enough things to spend all my money on."

"There's truth to that," Mrs. Zachary agreed.

"Yes," others said, nodding.

"Did I answer all right?" I asked Shea afterward.

"You said it just fine, son," he assured me.

"It wasn't altogether true, of course," I confessed. "I never cared much for harvest, and a wild, roaring river's a finer sight than any farm I ever lived on."

"And here I thought you might be losin' your wayfarin' ways."

"Not likely," I argued. "Too many places we've yet to see."

Chapter 10

Summer shone down in all its fury as we continued northward toward Ft. Hall. Behind us stretched a caravan of abandoned possessions. Ahead lay another bend, another narrowing trail climbing up one mountainside and down the next. Oxen grunted and mules moaned as they dragged their heavy loads ever onward. As for the rest of us, we silently endured each new obstacle. My hands were raw with blisters, the result of ceaseless chopping of fallen pines and cottonwoods. My shoulders glistened with sweat and reddened from overexposure to the intensity of the June sun. And long before the sun dipped into the western horizon, I collapsed on my blankets and let sleep ease my weariness.

I wasn't the only one worn down by the trail. I watched with dismay as the little ones stumbled along between the rumbling wagons. Their blank, haggard faces attested to the ordeal. There was no longer any softness or comfort to be found.

The trail grew no easier, either. Heat and terrain took a heavy toll. Horses went lame, and four oxen failed to rise to greet the trail. People suffered from a hundred miseries.

"Knew we'd miss Miz Brown," I grumbled as Shea and I dabbed berry paste on the worst of the sunburns. "Know a cure for bellyache, Tom?"

"A little mashed turkey foot or some parsnips can help. I got a little put by for the occasion."

And so we brewed up a concoction and mixed it with mint tea. I wouldn't swear that it cured anybody, but it seemed to bring out a little cheer. For the moment, at least.

Truth was, between exhaustion and dysentery, people had taken on a sour humor. Doing double guard duty didn't help, and Captain Martinson's effort to get the women to share cooking chores was a dismal failure. In fact, it brought about the biggest row of the whole journey.

Of all the families headed west with our company, none had more children than the Warners and Zacharys. As luck would have it, they traveled one behind the other, and their fourteen young ones were forever entangled in some manner of mischief. Ellen Warner was tall and broad-shouldered, and she tried to keep a tight rein on her family. That wasn't always possible. Mercy Zachary had turned over the little ones to her older girls and left Ollie to help his father.

Well, the trouble was Ollie spent more time running off with Nolan Warner than anything else. To top that, Miz Warner considered Modesty Zachary a poor example for her own girls, and spoke of it openly.

"Nobody's easier to rouse than a female comin' to the defense of its young," Shea declared, and Miz Warner should have taken heed. With the both families collected for dinner, meaning eighteen bodies, there was scant rations to begin with, and when Modesty invited Mallie Anderson over, sparks touched off a powder keg.

"She wants to invite company, let her lend a hand with the chores!" Mrs. Warner barked. "And let her ask somebody when it's your turn to supply the bacon and flour!"

That was reasonable enough, and Mercy Zachary might have swallowed such words for the sake of peace. But Mrs. Warner then continued.

"Of course, where I was raised, in a decent, God-fearing settlement, girls of fifteen weren't seen keeping company

119

with every boy they could wrap an arm around. Seems to me Modesty wouldn't suffer from some Bible reading."

"Oh?" Mrs. Zachary asked, rising to her feet. Anybody who saw her knew the storm was coming, but Miz Warner went ahead and started in on Ollie.

"Fool boy's forever landing others in trouble. Take that business with the Sioux Indians. Lost the company three good saddle horses, and close to got the littler Howell boy the same fate as his brother."

Even if it'd been Ollie's notion to ride off, Miz Warner should've seen saying so would be like waving a red flag in the face of an angry bull. Mercy Zachary threw aside her plate, rolled up her sleeves, and laid into Ellen Warner with a vengeance.

"Fight!" someone yelled, and the company came a running. Both husbands took a try of separating the brawling women, but Odell Zachary, who was scarce as big as I was and a full half head shy of either antagonist, limped off with a blackened eye, and Lane Warner got himself bashed with a frying pan.

The battle didn't stop with the women, either. Ollie and Nolan squared off, and the littler ones dove into each other behind the wagons.

"Stop it, please!" Captain Martinson cried, firing a pistol in the air.

"You stop it if you can, Cap'n," Hiram Dixon suggested.

The men did manage to pull the children off each other, and I stepped between Ollie and Nolan, getting their attention with my loaded revolver. As for their mothers, I wasn't half brave enough to wade into that tussle.

They fought for half an hour. Then, when they finally showed some signs of fatigue, Captain Martinson and the other men managed to pull them apart.

"Lord, what have we come to?" the captain asked. "Now we have mothers fighting like brawling . . ."

"I'd hold my tongue right there!" Mercy Zachary said,

squaring her jaw and doubling her fist. "I've gotten rather practiced at belting out retribution for those who slander my name, and I won't mind adding you to the list!"

"Now you know why those children are so wild!" Mrs. Warner screamed.

It was all the men could do to prevent a renewal of the conflict.

Flaring tempers would pass, though. I hoped so, anyway. Worse trouble lay ahead. I was riding along behind the Anderson wagon, keeping watch on a knot of children, when someone screamed a hundred feet behind me. I turned the big black and fought to move past the McIntosh wagon toward the trouble. The trail was far too narrow there to allow a horse to pass a wagon, so I dismounted, handed the reins to Mark Anderson, who happened to be nearby, then made my way along the narrow ledge of the trail back down the line.

The first hint of trouble was the Payne wagon. It was abandoned in the trail. I glanced around for some sign of the Paynes, for they rarely wandered far. Mr. Payne drove the wagon himself, and Mrs. Payne generally rode alongside or walked with the children.

"Hold on, Si!" I heard her call, so I squeezed between the oxen and the steep mountainside, passed the wagon, and continued along until I reached a cluster of people huddling beside the edge of the trail.

"It's Darby," Sully, the Payne's thirteen-year-old, announced.

I stepped through the others, then stared over the ledge at where seven-year-old Silas lay crumpled in the rocks.

"Get a rope," I instructed. "And move back. Won't do much good to have somebody else go over."

I don't know why it was, but the sound of somebody giving orders calmed the whole outfit. Sully produced a rope, and I tied one end to the Payne wagon, made sure Mr. Payne had the team in check, then tied the free end around my waist and started down the mountainside.

I was pretty sure-footed, and I might have been able to get down the slope on my own. There wasn't a chance in a hundred of getting little Silas back to the trail without help, though. I called to the boy, half expecting some sharp word or another in reply to my jests.

"Can't walk on the clouds, Si," I shouted. "Playing possum won't save you a whipping!"

But when I finally reached him, I saw he hadn't tumbled down the slope like I thought. He'd landed hard and fast, and his body was crumpled like a winter leaf. I bent over in an effort to hide my tears. Then I cradled the limp body in my arms and started back up the mountain.

"How is he?" Mrs. Payne called. "Is he hurt badly?"

I watched as her ears listened for sobs, as her eyes fell on limp hands and motionless feet.

"No!" she screamed when I lifted Silas up toward the waiting arms of his brothers. "No!"

"Happens," I said, searching for better words.

"Not my little boy," Mrs. Payne sobbed as she hugged the dead child.

I slipped out of the rope and carefully coiled it before setting it in the back of the wagon. The Paynes collected around Silas, and I set off to tell the lead wagons we'd need some time.

"That's hard news," Shea said when I told him. "There's a world of pain on this trail, Darby. Maybe you should drive for 'em today."

"Sure," I agreed, starting back down the line.

We buried Silas under a cairn of rocks. I helped Sully scratch his brother's name on one. We said prayers, remembering the boy who was always so curious about everything and now knew all the answers he ever would. And we continued along the trail.

Ft. Hall proved a welcome sight indeed. Its white walls and simple watchtower would provide the opportunity to replenish supplies, restore spirits, and most important of all, to make repairs. Nearly every wagon in the company suffered from a loose wheel or two. Most had loose planks or bad brakes.

The Scot trader, Angus MacLeod, welcomed us with bagpipes, and he turned over his forge to our use. I tied off my horse and made a dash for the well. I got only halfway when arms reached out and grabbed me. I spun around in an effort to free myself, but smaller arms clawed at my back, and a third attacker put my feet in a bear hug. I tottered a moment, then collapsed to the ground.

"Lord, it can't be!" I gasped when I blinked away the dust and found myself captured by the same Frey boys I'd helped dig out of the mountain snows a year and a half ago.

"Was thinking the same thing myself," Tim declared. "You've gone and grown up, Darby Prescott, but I see you're still wearing those bear claws."

"They get me through the worst of winter snows and summer heat," I declared.

I immediately wished I hadn't spoken of winter snows, for Tim frowned, and his mopheaded little brothers grew downright sour. The recollection of the frigid blizzard and the winter weeks we'd shared at the fort were clearly fresh in their minds.

"What are you doing here?" I finally asked. "Figured you off to Oregon with the first train through last summer."

"Yeah, me, too," Tim said, frowning. "Most of our folks signed on with this bunch or that. Ma got some work patching clothes, though."

"Besides," Miller, who was maybe ten now, said, "we didn't have money, and nobody much wanted a fresh wife if three boys came along in the bargain."

"Yeah," little Michael agreed.

"I'll bet we can find somebody willing to have your help," I declared. "Let me ask around."

"There are more than just us," Tim said. "Mostly trail orphans."

"We've got families who've suffered losses on the trail," I answered. "I'll bet we can take everybody."

"That'll be good news," Tim said, helping Michael and Miller to their feet. I then satisfied my thirst before leading the Freys toward the forge.

Ft. Hall became a beehive of activity. We stayed four days, making repairs and loading supplies. Shea announced most of the wagons too heavy for the rocky trail west along the Snake River, and Tim and I sawed a foot or two off most of them. The planks were used to replace others that were cracked or splintered.

Once the wagons were readied, Shea led Tim and I off into the mountains in search of elk. I believe our company wanted fresh meat almost as much as a rest, and though we'd managed a few brook trout and an occasional rabbit, elk steaks would truly revive the weary.

"Wouldn't hurt to get you boys some new britches, either," Shea remarked, pointing to our threadbare and ill-fitting clothes. "Elkhide's close to the best thing I ever saw to put up with rough life."

I agreed, though cotton trousers were a good deal better in the summer heat. I could tell what was in Shea's eyes, though. We were slowing down, and summer wouldn't last forever. Autumn winds would cut through my trousers as if they weren't there at all.

Shea had a nose for game, and he could scare up a few elk when no one else would believe there was game within forty miles. I never questioned his directions, even if they often seemed confused, and Tim soon accepted my confidence and adopted it for his own.

We located three elk toward late afternoon. They were drinking from a small pond enclosed by a stand of towering pines. Shea marked us each a target, and we dismounted, loaded our rifles, and took aim. He fired first, and we followed instantly. By the time the powder smoke passed, all three elk lay in the soft meadow grass.

I never had gotten used to butchering, but Tim took to it like he'd been born in a smokehouse. I did a fair job skinning the creatures, so I suppose it all balanced out in the end. We tied the meat behind our saddles and returned triumphantly to the fort. MacLeod was so impressed with our good fortune that he ordered a celebration, provided half a cask of spirits, and played his bagpipes while those who wished enjoyed a highland fling or two.

It was while fed to contentment and somewhat rested that Shea brought up the matter of the trail orphans. Actually, there were but eight needing homes, plus the Frey family. Bart Sawyer, a scruffy fifteen-year-old, was taken in immediately by the Schroeders. I think Mr. Shroeder would have taken the Freys as well, for he and his wife were young, and there was always more work than the two of them could manage.

The Sutherlands, a young English couple who were almost invisible most of the time, took in little Hunter Normile and his two sisters. Hunter was two years older than little Si Payne, and I thought sure the Paynes would take him in, but they found a better match for their already considerable family. Simon McAlister was orphaned when his trapper father fell victim to a fever, and the boy so closely resembled Silas, even in his name, that I suspected fate's hand hard at work.

I was a bit surprised when the Andersons adopted Matthew and Robert Murray. The Murrays were about the same ages as Miller and Michael Frey, and Mrs. Anderson was forever complaining of the trials of raising boys. She had Mallie and Mark half grown now, and here she was taking in two more.

As for the Freys, they paired up with the Whitsell family. Warren and Delia Whitsell weren't a lot older than I was, and they had a baby, Seth. They got more than a fair share

125

of advice from everyone, and I believe Delia in particular judged having a woman around who'd raised sons would put a stop to the meddlesome neighbors. Miller and Michael would help with chores, and Tim was old enough to stand a full watch or drive a wagon.

Tim was also a fast learner, and he picked up the trick of working hides straight away. The two of us tanned the elkhide while every other boy on the train looked on with envy. I soon had two or three of them trying their hand at the work, and in time all who so chose got the chance to join the labor.

I was showing the McIntosh boys how to soften the skin when Marietta appeared.

"Howdy, Etta," I said, grinning as she approached.

"Surprised you still recall who I am," she countered. "You haven't been around much lately."

"Been busy," I explained. "On the trail, I near collapsed as soon as we made camp, and I've been cutting down wagons or hunting the last few days."

"You could've said hello."

"Guess so," I confessed. "It's just there's been so much to do."

"Well, you've fed the train, got us ready for the trail, and even helped Tom Shea ensure those trail orphans a home. Seems all the orphans got taken in, in fact—except you."

"I've got a home," I argued.

"Do you?" she asked. "A couple of blankets isn't much of a home, not even a temporary one. And what kind of family is Shea? Half the time he's a puff of smoke off scouting the trail."

"That's just it," I told her. "So am I. We're brothers in a way you wouldn't understand. Our hearts are the same. Sometimes we talk without using words. We just know what's being felt, and we act on it."

"It's not like having a real family, a mother and father, brothers and sisters."

"I've got brothers and a sister," I insisted. "And Tom's as good a father as I could want."

"I was only thinking . . ." she began.

"Yes, I know," I said, smiling at her. "Thanks, Etta. But I'm a little too old for adopting. And far too set in my ways."

"But you'll still join us for dinner now and then?"

"Whenever I get the chance. Your cooking's improved, you know."

She pretended to wallop me across the head, but she only laughed. I matched her grin, then resumed my work.

Chapter 11

From Ft. Hall we turned west. Ahead of us lay 300 tortuous miles of dust-choked, rocky trail along the Snake River leading into Oregon proper. It meant a month and a half, maybe two, of hard traveling under the fiery summer sun, and I confess I grew weary just thinking of the journey.

The river itself, though, was a welcome source of relief. Its deep blue waters alternately cut steep canyons or broad valleys, but it was fed by small creeks and tributaries which quenched our thirst when the broader banks lay beyond our reach. The hills and mountainsides were well wooded with stands of cottonwood, pine, and willow. And the even grade provided our animals with a needed respite from the unrelenting hardships of the Bear River country.

As the towering peaks of the Rockies gave way to the Snake River Plain, so the Sioux and Cheyenne horsemen gave way to the gentler peoples of the Sawtooth country.

"Not much fear of Indian attack now," I told my relieved audience the first night out of Ft. Hall. "Truth is, you welcome what trade the Shoshonis and Nez Perce bring. Many a train's found shield from winter's bite in the comfort of an elk robe bartered off a Shoshoni band."

I recalled the Snake River country fondly. Always before

we'd found abundant game and good grazing. Shea and I hunted the hills and fished the streams, even in the heart of winter. But in the two summers since our last passage a new menace had come to plague the trail there.

Our first hint of trouble was the arrival of a single rider at the head of the train. Shea and I rode out to meet him. We didn't like what we saw.

"Lord, am I glad to find white men!" the rider declared.

I stared hard into the wild eyes of the stranger. His clothes were tattered, and his face and hands were blackened by powder smoke. His dark hair was oily and unkempt, and he had a smell about him that brought to mind a mound of horse dung swept from a cavalry stable.

"Found trouble, have you?" Shea asked.

"Indians," the rider said, coughing hoarsely as he fought to catch his breath. "Twenty, maybe more. Hit our wagons, cut us up proper."

"Indians?" Shea said, exchanging a nervous glance with me. "Which tribe?"

"Tribe?" the man cried. "How'd I know? You figure it matters, what with 'em cuttin' up my family this very minute? I need help. Ain't you comin'?"

The rider turned away from us and called directly to the company.

"I seen a boy no older'n ten cut down by the heathens!" he screamed. "Women carried off from their families! Please, help me save those that's left. May still be time. In God's name, come on!"

"What are we waiting for?" Melvin Bragg shouted. "I got kids myself!"

"I'll go," Uriah Anderson volunteered.

"And me!" another yelled.

"Shoot, we'll all of us go!" Niles Conway insisted. "We'll make short work of the murdering devils!"

Captain Martinson immediately enlisted a dozen men

and led them forward.

"Hold on a minute, Cap'n," Shea argued.

"There are men in need," the captain replied. "We can't ignore their needs."

"And what about us?" Shea asked. "Goin' to take yourselves off and leave the people to whatever comes?"

"He's right," Mrs. Frey said, warily gazing at the rider. "We're in danger as well."

"We'll send you six men," Captain Martinson announced. "I'll lead."

"You best stay with the train," Shea declared. "I'll take 'em. I know the country . . . and what to do about trouble."

"He's right," Mrs. Frey called.

"Cap'n, best you circle up the train till we're back," Shea added. "If we're a while comin' back, have Darby take a look. As to you, son," he said, staring at me with an intensity I'd never seen before, "read the trail close, and keep your nose to the wind so as to sniff out trouble."

"I will," I promised.

Shea then turned and led the other five men westward. I couldn't help noticing he seemed oddly uneasy.

"That was a mistake," Mrs. Frey announced once the men had galloped a hundred yards. "I know that man, and he's no part of any wagon train."

"What?" I gasped.

"His name's Glynn Hoover," she explained, speaking to Captain Martinson in particular. "I've seen him before. Two years back he offered to bring us food in return for four horses. We never saw either again. Last winter he put a knife through an American Fur Company man at Ft. Hall. He's the worst sort."

"Why didn't you say so?" Captain Martinson cried. "We've likely sent six men to their deaths?"

"He had a six-shot revolver in his hand," Mrs. Frey said, frowning as she saw my grief-stricken face. "He'd killed some for certain and likely gotten away. Tom Shea'll know what to do."

"What to do?" I shouted. "What can he do? They're surely riding into an ambush! I knew it smelled. Indian attack in this country? I knew!"

"So did he, Darby," Mrs. Frey said, resting a hand on my shoulder. "What'd he tell you? Use your nose? He knew it smelled rotten."

"We've got to warn him," I said, gazing anxiously westward.

"Yes," Martinson readily agreed. "But if it's as Mrs. Frey suspects, we're in danger here as well."

"Circle the wagons and watch for trouble," I suggested. "Just give me a couple of men to help Tom."

"I'll go," Bart Sawyer offered. "Nobody's apt to miss me, after all."

Bart was only fifteen, but hard living had aged him some. I nodded my agreement and offered him a spare saddle horse.

"Guess I'd best ride along to keep you youngsters out of trouble then," Ivar Shroeder said, slapping Bart on the back. Lars Bruning completed our party.

"Look after Bertha," he urged as he rode forward.

"Darby, don't you take any chances," the captain ordered. "You warn Shea, then get back here."

I nodded, knowing it was a doubtful thing. Then we urged our horses into a gallop and set off after the others.

Tom Shea was a whale of a man to have on your side in a fight, and most times I'd never worry. He had his ways of turning a game to his advantage, and I couldn't help agreeing with Mrs. Frey that he was suspicious of Hoover. There were others along, though, and if Tom had a failing, it was looking after others to his own disadvantage.

It was something we shared. Me, I would have ridden down the sun in my haste to catch the others, but there I

131

was, saddled with two Germans and Bart, the three of them less acquainted with a horse's rump than with a milking pail. I was forced to set a slow, if steady, pace, and we closed the distance only gradually.

In time we saw a rising column of smoke and broke directly toward that direction. I knew Shea well enough to know he'd circle a bit, maybe come at the trouble from behind. It wasn't like the old scout to rush a thing, especially when led by a stranger. I couldn't get the pistol Mrs. Frey had described out of my mind, though, and the notion of its blasting Tom Shea from the saddle sent shivers of dread through my whole being.

In the end, we came upon a pair of derelict wagons from the east while Shea's column slipped around from the west. There was a good deal of shooting and some horrific screams coming from the wagons, and if I hadn't known better, I would almost have imagined a massacre was in progress. In truth, I saw not a hint of a painted face. I did notice several crouching riflemen beneath one of the wagons, though, and a pair of others lurking in the nearby woods.

"Tom, no!" I suddenly shouted at the top of my lungs. "It's a trap!"

Instantly I turned the big black away from the wagons and waved my companions toward the safety of a nearby ravine. In minutes we dismounted, set our horses loose, and took shelter. Shea reacted quickly as well, but so did Glynn Hoover. Hoover discharged his pistol in the direction of Niles Conway, and Conway slumped across his saddle. Shea pulled his own gun and fired a split second later, toppling Hoover from his horse. Then the air exploded with gunfire, and a cloud of powder smoke swallowed our comrades on the edge of the far wood.

"Look there," Bart shouted, pointing toward the wagons. I saw with dismay dead men rise to join the ambush. A bloody corpse wearing a yellow bonnet raised a rifle and opened up with amazing accuracy. We had to duck as lead balls bounded off the rock rim of the ravine.

"And we're the rescuers," Bart grumbled as he rammed a ball down the barrel of his rifle and prepared to answer the gunfire.

"We have to be," I answered, swallowing hard as I at last located the rest of our people in the trees a hundred yards away. "There's nobody else."

"No, there isn't," Bruning agreed. "Got something in mind, do you?"

I felt the eyes of my companions resting heavily on my shoulders. Always before I'd followed Tom Shea into a fight, relying on his judgment, his skill to get us both through safely. Now it was suddenly the other way around, and I shuddered. Who was I, Darby Prescott, to lead anybody anywhere? I was barely eighteen, had but a shadow of a beard, and . . . Well, I told myself, of the four of us, I knew more about what needed doing than the others. I wiped my brow, collected my wits, and started down the ravine, taking care to watch the ambushers lest they circle around our flank.

The ravine covered all but the final hundred feet of our approach to the woods, but that stretch was open ground cut by deep ruts left by hundreds of westbound wagons. I searched the landscape for a more protected approach. There was none. I frowned, then pointed toward the trees.

"If we stay here, sooner or later they'll come around behind us," I explained to my companions. "A man moves fast enough toward those trees is likely to make it, especially if he doesn't go straight. It's a hard shot from those wagons, and I plan to keep their aim a little shaky. Bart, you go first. When you get there, tell Tom what's planned. The rest of us'll follow."

Bart nodded, took a final shot with his rifle, then made

133

ready for the run. I loaded my own rifle, took aim at the wagon, and waved Bart onward. I then blew a neat hole in the canvas cover, and my companions fired on the crouching riflemen.

Bart never hesitated, and though a few shots chased him across the open ground, none found its target. I sent Bruning next, then Schroeder. Finally, with legs that threatened to turn into mush, I made my own charge.

Fear, it's said, lends wings to a man's feet. So it was with me anyway. I raced across the ground fast as Snow ever carried me, dipping one way, then another as lead whirred and whined behind me. I could hear the shots nick leaves, fracture branches, and splinter rocks. When I stumbled into the cover of the cottonwoods, Bart grabbed my arms, and I fell behind a low rock wall that served to shield our small company from its enemies.

"I've seen stupider things in my life," Shea grumbled as he wrapped strips of cloth around Melvin Bragg's forehead.

"Stupid as following that Hoover fellow?" I asked as I reloaded my rifle.

"You know him?" Shea asked. "How?"

"Mrs. Frey," I explained. "Recognized him as a renegade."

"Thought as much," Shea muttered as he finished binding the wound. A short distance away Niles Conway lay moaning. Blood seeped through bandages on his shoulder.

"So what do we do now?" I asked.

Shea frowned, then gazed down the line of frightened men and boys. No one seemed eager to carry the fight to the enemy, and the renegades appeared no more willing to press the point. Still, they held the open ground, and we were trapped in the trees, horseless, and without provisions.

"Don't judge 'em to have a lot o' fight in 'em," Shea finally spoke. "If we could get around in their back, shoot 'em up some, they'd likely head for safer country."

"How do we get around there?" Bruning asked.

"Without getting shot," Bart added.

Shea sighed and again searched the faces. He found no flood of enthusiasm.

"Got to be done," he told us. "Take three of us. Who's the best shot?"

The men exchanged nervous glances. Then Ivar Schroeder lifted his rifle.

"I can shoot," he declared.

"Me, too," Bart added.

"Then you stay here and hold the wall," Shea ordered. "Darby, you, too."

"No, I'm going with you," I insisted. "I'm quick on my feet, and I've been in tight spots before, remember?"

"None like this!" he barked.

"Have they?" I asked, turning toward the others.

He frowned heavily, then pulled Uriah Anderson, Lane Warner, and Hiram Dixon off the line as well.

"Son, you figure you're mad as a scalded hornet?" he whispered as he led us along.

"Close," I answered.

"Well, you get that way in a hurry," he told me. "Be bitter hard, this kind o' fight."

I nodded. The five of us threaded our way through the trees a hundred yards until we skirted the fake massacre site. Then we raised our rifles and prepared to let loose a volley into the flank of our tormentors.

"Ready?" Shea asked, raising his arm.

We all nodded, and he dropped his arm. Immediately a volley of rifle balls cut through the back of the nearest wagon. A man stumbled out the back and fell face first onto the dusty ground. Another scrambled away, dragging one leg. Shea then whooped and charged the survivors. We followed, firing pistols at anything that moved.

135

I wasn't much of a shot with a handgun, and I emptied my Colt with little thought of hitting anything. Truth was, I'd shot elk and buffalo, but aside from killing a Sioux last summer, I'd never slain a man. Back then I had little time to consider things. When a man on horseback thunders down at you, you do what you can to keep his lance from ventilating your hide. Now, though, the fighting settled down some. I found myself crouching behind a flour barrel swapping shots with a slender fellow seventy yards or so away.

Shea had vanished. He was a wild man in that kind of melee, and his charge had already sent three of the renegades to flight. I located him in the back of the second wagon. He shot one ambusher from close range, then suddenly found himself trapped by two others. The first crept up behind him, and I shuddered.

"Not like this," I muttered as I finished reloading my rifle. I didn't stop to think before taking aim on the crouching gunman. I fired, and the man's head snapped back as if tugged by a rope.

I ducked to avoid an answering shot from my personal adversary across the way. A volley of rifle fire from the wood then sent him to flight. In another minute the last of the attackers fled, and the battle was concluded.

"Lord, help 'em," Bart cried as he made his way across the bloodstained ground, collecting firearms and assuring himself the dead were truly without life now. I stumbled over to the corpse in back of Shea's wagon and stared down at the would-be killer. His face was purple, and his eyeballs had turned back into their sockets. It was hard to tell much about him, except that he wasn't a whole lot older than me . . . and he was dead.

"Fair shot, Darby," Shea said, leading me away from the bloody scene. "Saved my life, you know."

"Guess I owed you one," I mumbled. "A dozen, in fact."

"Did a fair job this day."

"Sure. I'm good at killing, it appears."

"Son?"

"Man's got to be good at something, doesn't he?" I asked. I felt a tear trickle out of the corner of my eye, and though I rubbed it away, another quickly took its place.

"Told you it'd be a hard fight," he reminded me.

"Was, too," I added.

Bart and I then trotted off to recover our horses while Shea had another look at the wounded. Soon we would return to the train. I hoped the killing would pass in time, but I knew from experience that pain rarely did.

The renegades were not through with the Martinson train, it turned out. Even as we were trudging back to the company, gunshots exploded across the plain.

"Let's get mounted!" Shea barked, and we climbed atop our exhausted horses and coaxed them into a gallop. When we arrived at the circle of wagons, we were almost met with a volley ourselves.

"Lord, they're back!" Mrs. Martinson exclaimed.

Others shouted like phrases or yelled greetings. The wounded were helped down and into the waiting arms of loved ones. Shea and I turned our horses over to Marty, then sank into the grass and caught our breath.

"Looks like you had a time of it," Captain Martinson observed as he brought us cool cups of mint tea. "We had our own visit."

"Oh?" Shea asked, tensing.

"Six or seven of 'em," the captain explained. "Guess they thought all the men left with you. I dropped one myself. Two got as far as the Zachary wagon before Mercy let loose both barrels of her shotgun. Wasn't much to bury."

"Lord," I thought, envisioning the sight. Mercy? Was ever a woman so inappropriately named?

"Are they likely to come back?" Captain Martinson asked

as he sat beside us.

"Not many of 'em left," Shea noted. "No, it's more likely they'll wait for other game. We bloodied 'em considerable."

"Conway's shoulder looks bad."

"It'll get better," Shea assured us. "Bullet's got to be cut out, and the wound bound afterward. Best he not travel for a while. Hate to do it, but I judge we'll need to rest here a couple o' days."

"The horses had a hard run," the captain observed. "And we're all of us unsettled."

"Sure," Shea agreed, glancing at me. "All of us."

Chapter 12

I couldn't erase the memory of that day from my mind. I walked about the camp feeling strangely lost. I chopped firewood, fetched water, did anything I could find to keep my hands busy. It didn't help. I felt death closing in on me, somehow lurking in the distant hills, eager once again to snatch life from our company. And worst of all, the shadowy face was my own.

That night, as I tossed and turned in my blankets, a nightmare vision filled my dreams. I stood alone on a high cliff, surrounded by phantoms with long, jagged teeth.

"We've come for you," they called in deep, terrifying voices that echoed through my head. "Come, feel the sharp bite of our teeth."

Then they raised their bearlike hands, and I saw sharp talons akin to those of eagles. It seemed as if each of the creatures desired to tear at my heart. I had no weapon to fend off their attack. There was no escape. And I was all alone.

"No!" I cried out in the night. "Not this way!"

I then saw the renegade I'd shot turn toward me. His fiery eyes were filled with laughter, and he urged the phantoms on.

"Give him a taste of death," the renegade cried. "Let him feel your sting!"

I shivered from a sudden chill, and I covered my eyes. Sharp claws slashed my arms and forced me to see. A wave of blood washed the landscape, and a thousand terrifying moans drifted through the hills.

I screamed. Once, twice, three times. Then strong arms grabbed my shoulders and shook me awake.

"Darby, boy, wake up!" Tom Shea shouted. "Wake up!"

His hands weren't his own, though. In my senseless state I was being shaken by phantom devils, and I fought to free myself. Whatever words I muttered must have seemed the babbling of a lunatic, for as my eyes began to blink away the nightmare, I at last read the deep concern on my old friend's face.

"Son, there's nobody here," he whispered with a reassuring certainty. "Just us ole wayfarin' wagon train scouts."

"Tom?" I gasped, finally steadying myself.

"Who else'd be wakin' you in the middle o' the night, shakin' off the nightmares and bringin' you to your senses?"

"I'm all right," I told him as I shook off the lingering terror. "Sorry I woke you."

He nodded gravely, then relaxed his grip and returned to his own blankets. His eyes continued to betray their concern, though, and I swallowed hard.

"Was just a dream," I assured him. "Spirit ghosts."

"Happens sometimes," he mumbled. "Killin' comes hard."

"Yes," I agreed. "It tears at your soul."

"That's good," he told me. "Should be that way. Life's a precious thing, Darby. Takin' it away ought to be as tough a thing as a man ever has to do. But sometimes you don't have a lot o' choice."

"Yeah," I agreed. "Doesn't make it a bit easier, though."

He nodded his agreement, then sank into his blankets. I tried to do the same, but in truth I never altogether shut my eyes. I feared the nightmare would return.

Morning found me weary and no more free of my shadowy phantoms than the night before. The whole company seemed sour as if a funeral shroud was draped across us. Friends quarreled, and the slightest bit of nonsense would earn the little ones stern words—or worse.

"It'll be better when we get moving again," I told Shea as I doused our morning fire. "People need to put their efforts to some purpose."

"Be at least another day, maybe two," he replied. "Conway's shoulder's still bleedin', and Bragg's not on his feet yet, either."

"Two days?" I cried. "We'll half of us be at the other half's throats by then."

Captain Martinson took the news better.

"What this company needs is a lift of its spirits," he declared. "Know what tomorrow is, Darby?"

"No," I said, shaking my head. "Wednesday maybe?"

"Shea?" the captain asked, turning to Tom.

"Never had much use for calendars," he muttered. "Midsummer maybe. July."

"July fourth," Captain Martinson told us. "Independence Day. Long as we're held up, why not have a celebration of sorts."

"Sure," I responded. "Some dancing and singing might do the trick. Tom and I'll scare up some fresh meat, right?"

"Forgettin' our friends?" Shea asked.

"Forgetting nothing," I told him. "There aren't enough left to be much threat to the two of us, though. And I'm hungry for some elk, or maybe a buffalo. You game?"

"Tell the ladies to ready their stew pots," Shea told the captain. "Darby Prescott's goin' huntin'."

I forced a grin onto my face, and Shea seemed instantly to warm to the idea. In half an hour the two of us were riding south away from the river, our eyes searching out signs of game.

I'm not entirely sure what I hoped to find on the plain that day. Certainly not peace from the barrel of my rifle. Maybe I just needed to be away from the others a bit. Or possibly I needed the reassurance that Tom Shea was his same old self, master scout and surest shot in the West. If it was a father's comforting words I expected, they weren't forthcoming. Papa had never been much for soft words, either, and they weren't in Tom Shea. Instead he concentrated on the task at hand. We located a small band of buffalo, and each of us dropped a young bull from the fringe of the herd.

"Be full bellies tonight," Shea boasted as he started the skinning. "Good idea, this hunt."

"Was it?" I asked, shying away from the blood. "Gets easy, doesn't it, Tom?"

"What?" he asked.

"The killing. Buffs, elk, men."

"I never noticed it gettin' easy," he told me. "Truth is, I think it gets harder. Me, I hunt to eat, just like the eagle or the wolf. Figure that's how it's intended to be. Not so much pleasure in it. And as for killin' men, if there's a next time, you won't find it a bit easier to stomach no matter how low the fellow is you shoot. Takes a piece o' you away, son. You mourn some, just like when a friend dies. But you can't let it swallow you whole."

"It's not just the killing, you know," I told him, setting aside my skinning knife long enough to stare at his furrowed brow. "I've been thinking about something Marietta Martinson told me back at Ft. Hall."

"Oh? What was that?"

"She said I was the only orphan there that nobody had adopted. She was wrong, though."

"Was she?"

"You adopted me, Tom Shea, two whole years ago."

"I took in a partner, Darby."

"No, you've shown me the way, seen me through the hard times, taught me what I needed to know. Shoot, you call me son often enough. Can't be surprised I feel it. But the thing is, I don't sort out my feelings too good. Never can find the right words to tell you."

"Words don't count for much out here," he muttered. "I'd lot rather you drop the next fellow draws a bead on my back."

"That's the trouble," I told him. "I can't forget how close you came to getting killed. Everybody I ever counted on, ever . . . needed, even Snow, died on me."

"Your mama and papa, you mean. Darby, you're growin' tall now. Time you needed a pa to wipe your nose's been gone a long time."

"Fathers do more than that."

"A man sets out on his own path, though. Soon you'll take a little gal for a wife, raise a pack o' little ones. Shoot, I'll bet you have a regular tribe of 'em."

"Wayfarers don't take wives, remember?"

"Well, you're farm born and raised. And there's a call rides the wind sometimes. Call it a nestin' urge."

"You took a wife."

"Once," he said, swallowing hard as he began cutting away the buffalo's hide. I could tell he didn't want to share the story, but something in his eyes told me he would. It needed sharing, and I hungered to hear the great mystery of his life.

"She was Crow, wasn't she?" I asked. "The fellows at the ferry told me so. It's why we visited Two Blows last summer."

"She wasn't as old as you are," he explained. "Fifteen maybe. Too soft for the hard life I gave her. Too pretty for rough ways. Gave me a boy the first winter after we shared a lodge. He was like her, like you."

"Oh?"

"Liked music. Two Blows used to play a flute for him, and he'd hum along like nothin' you ever saw. He was quick-witted, too. You showed him a thing once, and he knew it. If he'd been white, he'd likely taken to schoolbooks and such. But bein' Crow, he hungered for the hunt, loved to ride, and he could notch an arrow and put it where he willed when he was only seven."

"What happened?" I asked. "Sickness, Ty hinted."

"Sioux," he told me. "I wasn't with 'em, you know. I never could plant my feet for long. Ole Two Blows and I'd led the young men after buffs. Sioux came, hit our camp. They tried to carry 'em off, but Cherry . . . that's what I always called her, cut one of 'em across the belly. They killed her quick. The boy, too. Was yet to see his ninth summer, Darby."

"Life cuts deep, doesn't it? It's so unfair."

"Sometimes it must appear so. Still, what happens happens. And you swallow your grief and head on down the trail."

"It's not that easy for me," I confessed.

"Didn't say a word 'bout it bein' easy," he said, gazing at me with swollen, red-streaked eyes. "Some men cut their fingers out o' grief. Others get drunk and howl at the moon. I've even known those who rode out swearin' to kill anybody who crossed their path. But in the end, none of it does you much good. Best to bury the dead, swallow your tears, and ride on."

I nodded, though I was a long way from being convinced. We spoke of it no more. There was work to do, and hungry mouths awaited our return.

We celebrated the Fourth of July with a buffalo feast, followed by singing and dancing and even a pageant of sorts. Some of the folks peppered their hair with flour and pretended to be this patriot or that. A batch of boys made themselves breechclouts from scraps of cloth and ran around half naked, howling and waving homemade tomahawks.

"Some Indians!" I complained. "Real ones sneak up on you quiet and run off your horses."

When it came my turn to join in, I dressed up in buckskins, shouldered my rifle, and did a fair job of impersonating Daniel Boone. As for Tom Shea, he wound up President Andrew Jackson!

I think just then everybody on the train needed to be somebody else, even if it was just for half a day. Etta played Dolly Madison, and Marty got to be the boy general, Lafayette.

"Now comes the hard part," Etta told me when the final scene was over. "I'll never get this flour out of my hair."

"Tom and I saw a spot where you can wash," I told her. "The creek widens, and there's a pool four or five feet deep. We took a turn at it yesterday so as to get the buffalo blood off us."

She greeted the news with a shout. Before I knew it, I was leading every female in the company to the pool.

I suppose it was bound to happen, considering boys are born curious, with a bit of the devil's tail thrown in. With all the females washing themselves at one time, there wasn't much of anybody to get after the boys, either. More than a few of them slipped past Captain Martinson's watchful eyes and spied on the bathers. I might never have known except Mrs. Frey spied Ollie Zachary's yellow hair hanging out of a tree and raised the alarm.

"Lord, you should've seen it, Darby," Mal Anderson told me later. "Never in my life saw so many women move so fast! Lucky for me I was across on the other side, in some rocks. Ollie and Marty were up in a tree, and they caught it proper. I'll bet they neither of 'em sit down for a month."

Ollie's eight-year-old brother Orion got it even worse, though. He blundered into a small army of girls and got himself dipped in honey, coated with sand, and salted with a few ants for good measure.

"You missed a fair time," Tim Frey declared when I shared his watch over the stock later that night. "It's a genuine treat to see some of the gals on this train after passin' all my time in a hayloft with two little brothers. That Enid Wagner's got a fine figure, and Modesty Zach-

145

ary, well, they made all her parts just right, don't you think?"

"I didn't have your view," I told him. "Considering the temperament of this camp right now, I'd keep such thoughts to myself. Miz Zachary's threatened to skin the next boy to spy on bathers, and I'd judge she's just the one to do it."

"Yeah, she's got blacksmith's arms, all right."

"Wouldn't say that too loud," I warned. "Hate to think I pulled you from that snow so Mercy Zachary could wring your neck."

He laughed loudly, then set off down the line of horses. I left him to tend the stock and returned to the small camp Shea and I occupied on the far edge of our encircled wagons.

"Was a fine day," Shea told me as I kicked off my boots.

"Yes," I agreed. "Captain Martinson was right about the celebrating. We needed a bit of laughing."

"You did a fair job dancin' with the Martinson girl. You look to've grown some."

"Maybe a bit," I said, grinning at the thought. "Isn't altogether satisfying, this getting older. You miss out on the pranks and devilment."

"Like watchin' the ladies takin' their baths?"

"Yeah," I confessed.

"Seems like I recall you doin' somethin' o' the sort a few years back."

"Jamie and I did," I said, recalling our skillful stalking of one particular beauty along the North Platte. Then Jamie fell in the river, and we were confronted by an angry uncle. That was four years ago now. It seemed like yesterday.

I took out my mouth organ and played a sad tune about leaving home. Home? The word had little meaning anymore. Pike County seemed a lifetime away now, and I hadn't found anywhere since that had provided much comfort.

"Awful sad melody, that," Shea observed as he rolled over

on his side. "Know anythin' livelier?"

"I don't feel real lively tonight," I said, pocketing the mouth organ. "I guess it's being in the play. I felt like a real part of the company today. But I'm not, am I?"

"Oh, I don't see how you can say that, Darby."

"We're scouts, Tom. We know the trail well enough, but its end doesn't mean the same thing to us. We only finish a job. There's no pot of gold waiting for us, no promised land of milk and honey. We'll just go along elsewhere."

"Startin' to feel the lonelies?" he asked.

"Yes," I admitted. "I guess it's part of a wayfarer's fate to get melancholy come July."

"Could be," he told me.

I lay back on my blanket and stared overhead at the thousands of stars twinkling in the blackness of the heavens. I felt terribly small, totally insignificant. And though I was exhausted, I couldn't seem to find any sleep. I rolled onto my right shoulder, then tried my left. I couldn't find a way to get comfortable, though.

"You'll want this sleep tomorrow," Shea warned.

"I know," I confessed. "It's just that, well, it seems too quiet to sleep."

"Too cold and empty, this plain sometimes," he whispered.

I gazed at him with surprise. It was fiery hot. And yet I understood what he meant. It wasn't a cold brought by the darkness. It was a chill carried by the remembering wind, the haunting moon. And though a man travel a million miles, it would still find him.

Tom Shea knew that. So did I.

Chapter 13

Our passage up the Snake River Valley seemed cursed by all manner of hazards. July rains stalked us like a clever hunter, lashing out whenever we faced a stream crossing or narrow trail. We found ourselves swinging north or south of the trail, carving out a new path where the old proved impassable. The times we marched fifteen miles in a single day were few and far between. Stock and company demanded days of rest, too, and for the first time on our long trek west other trains passed by.

"Those are the early ones," I noted. "They've got better wagons, the short-bedded sort. And they've got spare oxen."

"Fewer little ones, too," Shea grumbled. "Wager they don't spend so much time on foolishness like Bible readin' and prayer circles."

For my own part, I deemed us in need of considerable prayer. Nerves were beginning to fray, and the women squabbled among themselves most fearfully. The men were no better. Hiram Dixon three times invited neighbors to settle complaints with pistols. Captain Martinson managed to intervene, but when Dixon started in with Tom Shea, I thought for sure we'd be shy one member of the company.

"It's all your fault we're in this fix!" Dixon complained when he drove his wagon into a deep rut that trapped the front left wheel. "Ought to've followed Gaines to California.

Be rich by now!"

"You stump-headed bag o' prairie wind!" Shea answered from ten yards away. "I ought to take my skinnin' knife out and do us all a favor."

"Think you're able?" Dixon called, reaching for his pistol.

In less time than even I could have imagined, Shea raced his horse to the Dixon wagon, flung himself at Hiram Dixon, and the two of them fell into the bog below. The pistol discharged harmlessly. Tom Shea's fists, however, left their marks.

"Was bound to happen," Shea told me afterward. "But I merit it'll breed more discontent."

Perhaps it did, but we made better time on the morrow, and Dixon's puffed lips and sore jaw made complaining too painful.

We encountered a graver peril two days hence. Toward the middle of a bright summer morning a dark cloud came out of the north to engulf our company. A maddening buzzing assaulted our ears, and the next thing we knew horses were bolting and oxen bellowing. Mules whined and kicked. Then we ourselves were beset by what proved to be a huge swarm of locusts.

There's something in a man that can't abide insects, especially large ones that seem capable of penetrating every particle of clothing and getting into every crease and hollow a man possesses. I fought the monsters off my head and neck only to feel others creeping up my legs. I crushed one in my armpit. The big black leaped and shook, fighting to free itself from the plague. Nothing worked.

Elsewhere, wagons left the trail in every direction. Stock screamed in terror. Women threw off petticoats and slapped the hovering insects away. Small children rolled around in the grass, wailing as locusts clung to eyes and ears.

"Stop it!" Mercy Zachary shouted as she rescued her youngest daughter Molly from the clinging locusts. In madness, men fired pistols or cracked whips.

"To the creek!" Shea shouted, pointing to a muddy stream just ahead. Those still in the saddle urged their horses in that direction. Others abandoned wagons and families to seek what seemed the sole refuge from the hellish abomination. I tried to guide the big black there, but the horse had its own notions. It reared high in the air, gave a fierce shudder, and I tumbled earthward.

I hadn't been thrown from a horse often enough to know how to land properly. As it happened, I jammed my right ankle and battered my left side into every rock on the trail. As I lay, stunned, on the ground, the locusts burrowed their way into my hair, ate at my legs, crawled down my shirt, and generally infested me. I know of no comparable torture endured by mankind.

As I regained my senses, I stripped off my shirt, kicked off boots, and shed stockings. But as I slapped one locust or wriggled free of another, a third and a fourth took their place. I stumbled to my feet and rushed toward the creek screaming in the same manner as most of the rest of the band. A naked boy dashed by ahead of me, clawing away at the insects concealing his face and shoulders. Women carried their small children and shouted pleas for deliverance. I myself collected Linus and Logan Kimberly and dragged them along in the same way Ollie Zachary conducted his younger brothers.

I suppose it took five minutes to reach the water, but it seemed more like five hours. Every step was a torment, a brief passage through hell on earth. And when we plunged into the creek, I half thought to drown myself then and there. The water scattered the clinging insects, though, and I thrashed around in the shallow stream until all but a few, trapped beneath my trousers, had abandoned me.

"Lord, help us!" I gasped as I unbuttoned my trousers and pried the last unyielding locusts from my flesh. The surface of the creek was painted black with the drowned creatures, and the cloud continued to besiege our wagons.

If a party of renegades had attacked then, we would all surely have been killed—and some of us would have welcomed it. As it was, the locusts were our sole antagonist.

"I now know why the Pharaoh let Moses go," Marty remarked as he plucked locusts from his hair.

"That's not exactly how it was, Martin," Mr. Payne, the schoolmaster, objected.

"Then he was a fool for certain," Marty answered, dipping under the water to free himself from the insects. I had to agree. Give me a Sioux raid any day.

The cloud of locusts continued southward, and we finally emerged from it. Even so, it took hours to rid ourselves of the last defiant insects, and more time still to round up our discarded clothing. As for the horses and spare animals which had taken flight, we had no notion when the last of them would be tracked down and returned.

"How soon can we return to the trail?" a shaken Captain Martinson inquired.

"No hope of doin' it today," Shea announced. "Stock won't settle down enough. As for people, well, they're little better. Darby and I'll have a look after the saddle horses. In a bit," he added, prying a locust from my hair. "Be lucky to lose one more day. More likely two."

The captain and Shea exchanged scowls, then set off to inspect the damage.

It was worse than I imagined possible. Wagons had run into gullies, busting spokes or cracking yokes. Some of the mules and oxen had rubbed their hides raw straining to free themselves. Animals and humans alike suffered from nervous shudders and red blotches left by the insect bites. I was not the only one to have sprained an ankle. And little Eva Warner, just nine, had fallen beneath her wagon. A wheel had crushed her right leg. She'd bled herself white, and the leg itself showed signs of putrification.

"I bandaged it the best I know how," Marietta told the assembled Warners.

"Best you know, though," Shea added. "That leg's sure to come off."

"No!" Mrs. Warner cried. "Not my little girl!"

"Elsewise she'll die," Shea declared. "Ma'am, might happen anyway, but if you've the nerve to try, I've seen a body saved by sheddin' a limb."

"I have a book tells how it's done," Captain Martinson offered.

"Then it's best done now, while Eva's too feverish to feel it much," the girl's father argued. "Ellen?"

Mrs. Warner reluctantly nodded, and Captain Martinson turned to Shea.

"Can you do it?" the captain asked.

"I got no feel for the healin' arts," Shea replied. "Best see if one o' the women . . ."

"I'll do it," Mrs. Martinson said. "If Mr. Shea will find what herbs he knows of to help the fever."

"I know what to pick," I said. "Maybe Miz Warner would like to help."

"Yes," she said, eager to have some distraction. Enid and Selena, the elder Warner girls, came along as well. In no time we had the needed roots dug and such leaves and berries plucked as grew thereabouts. I then left Shea to help Mrs. Martinson and the captain while I set off with a half dozen men to collect the stock.

It took the rest of that day and two more besides to round up the scattered animals. Even so, we found ourselves short one pair of oxen and three saddle ponies. I suspected the ponies were beyond our reach, but the vanished oxen troubled me some. Shea and I rode out to have a look around, and what I spotted made me wary indeed. Two miles back of us along the trail a single wagon was drawn by oxen that were a bit too like our own to be mere coincidence. An old woman drove the wagon, but two gruff riders flanked it on either side.

"Likely strayed from another train," Shea muttered.

I judged the riders to have the kind of hungry eyes rarely found among emigrants, and I said as much.

"Good to be wary of strangers, Darby," Shea told me. "But they ride in plain sight. Renegades take to the shadows."

Sometimes, though, I thought as we returned to the company, a clever man paints a new face to mask his true intentions. Thus disguised, he walks in full view of his victims. Hadn't that been Lucien Reynaud's game?

I decided my fears were best swallowed, though. Little Eva Warren was only now breaking free of her fever, and there was too much work waiting. Wheels still wanted mending, and horses needed salve.

The morning of the fourth day we were camped at what we named Dead Locust Creek, I awoke to find the Martinson company busily preparing for the trail. Everyone sprang to his or her duties with rare eagerness. Even the stock seemed to want work.

"Guess we best take the lead, son," Shea told me as we packed up our belongings.

"You go along ahead," I told him. "Get the captain to ride along with you today. Me, I think I'll give a look to our back."

"Still worried 'bout those riders?" he asked.

"Aren't you?" I asked in turn.

"Well, I got to admit they didn't pass along by us like I expected. Wouldn't hurt to keep an eye open."

Thus I spent that first day back on the trail riding in a dust cloud behind the Cochranes. Tim Frey borrowed a spare horse and kept me company.

"Those locusts halfway drove me to distraction," Tim confessed. "Thought blizzards were hard."

"They are," I reminded him. "But those locusts . . ."

"Yeah," Tim said, laughing as I scratched under my arm. He'd pried a few of them from such places, too.

I began that day full of dread, but in truth it proved to

be a rather welcome change. Tim proved good company, for it had been a time since I shared so much time with someone roughly my own age. And if the dust sometimes threatened to choke us, and our bodies acquired an outer crust of the stuff, there was at day's end a stream to cleanse us.

"Any trouble from our shadow?" Shea asked when I joined him at the Martinsons' camp for dinner.

"Oh, they kept a respectable distance, but I felt their eyes on me," I explained. "Worries me some, Tom, but they didn't do anything out and out threatening."

"Likely they just want some company up the trail," he muttered. "Most'd come right up to a man and say so, though."

I nodded my agreement and made a note to share part of the night watch. As it happened, trouble didn't wait for darkness. As Mrs. Martinson spooned out portions of pork pie, she gazed around in dismay.

"Where's Marietta?" she asked. "That girl's wandered off before, but she's never been late for dinner."

"She and Agnes Payne went down to the creek to take a bath," Marty explained.

"When was that?" Captain Martinson asked.

"Don't know exactly," Marty answered. "They were down there when Bart Sawyer and I were swimming. Then they moved upstream a bit."

"To escape roving eyes, I'll bet," I added, grinning.

"Be along soon then," the captain declared. "Let's eat our dinner. I'll have a talk with Marietta later. And you, too, young man," he added, turning toward Marty.

We ate in a kind of nervous silence. I detected growing concern on the faces of the captain and his wife. Even Shea's forehead wrinkled up a bit. And when the Paynes appeared with word that Agnes hadn't returned from a walk to the river that afternoon, I rose.

"I know a place to look," I announced. "Coming, Tom?"

"Hold on, Darby," Shea called.

"Coming?" I asked again.

He nodded, and I led the way to our horses.

"Can't very well ride down on a fellow's camp and accuse him o' takin' those gals," Shea argued as I saddled the big black.

"Didn't mean to do it that way at all," I explained. "I'll find their trail and follow it. Then I'll watch a bit. Won't ride down on 'em till I'm sure."

"You sound pretty sure right now," he observed.

"Aren't you? I never knew Marietta Martinson, or the Payne girl either for that matter, to be gone with dark closing in. Men like that . . . no telling what they might do."

"Don't go losin' your head now, Darby," Shea warned. "There's a way to go about this."

"You lead, and I'll follow, Tom. Always have. But I can't sit around and wait. It's not in me."

He nodded his understanding, then flexed his dismembered left hand. Reluctantly he took the lead and started toward the creek. We led our horses along behind.

In the beginning, the creekbank was too muddied and torn by wagon and horse tracks to be much help. Upstream, beyond where the boys had been swimming, the sandy bank was less disturbed. Finally I spotted something in the dim light. It was one of Agnes Payne's stockings. Other articles of clothing lay nearby. A few feet beyond, the tracks of two heavily-burdened horses led eastward.

"Well?" I asked.

"Does look bad," Shea agreed. "Best we get some help."

"Do," I agreed. "I'm going on ahead. Just to scout things out," I said in answer to his worried gaze. "I'll wait for you before doing anything."

"It's best," he warned.

I climbed atop my black stallion and rode back up the trail toward where I knew the mysterious trailing wagon would rest. I found it easily. The old woman tended a kettle while a pair of ragged children fed the fire. The men were off to one side, arguing rather bitterly. I dismounted, tied the black to a cottonwood, and crept forward to listen. What I heard shook me down to my toes.

"Those two are of an age to fetch a price," a tall, heavily-bearded man spoke. "No time's to be lost. Many's the trapper down Ft. Hall way in summer, but come fall, they head for the tall country."

"Then it's settled," a second man said. "We leave 'em for Ft. Hall."

"Ah, Billy, won't hurt to give 'em a little practice," a heavyset fellow argued. "Just a little."

"You fool," the first one answered. "You kilt that little trail gal we got last month. Them boys may help Ma some, but they won't fetch spit in trade."

"I know a freighter who'll take 'em off our hands," the one called Billy declared. "Give us a keg o' flour and some shot."

"And the girls?" the heavyset one asked. "I'll only gentle 'em up some, boys."

"You can look at 'em," the tall man answered. "Only that."

The heavyset fellow moved toward a shelter made from the canvas wagon cover and flung one wall aside. Inside Marietta stood staring defiantly while a slender Agnes Payne huddled in one corner. The big man reached for Etta's hand, and I shuddered. Without thinking I started toward them. The sound of my footsteps in the tall grass drew the attention of the others, and the tall man called a challenge.

"Who's there?" he bellowed.

"Darby Prescott," I answered. "Of all the Martinson company. Come to invite you to our camp since you seem bound for the same destination."

The woman left her kettle long enough to call out a welcome. One of the men moved over to watch the urchins.

Their terrified eyes were all the warning I needed to watch my step.

"Truth is," the tall man said, "we just 'bout decided to turn back to Ft. Hall. Trail's been hard, and we hear the trappin's fair in the Teton country."

"Lots of Indians there," I told them as I inched my way toward the canvas. The fat man had vanished, and the white walls hid the girls from view.

"Oh, we've traded with the Sioux," the tall man told me. "We'll do fine. Thanks for the invite, but . . ."

"Those boys look thin," I interrupted, turning toward the fire. Then, as they moved to block my path, I spun around and dove into the shelter. The large man was caught unawares, and when he reached for a knife to challenge my entry, Marietta grabbed a frying pan and slammed it against his head.

"Poley?" the tall one called as his companion crashed into a chest filled with pottery.

"Get down," I told the girls as I drew out my revolver.

"Hey, what's goin' on in there?" Billy challenged, tearing open the canvas.

I pointed my pistol and cocked the hammer. He retreated nervously.

"Now," I said, assuring myself the fat man was senseless before stepping outside to face the three others. "We missed these girls. I guess I'll be taking them along home now. The boys at the fire, too. They don't seem any too eager to stay."

One of the youngsters made a move to escape, but the old woman reached out and grabbed his arm.

"You ain't goin' nowhere, mister," she announced. "My boys'd cut you in half 'fore you got ten feet from here."

"They've got better sense, I'm thinking," I said, waving my pistol at them. "I'd kill the first two soon as anybody reached for a gun, and I'd finish the third, and you, too, ma'am, before you could remember their names. Etta, get Agnes along toward our camp now. You boys are welcome to come, too."

The terrified youngsters didn't budge, but Marietta dragged Agnes away from the camp.

"Don't you figure we're entitled to anything for our trouble?" the tall man called. "Could've been Indians found those gals."

"Better it had been," I countered. "Boys?"

The one not held by the old woman suddenly made a break. I was amazed that, malnourished as he was, he managed to catch Marietta and Agnes in a single instant. The second boy fought to shake free, but the woman's stubborn grip held him captive still.

"Ma'am, don't force me to . . ." I began. Then the tall one drew a pocket pistol from his belt and aimed it at my head. I leaped away, firing my pistol as I went. My own shot was wide of its mark, but a rifle boomed out from the hillside, and the tall man fell back against a nearby pine. An expanding red circle spread across his chest.

"Sonny!" the old woman screamed, freeing her youthful captive as she rushed toward her fallen son. The other men, meanwhile, scrambled away, only to be caught in a wild volley from the hillside. The renegades were simply shot to pieces. The old woman then lifted a rifle and was dealt with in like manner. I sat a dozen feet away, watching in dumbfounded silence at the scene of madness enveloping the camp.

"You all right, Darby?" Captain Martinson called.

"Seems so," I answered, dusting myself off and staring at the carnage. Tom Shea then stepped from the trees and made his way to my side. He said nothing, just examined me for signs of injury and rested a heavy hand on my shoulder.

"Pretty stupid, I guess," I admitted. "You told me to wait."

"You got the gals out o' there," he mumbled.

"Only thing I knew to do," I explained. "Guess we're even

on lives saved now."

"Figured we would be, what with your knack for findin' trouble."

I forced a grin onto my face, and he slapped my back. Then Etta raced over, threw both arms around my neck, and half choked me to death.

"Never knew you had that kind of talent with a frying pan," I told her once I caught my breath.

"You could've got yourself killed," she scolded me. "Next time . . ."

"Planning on getting into this sort of fix again, are you?"

She scowled, hugged me again, then led the way back to camp.

Chapter 14

Captain Martinson and a handful of others stayed to bury the dead. The fat man recovered enough to be hung. There wasn't much sympathy for him in our camp after Nick and Tommy Hull, the ragged young prisoners, explained their weeks of torment. As for the Hulls, Captain Martinson agreed to look after them until they could join an uncle in The Dalles.

"Don't know that I wasn't rescued from one fate only to be subjected to a worse one," Marietta complained to me. "One brother's bad enough. Three's sure to be the end of me."

In truth, she spoiled the newcomers shamefully. Etta was either baking up some treat for them or sewing a new shirt most every day for a week.

"Can't have them running around naked," she declared.

"Don't see why you don't just admit it," I replied. "You've got a natural talent for mama henning, and misfits draw extra attention."

"Oh?"

"Sure. You've done your share of looking after me, haven't you?"

She laughed, then declared I was in need of more help than she could provide.

"Well, you're certain to have better luck with the Hull

boys," I told her. "They might not rescue you next time renegades ride down to the river."

"Rescue me?" she asked. "Was me brained the fat one. You nearly got us all shot!"

I scowled heavily. She might be closer to the truth than I cared to admit, though. I wondered about it. Nobody else did, however. As I walked about the train, I couldn't help noticing the admiring glances of the younger boys. Girls pointed and whispered. Even their parents gave me approving nods they had so far withheld.

I judged it all the doing of Tim and Marty. They hadn't either one been there, of course, but they told a story so full of heroic boasts and brave exploits that I myself began to believe it. I walked a little straighter, and when questioned about this detail or that, I shook my head and pretended modesty. Actually I remembered almost nothing of what had happened. I was too worried about Marietta at first and later too scared to take note of what had happened.

Those final days of July flew by. Storms continued to slow our progress, and the trail was often blocked by swollen streams or rockslides. We found the grass a bit thin sometimes. Fresh meat was still to be found, but it often required Tom Shea and I a whole day scouring the hills to scare up a deer. Once or twice we contented ourselves with a few rabbits, and we came back empty-handed a few times.

I hated those days. We always read the disappointed eyes of the company. Soon our hearts were as heavy as theirs. What a delight venison was to people who'd eaten salt pork and beans until the former tasted like leather and the latter resembled river pebbles!

There was only one solution when despair threatened to devour our spirits, and Captain Martinson arrived at it immediately. We would halt our travels early and have a celebration. While children scoured the hillsides for those berries which appeared late in the season, Shea and I led what men who could be spared into the surrounding hills and hollows. We shot rabbits, squirrels, and two deer. After dressing the meat, we turned the cooking over to the women and busied ourselves building fires.

At no time were fresh meat or fresh-baked pies more welcome. Full bellies bred contentment. But to truly raise our spirits, we relied on the evening's entertainment. In the beginning, there was singing. Dancing followed. I drew out my mouth organ and shared in the music-making, but Marietta quickly put a stop to it.

"I can't dance without a partner," she told me. "Come on."

"But there's little enough music now," I complained, pointing to where Mr. Bruning blew notes on his trumpet and Mr. Whitsell played his fiddle while Captain Martinson called the steps.

"I don't care," she insisted. "You owe me a dance for bashing that renegade! I collect my debts, Darby Prescott."

"I can't see how I'm the one owes you," I argued. "Was me rushed in there to save you and Agnes."

"Well, I admit Marty and Tim make a good tale out of that, but I was there, remember? And I say . . ."

"Too much," I objected. "If you won't talk anymore, I'll do my best not to stomp on your toes. Afterward, though, I play."

She frowned heavily, then took my arm, and we joined a promenade. Soon we were swinging around, bowing right and left, and doing a fair job of keeping up with our elders.

When the dance concluded, I clapped, bowed to Etta, and reached for my mouth organ. She snatched it away and stared hard at my startled face.

"One isn't enough," she told me. "I've spent the last month slaving away like a hired cook, with dust coating every inch of me, listening to oxen moan, putting up with a brother's pranks, and now hearing you'd rather blow notes on this fool piece of brass than dance with me! Well, if you ever want to see this mouth organ again, you'd better show me some high stepping."

Some of the women applauded. Malcolm Anderson offered to take my place. Tim and Marty offered to saddle my horse for the getaway.

"I'm not altogether ugly," Marietta declared.

"Never said you were," I replied. "It's just that my ankle's not been right since our run-in with those locusts, and I . . ."

"Your ankle's been well enough to chase after squirrels and rabbits," she countered, taking my arm as the musicians resumed. And so I led her across the dance floor once more. And again after that. In all we danced more than an hour. By then my ankle really was hurting, and even Etta noticed my limp.

"Well, I guess you win," she grumbled. "Here's your fool mouth organ."

I took the instrument and started for the empty chair beside Warren Whitsell. Then I motioned her over.

"I wouldn't mind some company," I told her. She grinned, rolled a log over, and sat at my side while I blew tunes for the others.

We passed another hour like that. Then Marietta danced a bit with Tim and Bart Sawyer. She even talked Marty into one dance. I couldn't help grinning when the Hull boys invited her afterward to give them a try.

"That's enough!" she cried, marching to my side and pulling me to my feet. "Time for a walk."

I'd been enjoying the music, and my ankle was still a little stiff. There was no chance to argue, though. Etta simply stormed off toward the edge of camp, hauling me along as if I were an afterthought. We passed the picketed horses, nodded to Sully Payne, who was keeping watch, and continued to where a small pond formed beside a small spring.

"It's nice here," she said, sitting atop a fallen tree and

motioning for me to join her. "Quiet."

"You can still hear the music from our camp if you listen real good," I told her.

"Been a while since we walked out and gazed at the stars, Darby."

"Yes," I admitted. "Doesn't seem like there's been much time for such things lately. Shoot, before tonight I hadn't played my mouth organ in better'n two weeks."

"Sitting out here, it seems like we're the only people in the entire world. It's a lonely place, this plain of yours."

"Valley," I explained. "Lonely? No, there are all sorts of birds and animals about."

"I'm not talking about buffalo!"

"Not many of them hereabouts," I argued. "But deer, yes, and lots of . . ."

"Stop it, Darby. You know what I mean. I need to share things. So do you. I feel it when we're together."

"Do you? Etta, I think maybe you're misunderstanding things some."

"You do a fair job of hiding sometimes, Darby, but you can't mask your feelings. I can feel your hands trembling right now," she said, gripping my wrists. "Maybe you've been living wild of late, but nobody raised in the wilds can play Mozart. Once you had a home, and you weren't so different from the rest of us. I'd like to see you that way again. With me and my family maybe. Then later on we could . . ."

"Etta, I like you," I confessed, squeezing her hands. "As much as about anybody I've met. It's fun talking things over with you, looking at the moon and stars, even dancing. But you don't know me."

"Don't I?"

"No," I said, releasing my grip on her hands and walking away. I stopped beside the pond and splashed cool water on my face. It seemed to cool a growing fever.

"Darby, I want to know you. Tell me about yourself. Tell

me about your dreams."

"I quit dreaming," I answered. "Long ago. Now I go where the wind blows me, and I do my best to stay clear of bear claws and rockslides. And locusts."

"And farmgirls?" she asked.

"Them especially," I said, matching her grin. "I can't help you know me 'cause I don't know myself. Shea calls us wayfarers on account of we don't know where we're going, or even why. Guess that's as good a word as another. I do know most of the people I get attached to don't live long, and it's made me cautious about making friends."

"So, I'm not even a friend?"

"Yes, you are one," I said, staring at my feet. "A good one, I think. But as to there being more to it, you've got to understand. It's not in me."

"That's a shame, Darby. Being lonely's a hard way to be."

"I know," I agreed. A frown spread across my face, and a shiver worked its way through my entire body. I wanted to sigh, but I held myself in check.

She walked over and clutched my hand. We walked around and around the pond, neither of us speaking a word. Then I took out my mouth organ and played a somber tune. It was, like most of the trail tunes I knew, a sad tale of leaving home and loved ones for the uncertainties of a mist-shrouded future. She hummed along, then struck up the words.

"Oh, hear me, my darling, I'm bound for the west,
Don't cry for me, dearest, just pray for the best."

It was the way we all felt setting out for Oregon back in '48. Like Marietta, too, I judged from the pale expression on her face.

"Won't be long 'fore you're clearing land, building a house," I whispered. "Me and Shea'll likely be riding into the mountains."

165

"It doesn't have to be that way," she declared.

"No, but I figure it will be," I explained. "It's the life I know best, you see. And if it's lonely sometimes, well, that passes."

She rested her head on my shoulder, and I stroked her long, soft hair. I could feel something new and special flowing through her, something she was offering to share. I yearned, as always, for that special belonging Marietta Martinson was freely offering. Oh, how I wanted to accept! But I finally stepped away and pointed toward our camp.

"Time we headed back," I told her. "Your family's sure to worry if you're out late."

"I'm in good hands," she countered.

"And I'd as soon not be in theirs," I said, laughing. "Hasn't been so long ago they hung that renegade. Wouldn't want to share his fate."

"You just can't admit it, can you?" she complained. "You've got strong feelings, too. I know it."

"Come on," I said, waving her along. "Let's get back."

I judge I returned with Marietta only moments before the captain would have had half the company out searching.

"Told you she was safe, Pa," Marty said. "I saw her walk off with Darby."

"Where were you two?" the captain asked.

"Had a look at the horses," I explained. "Then we watched the stars a bit."

"Marietta, best give your ma a hand," the captain commanded. "Darby, I'll have words for you later."

"Yes, sir," I said, figuring he would complain about our leaving camp after dark. Marietta squeezed my hand in farewell, then hurried to find her mother. I accompanied Tom Shea to the small camp we'd made just ahead of the train.

"Have a fine time of it tonight, did you, son?" Shea asked as we approached our blankets.

"Yes," I admitted. "Leg's a bit sore, but the dancing did stir my heart some. And Etta's good company."

"What'd you two do?"

"We sang some songs, and we talked. Nothing much else you can do hereabouts."

"Growin' fond o' that gal, are you?"

"Tom, she's a fine friend. Reminds me of my sister Mary. Oh, sometimes she turns downright serious, but mostly she talks about the trail and the future."

"Future?"

"Well, I suppose she's put all manner of strange notions about us in her head. But I'm not ready to take a woman into my winter cabin, am I?"

"You'd have to answer that yourself."

"How'll I know?"

"Don't know words to explain it, but you will. It's a natural thing, you know. Call it a nestin' instinct."

"You knew when you married the Crow girl, didn't you?"

"I knew," he said, scowling.

"How?"

"Because I couldn't breathe when we were apart, Darby. Because we were like two branches of the same tree. Wasn't any thinking to do. We knew, the both of us, that we'd share a lodge. Was meant to be."

I nodded, though I understood very little of it.

Captain Martinson appeared moments later, though, and his sharp words tore me away from the mysteries of women and love.

"Don't get me wrong," the captain said in conclusion. "I like you, Darby, and I respect your efforts on the trail. You're a fine scout and a good man. But I wouldn't want you to hurry things where Marietta is concerned."

"Sir?"

"I know it's the frontier way to rush everything. Boys just naturally seem to grow taller here sooner. Youngsters like Bart and Tim seem in their twenties. But where Marietta is concerned, I expect caution. I simply won't have it otherwise!"

"Yes, sir," I responded. "You know, I like her, Captain, but I've never spoken to her of anything more serious than the way Mt. Hood looks at autumn sunrise. Truth is, I don't know enough about the future to speak of it. Half the time when we're together I don't know what I'll say or why. But I've never done anything to lead her to think . . ."

"You don't have to say it," the captain told me. "A woman judges a man's actions more than his words. Your going after her that afternoon at Dead Locust Creek spelled it all out."

"I went after Agnes Payne, too, but she hasn't dragged me around camp, telling me how I ought to feel."

"And Marietta has?" he asked with a frown."

"Well, I guess that's a bit strong," I confessed. "She does set her mind to things, though, and it's hard to discourage her."

"You'll try, though, won't you, Darby?"

"That's what you want, isn't it?"

"Yes, son. It's what's best. Take this advice from a man who this once will step into the shoes your father ought to be wearing. Darby, you're a farmboy, or were born one at any rate. Any farmer knows that before he plants seed, he's got to clear the land and plow the fields. Before winter comes, he'll need a cabin."

"I don't think I understand," I told him.

"It's pretty simple," he insisted. "You have a lot of preparing to do before taking on heavy burdens. Ease into things. Don't give way to sudden passion."

"I won't," I promised. After all, I had no notion of what he meant by sudden passion!

Captain Martinson retired to the main camp, and I tried to make some sense of everything. It was hard, what with me not understanding half of it. The captain and Etta both wanted to make something serious out of each smile or casual nod. And Marty didn't help things the next day when he trotted around, shouting how I was ready to declare myself to Marietta any hour. Finally Tom Shea put an end to that by riding over, yanking Marty onto his horse, and riding out to where I led the train westward.

"Boy's got something to share with you," Shea said, gripping Marty by the shoulders.

"Was just tellin' folks you and Etta might get married," Marty explained.

"Little fool," I cried. "That's not true at all."

"She writes about it in her diary, and I peek," Marty explained. "Didn't mean anything. Figured you knew."

"Isn't a thing to laugh about, even if it's true," Shea scolded. "Pitiful rare these days for folks to take each other to heart When it happens it ought to be respected. Understand?"

Marty squirmed and squealed as Shea held him by the shirt collar over a steep ravine. He promised never to repeat his mistake, and Shea dropped him to safer ground.

"Sorry if it troubled you, Darby," Marty said as he brushed himself off and turned back toward the approaching wagons. "Didn't mean anything."

"Go on," I said, waving the twelve-year-old along.

"Might be best if we stayed ahead o' the train a few days," Shea suggested once Marty was out of earshot.

"Was thinking the same thing," I told him. "Maybe we can even get some hunting in."

"Could be," he agreed.

And so I contented myself with the howling wind, Shea's snoring, and the big black's restless stomping for company. The stars found only my weary eyes staring overhead at night. And more than ever, I was lonely.

Chapter 15

The trail rolled ever westward toward the Snake's junction with the Boise River at the fur trading post of Ft. Boise. The last hundred miles Shea and I scouted the path ahead, keeping an eye out for trouble and hunting when the opportunity afforded itself. It was a rather uneventful time for the train. No renegades or floods hampered our progress, and oxen plodded along wearily as the August sun blazed down on man and beast alike.

The strain of those months on the march showed. Two horses went lame, and nearly everyone was now afoot. The few spare oxen left to us were set to work daily in hopes some other poor creature might recover its strength if rested. None did, and finally every ox took its place in one yoke or another.

I rarely got so much as a glimpse of Marietta. Each two days Shea sent me back with fresh meat or instructions to Captain Martinson, and once or twice we spoke. More often I nodded silently in her direction as I passed along my news or unpacked the meat from the back of a pack horse.

"Best you be along back to Shea," the captain said whenever I eyed his daughter. "Tell him to keep the road clear. We have some time to make up."

Perhaps we did, but the company's pace fell to a mere ten

miles per day as we approached Ft. Boise. Wagons groaned from hard use, and breakdowns slowed our progress even more.

"I'm a fool to bring pilgrims up this trail!" Shea grumbled as we gazed down at the procession of white canvas snaking its way toward us. "Give me a mule train anyday."

"You came west yourself once," I reminded him.

"Was never half the fool those folks are," he declared. "Why, it's plain to see the McIntosh wagon's done for, and those Germans near the back that took in young Bart have a bad wheel."

"I know you'd have them abandon their wagons and pair up with somebody else," I said, frowning. "Maybe it's good sense. But Mrs. McIntosh's got a lifetime's treasures with her, and Mr. Schroeder and Bart'll nurse that wheel till we get to Ft. Boise and fix it proper."

"Taken the whole batch to heat, haven't you, Darby?" he asked.

"Disappointed in me? Think maybe I'd grown as hard-hearted as Tom Shea, what with wintering in the mountains and all?"

"Mountain's a good teacher, all right."

"You'd have me believe the lot of 'em could sink in a hole and you'd never know the difference. Tom, you old fraud, I know you. Remember, you took in an orphan farmboy two winters back, and I've seen how you take care to cut the little ones an extra slice of venison."

"Never said I was without my faults," he said, grinning. "And me?"

"You got enough for an army, boy. Lucky I'm a tolerant sort, eh?"

By and by, Shea would offer some of the older boys a horse to ride. He'd done much the same with me once. Occasionally Tim Frey and his brothers, Bart Sawyer, or Marty would join us for a day or so. I took advantage of those times, and we usually had a hunt, swam in the river, and fished for brook trout. It was a rare chance to laugh and shout away the fatigue. And to be young. I do believe Tom Shea enjoyed those times even more than the rest of us. Afterward he always slept soundly. Other days I would find him sitting in the moonlight, staring at his missing fingers and remembering.

Being off to ourselves most of the time had its drawbacks, though. Neither of us took much care with our appearance, and Shea took on a rather wild look. His beard fell down onto his chest, and his oily brown hair curled under his hat and stretched down over his collar. Most days he wore only a pair of buckskin breeches, and his hard, leathery shoulders browned until you would have thought him an Indian sure except his chest was haired over, and his face bearded.

Summer worked a spell on me, too. My hair grew lighter, a sort of prairie grass yellow laced with strands of brown. It grew down almost to my eyes in front, swallowed my ears, and flowed down my back. A scraggly beard spread across my cheeks, and my skin was nigh as bronze as Shea's.

"Think I could pass for Shoshoni?" I asked as we rode along the river.

"Ute maybe," he replied. "Tall for Shoshoni. Might make a Crow of you, Darby. Once you get a little more sour. You still got too much white boy in you."

"Think so, Tom?"

"Not altogether a bad thing, you know. Might be you want to go back to civilized ways someday. Maybe not farmin', but tradin' or such."

"Like run a ferry or a store like Burkett?" I asked. "Guess there's worse fates, Tom, but I've got a mountain heart. You said so yourself, remember?"

He nodded, and I detected a trace of a grin. Afterward he nudged his horse into a gallop, and we rode briskly westward.

August was half gone when we reached Ft. Boise. Shea

rode on ahead to speak to the trader, Duncan Macilvain, a fellow Scot who greeted the rest of us with bagpipes and a highland song. The two of them hopped about like a pair of fools, joined by the dozen other occupants of the little trading post.

I stepped down from my horse in time to be lifted bodily by bespectacled, gray-haired Molly Bostwick, who took in laundry and tended a handful of strays at the trading post. A winter and a half back she'd done a fair job of thawing me out when Shea and I'd got ourselves caught in a blizzard crossing the river. I nodded to Sheila Brooke, the Paget brothers, and slapped young Jubal Boyd on the back. It was like seeing long-lost family.

"You must know every trail orphan west of Laramie!" Marietta exclaimed when she pried me away from Jubal's firm grip.

"We orphans got to look after each other," I explained as I introduced her to the others. Sheila offered to show Marietta around, but Etta declined.

"Why don't you do it?" she asked me.

"Thinkin' o' takin' to tepee livin', Darby?" Jubal asked, grinning so that his fourteen-year-old eyes squinted and blinked. "Bet she'll cost you three horses."

"Horses!" Marietta yelled. "Why, you little . . ."

The words were wasted on Jubal. He was quick as a lizard and well out of reach before Marietta could locate an appropriate club.

"You'll have dinner with us, won't you?" Sheila asked. "Miz Molly's been shinin' up her piano ever since Shea rode in. Been a time since we had anybody play it who knew how."

"Can't say for certain," I said, gazing at Shea. "We been keeping ahead of the train."

"He won't be ridin' anywhere tonight," Sheila assured me. "Mac's already opened a bottle, and the two of 'em's sure to empty it. You can bring *her* along, if you've a mind. There's

173

food enough if she won't eat a lot."

"Care to come?" I asked, turning to Etta. Shea was puffed up like something fierce, and I believe she'd hit Sheila except for the fear Sheila'd surely have struck back. It wasn't an idle fear, either. Sheila might not be much bigger than Jubal, but she was coiled up like a rattlesnake, and I figured her to have as nasty a bite as a diamondback.

If the two of them had set upon each other, it would have been a close call who'd won. As it happened, Miz Molly summoned Sheila to help tend the store counter, and Captain Martinson called for Etta to help her mother.

"I thought maybe you'd lend the smith a hand, Darby," the captain said to me. "Later on maybe you could gather up some of the boys and fish the river. Macilvain says there are trout there just waiting to bite a hook."

"Thought I might do some visiting," I explained.

"Rather you tend your duties," he barked. "Marietta's apt to be occupied, too."

"Yes, sir," I told him. I then set off to the stable where Duncan Macilvain had set up a small forge. An old trapper named Hicks was busy pounding out horseshoes on his anvil when I arrived. A line of people stretched halfway around the side of the building. Each one held some piece of harness or leaned against a bad wheel. The smith gazed at the line, frowned, and hurried his work.

Hicks spent the better part of the day slaving over the forge in a sweltering heat that surely matched the fires of perdition. Most of that time I was nearby, either stoking the fire or working the bellows. I hammered a bit of iron as well when Hicks retired to douse himself with a pail of well water.

"Know your way around an anvil, don't you?" he asked as I reshaped a bent rim.

"I used to help my brother back in Illinois. He wasn't a regular smith, understand, but he made horseshoes and worked on harness sometimes."

"Don't have the hands for rough work," Hicks observed. "Fingers too skinny. Look at mine."

His hands were flattened out as if he'd taken a hammer to them, and his long, puffy fingers reminded me of German sausages. He was a powerful man, stout like a pine stump, and if he carried an unfortunate odor, it was honestly come by through toil and effort.

"Sometimes," I told him, "a man does things he's not born to. Mama always fretted that when I lifted a hammer I'd take off a finger or such. She supposed I'd be a musician, I think, or maybe a lawyer. I took to books early."

"You're the one Jubal says plays Molly's piano, aren't you?"

"Was here a couple of winters ago," I explained.

"And she had to thaw you out in a tub," Hicks added with a hearty laugh. "That was a tale, son. You woke up plumb naked thinkin' you'd likely been called to the Almighty. Least St. Pete allows you a robe, or so I've heard."

"Wasn't the best way to meet a person, I'll admit," I said, grinning.

"Molly's a good 'un."

"Saved my life, and others as well."

"Set my cap for her, you know," the smith explained. "She's playin' it shy for now, but she'll come 'round. Woman wants a man, don't you know?"

"I'm not sure Molly needs much of anything."

"Everybody needs company, boy. Winter chills need a bit o' comfortin'."

I thought back to the icy touch of the wind cutting through me and nodded. Shea wouldn't agree, of course. He needed nothing, or so he liked to say. If it was altogether true, he never would've cut off his fingers.

We called it a day late in the afternoon. I don't think Hicks could lift his arms, and I was sweated down to the bone. I staggered out of the forge and ran right into Molly Bostwick.

"Dear Lord, what've they done to you, Darby Prescott?" she cried. "Look to've been tortured by devils. Your forehead's afire, and your shirt's soaked."

"Far cry from how you found me last time," I told her as I wiped my forehead.

"Well, I threw you in my tub and scrubbed you then. Doesn't look to me like you've had a bath since."

"Was working with Hicks at the forge," I explained. "Too much work with the heat and all."

"Judd Hicks, you old scoundrel!" Molly barked. "Keepin' a boy at his work when there's a river to swim. You know he's been two years with Tom Shea. That old mountain goat sure hasn't give him leave to run about. I'd say he's due a holiday."

"I'm supposed to take some of the boys to the river," I said, gazing around nervously. Captain Martinson was probably cross with me for not doing so already. Soon it would be time to cook dinner. Trout not caught couldn't be eaten.

"Jubal took 'em down an hour ago," Molly said, shaking her head. "Made himself some friends. The Pagets are a bit old for him, and Sheila judges him poor company. She's right more often than not."

"Well, I'd best join them," I declared, turning toward the junction of the two rivers.

"While you're down there, why not have a wash?" Molly suggested, passing a cake of soap to me. "Scrub good, too. I cleaned up my piano. Don't want horse sweat and traildust all over it."

"Yes, ma'am," I answered as I left.

I arrived at the river to discover Jubal had identified all the best spots for hooking trout. Hooks and lines were doled out, and now three baskets of trout awaited the cook fires. Meanwhile women busied themselves washing clothes while downstream men and boys washed a month's accumulated filth off their bodies. The women would do their bathing after dark when the view from the trading post would offer less temptation to the hunters and trappers who frequented the place in summer.

"Never in my life saw anything to match it," Niles Conway said as he scrubbed his tender shoulder.

"Not such a bad scar," I observed.

"Wasn't talking about that, Darby," he answered, laughing loudly. "Look at the river."

I did and laughed. A dark muddy sludge washed up on the green banks. We'd muddied the river with three hundred miles of Snake River dirt mixed in with sweat and perhaps a few tears.

"Only right to leave the trail behind 'fore passin' over into the Promised Land," Hiram Dixon called. "Yonder lies Oregon proper, eh, Darby? We're almost there."

"Closer," I told them all. "Long ways yet, though. Ought to beat winter to the Willamette just the same."

"I hoped to do some fall planting," Dixon grumbled. "Bad luck we've had so many animals go lame."

"We've had good fortune," I argued. "Not buried half the people I did coming West back in '48."

"Buried enough," Stephen Payne declared, and I nodded sadly. Simon McAlister eased his way over to his new father and offered a comforting hand, and Payne's sour gaze passed.

We frolicked around the river another hour. Then Captain Martinson declared the fish ready, and most everybody scrambled into clothes and set off for the feast. I slipped away to the fort. Molly had a kettle of stew bubbling on her stove. Jubal had a change of clothing at hand, for Molly deemed my dusty trail clothes a danger to her piano. I changed in the back room and reappeared in time to squeeze between Jubal and Tom Shea on one side of a long table. To my surprise the Martinsons appeared and occupied the opposite bench. Only the Hull boys were missing. The Pagets and Sheila helped serve, then took station where space allowed.

"Oh, what a treat!" Mrs. Martinson said when she gazed at the stew. "Vegetables. Carrots and peas. Potatoes and onions."

"Onions grow wild hereabouts," Clark Paget explained. "Darby knows where. Turnips, too, and other things."

"The potatoes, peas, and carrots come from my garden," Molly explained. "Sheila and I tend it like a child, it and the piano. They're about the only civilization we have at Ft. Boise."

"Ah, Molly, we read the Bible and do our lessons," Jubal complained. "That's about as civilized as a body can stand. Darby, you don't do any such nonsense out on the trail, do you? Scout's not got any need o' readin'."

"Got to read lots of things," I argued. "Sometimes you have to sign contracts. Best know what they say. There's guidebooks come along, too. Some offer a helpful hint. Most are pure nonsense. You've a need to know one from the other."

"Maybe," Jubal conceded. "But there's so much adventure. You hunt and fish, live off the land. There are Indians to treat with, new places to see . . ."

"Mostly it's hard work," I said, grinning as Shea flashed a mischievous smile in my direction. "But there are times, well, like when we met up with a herd of grizzlies."

"A what?" Henry Paget asked. "Grizzlies don't travel in herds."

"They do in the Rockies," I explained. "Hundreds. Rumble down on you like buffs except instead of stampeding away, they come at you with those monstrous claws and . . ."

"Please, that's enough," Mrs. Martinson pleaded. "Darby, we needn't know all the particulars."

But the others egged me on, and I spun a wondrous adventure of tackling the grizzly herd. It was a shameless lie, but everyone seemed to enjoy it.

"You know, I might give scoutin' a try once my tradin'

days are over," Jubal declared. "Figure in a couple of years you'll need a new partner, Tom?"

"Never can tell," Shea answered. "This one I got now's partial to pretty gals. Bet he'll want to take a little Shoshoni gal into our winter lodge."

"He's a bit young, don't you think?" Mrs. Martinson asked. "And with young ones present, I wish you wouldn't talk of such matters, Mr. Shea."

"Sorry, ma'am," Shea apologized.

For a time the conversation shifted to gardening. Then Captain Martinson narrated our eventful journey. I took a turn at the piano afterward, and the others sang with rare enthusiasm. I found the keys warm to my touch, and I knew I would miss that part of myself that loved a melody once we were back on the trail.

"You could stay here, Darby," Molly told me. "Judd needs help at the forge, and he says you'd do. Jubal'd be happy of the company."

"I've got a job," I explained. "And I want to see my sister in a bit."

"Well, I can well understand," she said. "Just watch out you don't let Tom Shea lead you too deep into those mountains o' his. I like to hear good music, and you've got the gift of the angels with a song, Darby."

"Thanks," I said, feeling a bit self-conscious with everyone gazing at me.

I played close to an hour in all. Then my fingers told me it was enough. I thanked Molly for dinner and escaped out the back door. Marietta was waiting there.

"Thought you'd sneak out," she said with a frown. "Forget I was alive? You've hardly spoken to me in weeks."

"Not much to say."

"Was once. I thought we were friends. You've grown so distant."

"It's how I am," I said, shrugging my shoulders. "Lots of trail left."

"Papa spoke to you, didn't he?"

"Yes," I confessed.

"Darby, I miss our talks. It gets so lonely, especially with Nick and Tommy around."

"I know it's hard, Etta, but this is a new trail for me. I don't understand much of it. I figure maybe your papa might know what's best."

"Talking never hurt anybody."

"I don't know I could be content to talk forever, Etta. Not when the stars are all out, and the moonlight dances on your hair."

"I like you, too, Darby."

She walked over and rested her head on my shoulder. I felt closer to her than to anyone since Mama died. Something warm and wonderful seemed to be flowing through me.

No! I thought. The captain's right to urge caution. A wayfarer blows with the wind. And a Rocky Mountain winter's no time to take a wife.

I made my escape silently. In minutes I reached the loft Judd Hicks had offered Shea and I for the duration of our stay. I kicked off my boots, shed my clothes, and dove into the hay.

Come morning, I rose early. Shea was still snoring away in the hay nearby. I thought to wake him, but the scent of spirits was strong on his breath. I deemed it likely he needed sleep.

As for myself, I deemed my return to civilization merited a bit of cleaning up. I had Sheila cut back my hair, and I used a razor to erase my whiskers. When I finished, I was reborn. My eyes, now freed from their shaggy overhang, were deeper than I'd noticed, and my face was almost solemn. Even with the whiskers shaved off, I looked older. And for the first time I noticed small delicate brown hairs sprouting on my chest.

"It's time," Shea called from behind me. "Been standin'

tall awhile. Size and such comes."

"Sure," I said, remembering what Captain Martinson had said. The frontier did hurry a man along. It was at the same time both a comfort and a trial.

Chapter 16

We didn't stay long at Ft. Boise. Once wagons were repaired and stock rested, we began preparations for crossing the Snake. The first hints of autumn came on the midnight wind, and everyone seemed filled with sudden urgency.

"Use the crossing upstream," Macilvain advised. "Other's shallow, but the mud can bog down your wheels and leave the current to work her tricks."

Shea nodded, and together we led the company a mile upstream to where the river seemed to narrow prior to making a wide bend. I tried the crossing myself first. It proved no more than three and a half feet deep there, but the current was swift enough to give the big black a nervous moment or two.

"What d'you think, Darby?" Shea called from the far bank when I reached the other side.

"Best we string some lines," I suggested. "Give folks something to hold onto. And the little ones are sure to need some looking after."

"Can the wagons make it?" he asked.

"Oh, if the oxen can, the wagons'll make out. Might be a good idea to float what supplies need to be kept dry across. Wet flour's not much for lasting."

And so we halted the crossing long enough to construct a

pair of rafts. Casks and barrels were loaded onto one, and it was hauled across the Snake with poles. Two ropes on either side kept the raft on course, and the ride across was fine as a ferry trip. The wagons were driven across, each in turn. The rocky streambed jostled everything and everyone aboard, and I daresay some wished they had chosen to ride the raft instead. Little Aurora Dixon was sitting beside her mother in the bed when water swept her away. I was watching and couldn't believe my eyes! It was as if the river reached out and snatched the nine-year-old.

She would surely have drowned had not Tim Frey flung himself into the stream. He swam like a fish anyway, but just then he had the whole company cheering him on. Tim grabbed Aurora's bobbing head just in time, then splashed back to shore. A bit of pounding on her back emptied her lungs of water, and she soon regained her color.

Henrietta Normile wasn't so fortunate. She, her brother, and her sister were taken in by the Sutherlands back at Ft. Hall. She was a pleasant-looking little thing, all nutmeg hair and emerald eyes. After Aurora's misadventure, Shea had warned the children ought to be tied to the wagons. The Sutherlands were new at looking after youngsters, though, and they ignored the advice. The river slapped at the wagon fiercely, and suddenly the Normiles were in the water. Hunter, the eldest, managed to swim ashore with little Hyacinth. Henrietta was simply swallowed by the foaming current.

"It's hard losing one so young," Mrs. Sutherland remarked when we finally located Henrietta's body an hour or so later, washed onto the bank downstream.

"So near the end of the trail, too," Marietta observed.

"Death's as hard one place as another," Shea grumbled. "We got work waitin', friends."

He was only saying the truth, but I think the company thought less of him for it. Or maybe they blamed us for picking the crossing.

"It's a scout's lot to take the blame," Shea told me while we helped Hunter dig a grave for his sister. "Sometimes, though, I wonder that they can't see we grieve just the same as they do."

"Difference is we know what's ahead," I reminded him. "Nobody wants to get himself trapped in the Cascades by winter snows."

"We won't, will we?" Hunter asked.

"Not unless we turn stupid," Shea answered, lifting the boy's chin. "Or we spend too much time talkin'."

I took the hint and resumed digging. We set Henrietta in the soft sand beside the river and marked her grave with rocks shaped like a cross. We read some verse, sang a hymn, and swallowed our sadness. It was the only way to face death on the trail.

The country north of the Snake River crossing was a rather faceless plain. It offered no obstacle to our progress, and in two days time we were camped on the banks of the Malheur River. Ahead lay a series of low mountain ranges leading first to the Blue Mountains and then on to the Cascades. The final four hundred miles of our journey were the most difficult, for we had to cross the most rugged mountains on the continent, ford raging rivers, and traverse in-between a dry, treeless plain that offered scant shade and less water.

It was a foreboding prospect even for a train in high spirits with sound stock. Weariness now sapped the company's strength, and animals grew weaker each morning. The children were pale and thin. Nerves were raw, and almost daily Captain Martinson had to separate some pair when tempers exploded into a fistfight.

"If we reach the Willamette tomorrow, it won't be soon enough for my taste," Mrs. Frey told me. "I've been three years on my way here, lost half my family along the way, and it seems I'm no nearer to trail's end than when I first left St. Louis."

Others felt much the same. I recalled my own exasperation as the monotony of trail life gnawed at my soul. This time even tunes from my mouth organ or a bit of dancing in the evening wouldn't hold despair at bay.

"I wish there was a shorter way," I told Shea as we walked along the banks of the Malheur that evening.

"Why, there is!" a voice called from the darkness.

"Hold still!" Hiram Dixon shouted as he shouldered his musket. Since our trouble on the Snake and at Independence Rock, no one took guard duty lightly, and Dixon was in a foul mood besides.

"Friends, I mean you no harm," the voice called to a growing crowd. "Name's Pembroke, Joshua Pembroke, and I've come to deliver you from your trials."

Bart Sawyer lit a torch and lifted it high so as to illuminate the far bank of the river. A single horseman then splashed across the shallow stream and entered our camp.

"What business have you with us?" Shea asked as Pembroke rolled off his horse.

"I've come to spare you the Blue Mountains and the Cayuse Indians," Pembroke declared. "You've heard how the Cayuse murdered the good reverend Marcus Whitman and his wife, not to mention those poor innocents taken in by their generosity. Well, no more bloodthirsty tribe ever breathed, and there's others besides. Nez Perce and Umatilla."

The men exchanged anxious looks, and women drew their little ones close.

"I come to take you another way," Pembroke explained. "Five years ago a mountain man name o' Steve Meeks cut a trail west to the Willamette across gentle valleys and good grass. No mountains to speak of. You follow the trail to the Deschutes River, then north to The Dalles. Cuts a month's travelin' in half."

"And what would this shortcut cost us?" Captain Martinson asked.

"Trail's free, though I'd have to charge you for my time if I was to guide you across," Pembroke explained. "Fifty dollars for the first wagon. Five apiece thereafter."

"Do you know this trail, Mr. Shea?" the captain asked.

Shea eyed Pembroke coldly, then drew out a knife and cut a slice of dried venison to chew on.

"Meeks cut-off," Shea muttered. "Sure, I know of it."

"And?" Captain Martinson asked.

"Steve Meeks was a fair trapper, folks, and as honest a man as you could meet. Saw folks sufferin' on the hard crossin' north to the Columbia and 'round past Mt. Hood. He knew the Cascades, and he cut a trail west as this fellow claims. Sold folks maps or guided 'em through himself. A thousand or more turned that way. Most wished they hadn't."

"What happened?" I asked.

"Meeks was a loner," Shea explained. "He never took a whole party o' folks anywhere. He didn't know they'd need so much water, and he never figured the lead animals'd eat all the forage. Didn't mean to take 'em into a wilderness that'd swallow their hopes and leave most of 'em staggerin' into The Dalles in the dead o' winter with nary a shirt on their back nor shoes on their feet. Two dozen of 'em never did get to trail's end, and them that did were months gettin' there. They call that trail Meeks's Misery, or the Trail o' Graves. It's not a route I'd choose."

"So you say," Pembroke declared. "I was there, with the first train, and I want to tell you it was everything promised. If other folks had their troubles, well, maybe they started late or were shy on sense. I only know I was in Oregon City three weeks after takin' to Meeks's cut-off."

"Three weeks!" Mercy Zachary cried. "Glory! Mr. Shea, you say we're a month or more away by your route. It's early. Couldn't what he says be true?"

"I had my say," Shea said, shaking his head in frustration.

"He's never been that way," Pembroke declared. "I have. What's more, I have mapped the entire passage. Here," he added, drawing out a map and spreading it in front of Captain Martinson. The whole company crowded forward to get a glimpse, and Pembroke took advantage of the opportunity to extol the merits of his route.

"A dry trail?" Uriah Anderson asked. "Why, you show rivers aplenty."

"It's clearly shorter, Martin," Melvil Bragg agreed. "Surely we should consider it."

"Then a vote is in order," the captain announced.

"Wait!" I pleaded. "Won't you listen to Shea? He knows!"

"We've got a map, Darby," the captain explained. "We can choose for ourselves."

"A map!" I yelled. "Maps don't feel the heat or choke on the dust. They don't bleed and they don't starve. If it's such a wondrous route, why haven't others gone that way? You're not blind. See if you notice any wagon ruts headed west along the Malheur. There aren't any."

"But the Indians!" Mrs. Anderson cried. "Have you forgotten the Howell boy?"

"I've been up this trail," I said, gazing at Shea with pleading eyes. He seemed unwilling to help, though, so I went on. "I've heard of the Whitman massacre, but that was way north of the Columbia. The Umatillas brought us food, and the Nez Perce, why don't you remember the white horse I used to ride? They gave it to me."

"Times can change all that," Pembroke declared. "This has been a troubled year in the Wallowa. One whole train was wiped out."

"I don't believe a word of it," I grumbled. "Shea, tell 'em. Tom, please?"

"Well?" the captain asked. "We're ready to vote."

"I said it all," Shea said, pacing back and forth. "I never traveled it, true enough, but I buried some that did. You won't need Indians or renegades to kill you goin' that way.

Trail's hard enough to do the job itself. It's less'n four hundred miles more. Don't go gettin' yourselves buried now, when you're close to the end."

"Listen to him," I urged.

"Think of the weeks you'll save!" Pembroke shouted. "The miles."

"No, think o' your little ones," Shea answered. "That road'll get some of 'em killed. Maybe all o' you."

"It's uncommon cruel of you to speak that way," Mrs. Kimberly said, holding her little girl Susan tightly.

"Dyin's a lot more cruel," Shea reminded her. "It's your choice to make, folks, but I wouldn't wish that trail on a Platte River card shark."

We were battling long odds. Fatigue and folly are brothers, and the good sense in our words fell on deaf ears. The company voted to follow Pembroke, and between them they paid out fifty dollars to hire him as guide.

"You have to do something," I told Shea when we made camp that night. "You couldn't be mistaken about the cutoff, could you? The grass could be better. Maybe they've had rain."

"Ocean o' rain wouldn't make that country fit for a wagon train," he assured me.

"You should've spoken stronger."

"No, son, it's for them to choose. A scout's nothin' but a guide. The company's got the reins, don't you see?"

I didn't. I only knew our friends were about to set out on a foolhardy course, and I was unable to stop them. Or was I? A notion crept into my mind, and I set to work making plans.

A year before I never would have undertaken such a scheme. I expected Tom Shea to do what was needed, and I followed his lead always. But when a man's chest sprouts hair and his voice deepens, he can't always rely on somebody else to do his acting. So I decided to thwart the plans of Joshua Pembroke and insure the safety of the Martinson company.

Pembroke himself cooperated wonderfully. He stayed well past midnight in the camp, sharing stories and taking long sips from a pocket flask. He had the fifty dollars in his coat pocket, and he wasn't worried about anything. He spread his blankets out near the edge of camp and left his horse to graze.

Running the horse off across the Malheur was easiest. The animal didn't seem to take to camp life, and when I waved my hat and slapped its rump, it galloped off in an instant.

Next I crept up to Pembroke, laid a solid whack on his forehead with a length of pine, and dragged him to a rocky thicket downstream. After taking care to hide our tracks, I bound the would-be scout head and foot, then gagged him. I sat with him until he regained consciousness, then urged he lay low.

"I'll come back later this morning and free you if you do as I say," I explained. "You cause any trouble, I'll come back and skin you. Understand?"

Pembroke was furious, but he had little choice. He tried to loosen his ropes, only to find them tightening instead. He finally nodded and rolled over against a large boulder. I made a hasty departure, glad to use what darkness remained to conceal my activities.

"Where you been?" Shea asked when I crawled back to my blankets.

"Guess I'm not so good a raider as I imagined," I told him. "Been having a look at the horses. With this Pembroke suddenly popping up, no telling what other surprises lurk nearby."

"Don't care to tell me the truth, eh?"

"Thought I just did," I said, nervously slipping off my shoes and wriggling out of my trousers.

"Don't ever take to Pembroke's trade," Shea advised. "You aren't cut out for lyin', son. But I'll let it pass. You'll tell me when you've got a mind, I suspect."

I suspected otherwise.

When morning broke upon the camp, the company hurried about its chores as always. It was close to an hour later when someone discovered Pembroke's horse and belongings, together with the man himself, had vanished.

"Can't be!" Mr. Dixon cried. "He was going to lead us through the short way."

"Maybe he's ridden ahead a ways, like Darby and Shea do," Marty suggested. "We could have a look."

"Shea?" Captain Martinson called.

"I'll ride on ahead," Shea promised, "but I won't find him. If you ask me, he took your money and rode for high ground. He's not near the fool to go that way himself."

"Maybe he's gone down to the river," Sully Payne said. "I'll go see."

"Can't imagine him just running off like that," Dixon declared. "He seemed so certain the cut-off would prove our salvation."

"Took your cash and ran," Shea grumbled. "Did you all a service by my way o' thinkin'. Now we can get along with our journey."

"Along the cut-off?" Dixon asked.

"I don't know I can get you to Oregon City safe and sound, but I sure won't that way," Shea explained. "Sorry to see you lose fifty dollars, but it might prove a bargain."

"You will have a look, though?" Captain Martinson asked.

"Sure," Shea agreed. "Darby, let's ride. We got a fellow up and vanished."

I knew better, of course. When I could, I slipped away and returned to the rocks. By then the whole train was rolling north toward the Blue Mountains. I nodded with approval as I kept well out of view. Then I rode to the rocks and freed my captive.

"What manner o' craziness got into you, boy?" Pembroke

cried. "You've near killed me! Why? Can't be for my horse as you've got a better one. You didn't take my money."

"You came by that fair enough as I see it," I explained. "But I couldn't let you lead my friends to their deaths."

"There's other ways o' persuadin' a man than bashin' in his head," Pembroke argued. "They all gone, are they? Well, I do suppose I've done all right. Fifty dollars'll keep me in whiskey through winter. And there'll be more trains comin' through."

Unfortunately he was right, and some were sure to follow him down Meeks's cut-off. Nevertheless, that was not my affair. I'd done what I could.

"Where's my horse?" Pembroke called as I turned to leave.

"Off grazing most likely. He'll come back to the river when he's thirsty, I imagine. You can catch him then. If not, I imagine you can buy a horse with fifty dollars."

"And my gun's gone, too."

"Don't know I trust you enough to leave you a loaded pistol. It's on the other side of the river, hanging in the lower branches of a small cottonwood. You'll find it easy enough."

"You thought it out just fine, boy," Pembroke muttered. "Shame you couldn't turn to my line o' work. You got too honest a face, though, and you'd go soft-hearted on me sure. 'Least you left me the flask. Off with you!"

"I never outstay my welcome," I said, mounting the big black and charging off to the north. I barely left the rocks when Shea rode up behind.

"Strange way o' scoutin' the trail ahead," he observed.

"Had some business to conclude," I told him.

"Saw that. Not like you to sneak up behind a man and club him, Darby."

"Only way to keep the train on the trail," I explained.

"Know that. And I'd call what you done a rare display o' good sense."

"Doesn't feel that way, Tom. I've got a sour taste in my mouth."

"Little honey'll take care o' that," he advised. "Now, why don't you strike up a tune on that mouth organ. I got a hunger for music."

"Me, too," I told him as I complied with his request. So I took my mouth organ and played—first for him and later for everybody.

We kept to the trail as Shea advised, and we left it only to hunt or trade with the Indians. Soon we were climbing into the reddish hills, past the tall pines and the stout oaks. We camped beside a great bend in the now northward-flowing Snake River, and I sighed. Tomorrow we would bid a final farewell to the Snake, our old friend, and head into the Blue Mountains.

Chapter 17

The easy trail soon seemed like a distant memory. Daily we faced steeper grades, and the groans of wagons blended with the moans of passengers, filling the air with a daunting wail. We pressed on to limits of endurance, fearing October might find us in the Cascades. When camp was made, dinner was hurriedly cooked, pots were scrubbed, after which the entire company, save the guards, took to their blankets.

We began to lose animals, too. Oxen refused to respond to prods and pleas. They merely collapsed in the dusty earth and accepted the peace death would bring. Horses and mules went down. We were forced to abandon the Cochrane wagon in order to pair their surviving ox with that of the Brunings. Shea and I lent our pack horses to help wagons transit the roughest of the slopes. Even so, I figured we all might be afoot before we crossed the Grand Ronde River and traversed the Blue Mountains.

"What've we done wrong?" I asked Shea. "We had an early start, and we've made fair progress. Why is it I feel we're coming to a bad end?"

"Don't know," he grumbled. "I feel it, too, though. Sometimes the wind blows against you. Hard to say why, but it does. Nothin' much to do but keep movin'."

And yet as we crossed that dry, difficult country, we marvelled at its beauty. Seas of wildflowers clung to the slopes of mountains, and the distant peaks etched a jagged backdrop for our desperate pageant. At river crossings we took every precaution against another drowning. And Shea saw every barrel and cask set aside for water filled to its rim.

"All we do nowadays is fill water barrels," Marty complained bitterly.

"You'll be glad of that water in a day or two," I answered.

Indeed we were, for though we could see rain falling on the distant mountains, none came our way. What creeks were at hand often had a hard, alkali taste and would sicken man and beast. We came to long for the sight of a boggy streambed or a river. In spite of the perils faced there, at least we could satisfy our thirst.

For weeks now I had been so completely a member of the company that I had almost forgotten the burdens borne by a scout. In such trying times, those burdens weighed heavily. Shea and I were needed in a hundred places each moment. I might be salving a horse's injured tendon while he was off inspecting the trail ahead. Then one of us would help urge a reluctant team up a steep incline while the other shot fresh game for the table. Between locating stands of willow where firewood could be cut or concocting a cure for the stomach cramps, I was never idle. And it was worse for Shea.

I never once heard him complain, not even when a band of women stripped our camp of every blanket or skin worth having.

"The children are cold," Marietta told me later. "It was thought you men were used to rough living and wouldn't mind."

"You should've asked," I barked. "A man doesn't take kindly to having his camp plundered, especially by those he thought were his friends."

Shea took it better.

"Pilgrims," he growled. "Got to expect anythin' of 'em.

Next they'll want the horses. Be glad you're not left bone naked, Darby. They might've taken your trousers."

I muttered a reply under my breath, and I was less than friendly the next day as we headed to the Burnt River crossing. Truth was, they could have had anything I owned by asking. But taking a man's belongings without asking was stealing any way you put it. I ended up saying as much to Captain Martinson.

"I'll see everything's returned," he promised. "It's just the trail, Darby. The night's grown chilly, and some didn't bring much to begin with. A lot of the blankets have been cut up and sewn into shirts and trousers. Children wear out clothes, you know, and they outgrow them as well. Others have left the heavier woolens behind to lighten their wagons. A mother and father can suffer the worst themselves, but their hearts break watching a little one shiver away the night."

"Let 'em keep the blankets," I grumbled. "Lord knows Shea and I've brought 'em elkhides and buffalo coats. It's the not asking that tears at you. I know some of the little ones better'n I know my own brothers and sister. I wouldn't have 'em freeze. But it seems that not a one of 'em's got like feelings for me and Tom."

"It's not that way at all," the captain argued.

"Words don't make it so," I replied. "You read a man's heart through his deeds."

And having said that, I left.

The climb to the crossing left man and beast bone weary. The trail was blocked in three places by boulders that were only removed by the considerable efforts of three mule teams. A fallen tree was more easily removed, and the resulting firewood at least helped cook a warm supper.

Burnt River crossing itself was a considerable trial. Both banks were steep, with little enough riverbed between to first slow a team and then allow it to dig in for the hard climb back up. To make matters worse, the sun blazed down in all its fury, adding a fiery yellow tint to the clouds of choking dust raised by our efforts.

"Burnt River, eh?" Marty cried as we put our shoulders to the back of the Martinson wagon in hopes of getting it up the far bank. "Good name. It's hot enough here to burn water."

I couldn't help agreeing. I felt myself melting, and sweat soaked every inch of my clothing. My hair fell across my forehead like an overused mop, and I longed for the cooling waters of the Snake or even the stagnant pools that made up the North Platte come summer.

In spite of the dust and the heat, we got the first nine wagons down to the river and then back up to the trail. The tenth to try was the Dixon wagon, and a sorrier excuse for a vehicle never touched wheel to trail. Borrowed horses started downhill, but Mr. Dixon couldn't control them. They sensed it and made a break to the left. Harness snapped, and Dixon pulled the brake. The sudden stop froze the front wheels, and the back of the wagon rose off the ground. Next thing you knew, the wagon shook itself to pieces, then rolled over and crashed into the rocks below.

I deemed it a miracle Dixon himself jumped clear, but the family's belongings were scattered everywhere, and there was no hope of salvaging the wagon. Shea and I had a half hour's ride just to catch the breakaway horses.

Returning, I found myself gazing upon the saddest sight in memory. Mrs. Dixon and the four girls were digging through the splinters to rescue what they could from the calamity. Precious belongings hauled two-thirds of the way across the nation were now but shattered shards of glass or scraps of torn cloth.

"We've got some bit of room in our wagon still," Mr. McIntosh offered as his boys, Randy and Ray, helped sift through the wreck.

"You're welcome to share what little clothes I have," Mrs. McIntosh added. "I've a good sewing kit, too, Teresa.

Perhaps we can mend some of the things."

Mrs. Dixon nodded grimly.

"I'd appreciate your carrying along what we can't carry," Dixon said, mustering a defiantly erect posture. "We're all strong and can walk what trail remains."

"Still, you can't sleep out in the open," Randy claimed. "We can hunt, maybe make you a tent of buckskins."

Others offered assorted bits and pieces, and the Dixons began to cheer.

The Whitsells and Sutherlands managed the crossing with better luck, though it was not a bit easier with pieces of the Dixon wreck breaking loose and floating downstream to annoy the animals or hinder the wagons. The Schroeder wagon's right rear wheel managed to wedge a plank between its spokes, and before Mr. Schroeder could halt his team, that wheel disemboweled itself. The wagon bed crashed into the streambed, and only quick handling of the horses by Bart Sawyer prevented a real disaster.

As it was, the wheel was clearly finished. Bart and I cut the back of the bed away, leaving little more than an oxcart. But it was enough to haul the Schroeders and their meager possessions.

"One of the blessings of having so little is that there isn't much to lose," Mrs. Schroeder said as she clutched her husband's strong arm. "Come, Bart, there is work to do."

Bart trotted after the young Germans as always, and soon the half-wagon was bobbing up the embankment to join the others.

We shared a meager dinner that night on the north bank of the river. The whole company seemed rather grim, and even my mouth organ was unable to raise a song from them. Shea tried a tale, but no one had ears for it. The night was colder than usual, too, and even I, camped a quarter mile away, could hear the cries of the little children.

"Winter's comin'," Shea whispered when I sat up.

"Early, don't you think?" I asked.

"Does that sometimes," he mumbled. "Mostly when you don't need it. We'll cut down some more o' the wagons tomorrow, make carts of 'em like you did the Schroeders' rig. Maybe that'll hurry us along."

But cutting back the beds meant leaving more belongings, and the families refused.

"It can't be much farther," Mrs. Payne insisted. "Our oxen will last."

Wishing a thing doesn't make it so, though. In three days' time we traversed the first pass leading toward the Blue Mountains, and the Payne team and others were nearly finished. We were half a week shy of the Grand Ronde when the first ox went down, and a dozen more fell by sunset. Mules and horses were nigh as bad off, and the train suddenly came to a halt.

"We'll pray for salvation," Captain Martinson declared, and the wagons were circled, stock was rested, and prayers were said. The break allowed a few of the animals to graze, and a handful seemed stronger. Most had traveled their final mile, though. It looked to all the world as if we'd most of us walk the final stretch of the trail.

"Should've cut down the wagons," Captain Martinson admitted. "Ought to listen to those who've come this way before."

"Ought to've gone with Pembroke," Mr. Dixon objected. "Or without him. That cut-off was gentle grade, he said. I'd have my wagon yet."

"Maybe we should've gone with Gaines to California," Uriah Anderson suggested. "Oregon is proving to be a hard country. Now we're apt to lose everything and be late to the Willamette as well. What folly have we brought ourselves to?"

I watched in disbelief as trail-hardened men broke down and wept. I saw good friends fight over scraps of firewood. Boys squared off and flayed away at each other with a heretofore unknown meanness. It was a nightmare, and I climbed atop the big black and fled the place.

I'm not certain how far I rode. I had no real direction. I simply gave the powerful horse his head, and he did the rest. I topped one ridge after another, swept across grassy valleys and through muddy streams. When finally the big horse tired, I climbed down from the saddle and collapsed near a small spring.

"Lord, what've we become?" I cried as I dipped my head in a small pool. As the surface calmed, I stared at the stubble-cheeked face reflected in the water. My eyes were wild, and my face had thinned so that I appeared half-crazed. "And now I'm talking to shadows," I muttered.

I then heard my horse stomp the ground nervously. Glancing back, I saw three bare-chested bronze-skinned boys appear from nowhere to grab the big black. I leaped to my feet, drew my pistol, and might have fired had not a faintly familiar voice called out, "What greeting is this, Bearkiller?"

I turned and gazed into the eyes of the young Nez Perce warrior, Flies Over The Mountains. He sat atop a spotted stallion, and his amused gaze forced a smile onto my face. I stuffed my gun in my belt and offered my hand in friendship. Flies Over reached down and pulled me up onto his horse's back, and the young Nez Perce riders whooped their approval.

"Two snows have come and gone, and the bears in this valley have been safe," Flies Over said, laughing. "Come now. We will celebrate your return."

"You speak better English," I observed.

"We have had many visitors," he explained. "Others travel the white man's road."

"Yes," I said, nodding. "I travel with such a company. I must return to them. They need food for their table and hides to keep off the winter chill."

Flies Over turned to his companions and spoke to them in their native tongue. One of the boys rattled off a considerable answer, and Flies Over frowned.

"Your people will not starve," he promised. "I will send word to my grandfather. Now we will test this black horse of yours. He runs faster than the white pony you rode from our camp?"

"No horse will ever match Snow," I said, swallowing my sadness as I hopped down and stumbled to where the black stood pawing the ground. "He couldn't outrun a Sioux arrow, though. I am sad to tell you he rides no more."

"Ah, I see it in your eyes," Flies over told me. "And in your heart. We will find you another."

"Flies Over, my brother, others are more in need than I am," I explained. "If you have horses to spare, the people with the wagons would buy them."

"Buy? What use have I for the white man's paper? Have they things to trade?"

"Maybe," I said, wondering what an independent folk like the Nez Perce could want. "Come. Bring the horses to the camp. We will see."

Flies Over barked a command to his companions, and the three boys turned and rode away. He then motioned for me to lead the way, and I turned back toward our camp.

I've never put a lot of stock in prayer, but many among the Martinson company were quick to point out the Nez Perce found me the day we halted our journey and besieged the Lord with pleas. And after all, Flies Over and his people were well south and east of their usual camps, led there by a buffalo herd.

The Nez Perce provided all we needed. There were heavy robes to fend off winter chills, and fresh meat for hungry bellies. Best of all, Flies Over led twenty stout horses into our midst. In return, the Indians accepted glass baubles and yellow bonnets, a few steel knives, and some hatchets. We gave all we could spare, and I judge they did the same. There was a sense of kinship among us all, and we concluded the trade by singing and dancing together around a roaring fire.

"And these were the Indians Pembroke warned us about?" a changed Hiram Dixon asked. "God's angels, I'd deem them."

Others felt much the same. As for myself, I offered Flies Over my single possession, the great black stallion. He responded by giving me a beautiful stallion of a breed Shea told me they called the Appaloosa. The horse was a beauty, with a white trunk peppered with brown spots, a painted face, and a spirit that instantly reminded me of Snow.

"He is called Shadow," Flies Over told me, and I agreed the name fit. After the briefest of rides, I was convinced Shadow could chase the sun across the heavens.

We concluded our bargain by smoking the pipe, and Flies Over spoke of hunting buffalo and stalking deer. For my part, I talked of the bear slain in the Absaroka country and my encounter with the white buffalo.

"You must ride to the hunt with us, Bearkiller," he insisted. "We will have much meat to last us through the cold months, for surely the buffalo have drawn us to you. Your brother, the buffalo spirit, has heard your prayers and answered by bringing your brothers."

"We've got a hard trail ahead, and I'm needed," I argued.

"They need meat, too," Flies Over reminded me, and I agreed to ride at his side.

"Do you good to taste the bite of the wind," Shea said when I told him. "You catch up when you can. Won't be hard trackin' us down. A snake'll move faster than wagons pulled by ponies."

He grinned when he spoke, and I knew he'd as soon be going along with us.

I was gone three days riding after the buffs. My rifle dropped three while the Nez Perce dropped two dozen. I gave away heads and tails and bones to those who helped with the skinning, and some of the meat I gave to Flies Over to smoke and share with those in need come winter.

"I would help your people in time of need as you have helped mine," I explained.

"Perhaps you will come again when the snows fall," he said, nodding as if he knew I would. "This meat we will save for that time."

"Oh, there are always elk to shoot come winter," I told him. "You use it as you see fit. Now it's time for me to return to my people. Perhaps you can spare a horse to carry the hides and the meat. I'll let him go, and he will surely find his way home."

"I will ride with you," he insisted. "Perhaps you will kill another bear for me."

"Hope not," I said, laughing. "Don't have all that many places left for a bear to mark me."

He touched the faint scars on my chest and grinned. But the next day, as we headed north along the rutted trail, he seemed downhearted. I asked him why, and he frowned.

"I think of my brother lost among the crazy people," he answered. "These white ones cut the trees and dirty the streams. They scratch the earth for food when it is all around them. Come to your brother this winter. Our mountains are tall and strong, as are our people."

"I won't be with the crazies," I assured him. "I'll be with Tom Shea. Who knows? We might just be through here. But I can't be sure. I never know where my trail will lead."

"A man has need of a home," he told me.

"Yes, he does," I agreed. "But a home isn't always a place. Sometimes it's people. So I have a home of sorts."

I could tell he didn't believe it. When I turned to ride the final half mile to the train alone, I wondered if I was sure myself.

Chapter 18

The Nez Perce ponies were never intended as draft animals, but they were fresh, and now that most of the wagons had been cut down to a shadow of their original size, the horses sufficed to pull half our wagons over the difficult terrain leading to the Blue Mountains. We had enough oxen and mules left to haul the rest. Shea ordered rests each three or four miles to allow the teams a bit of water and forage, and I think to let the rest of the company catch their breath. Then it was onward again.

Rolling through the Baker Valley, with its muddy creeks and broad stretches of treeless plain, I couldn't help staring ahead at the approaching foothills of the Blue Mountains. Nothing they had seen along the way could prepare emigrants for the steep and treacherous trail to come.

"Wish we were early," Shea muttered when we started up a steep slope. "Grass's thin, and the springs've gone dry."

"Yes," I mumbled in reply. "But what choice is there?"

The Blue Mountains were, indeed, a cruel ordeal. When Shea and I returned to the main camp that night, the others crowded around to ask about the hazards that lurked in the distant slopes. I pretended fatigue, but I think they read the dread in my sorrowful eyes.

"We'll make it," Captain Martinson declared. "We're close now to trail's end."

But even the captain was muted by the daunting nature of the terrain. The trail wound along narrow ledges, and the slightest mistake could send a wagon tumbling off the edge to a rocky death far below. Rocks cluttered the trail, inviting injury and abuse to animal and man alike. And there were stretches when the trail rose or fell hundreds of feet in a mere twenty yards.

"It's almost perpendicular!" Mrs. Martinson gasped when she beheld a particularly nasty descent.

"How's it possible to get a wagon down that?" the captain asked. "It's straight down!"

"Use a team to slow the wagon," Shea advised. "Maybe two."

"And when it's worse?" Hiram Dixon asked.

"Use ropes tied to trees," I told them. "Lower yourself slow and easy."

"That'll take forever," Niles Conway objected. "Isn't there another path?"

"Several," Shea explained. "This is the best."

We discovered other ways of slowing wagons. Sometimes we would tie heavy pine logs in front of the wheels to add weight and drag. The rocky trail itself often kept wheels from spinning out of control or burning through the brake. The horses in particular developed a method of zigzagging along the path. They gained better footing, and the wagon wheels never had a chance to spin out of control.

A few drivers continued to direct their teams from atop wagons, but most now walked alongside, alternately urging their teams onward or counseling caution with cool, steady voices. Sometimes a firm hand on a bit of harness kept a horse from panicking.

As to riding in the wagon beds, only the sick or indisposed tried it. Anyone fit to walk spread out in clusters between wagons or on either side when the width of the trail allowed it. Only Shea and I rode, for we often made four and five trips from the vanguard to the tail of the train each day, warning of peril ahead and insuring the last wagons didn't stray too far. I walked sometimes, too. Some days I would pass a bit of the afternoon with Tim Frey or the Martinsons. In those scant moments we would speak of the Willamette or dream of a deep river where we could satisfy our thirst and wash the dust from our clothes and our hides.

"Lord, what's become of the rains?" Mr. Payne cried as our water barrels went dry.

"Can't go on without water!" his wife exclaimed.

We scooped up a bit of muddy liquid from streams or springs, but it wasn't suitable to drink. We tried digging wells, but the rocky ground frustrated our every effort.

"Best suck on a stone when you walk," Shea suggested. "And keep on the trail. Water's sure to be ahead."

I began to doubt it, though. The Blue Mountains, though as grand and beautiful as any we'd encountered, proved miserly in meeting our daily needs. Wood was often scarce, and as to water, we had begun to doubt it existed.

"Pray for rain," Captain Martinson shouted whenever we spotted a dark cloud.

But what came instead was a frightful hailstorm that slashed great gaping holes in the canvas covers of our wagons and left man and beast sorely battered. Frozen stones the size of cherries whipped through the air like musket balls. Even so, we dashed about gathering them in our hats and filling the nearest empty barrel.

"The world's gone mad!" Mercy Zachary screamed as her youngsters threw off their clothes and let the cold globs of moisture bombard dusty flesh. And when the storm passed, horses and mules licked droplets from wagon wheels or harness while oxen touched their tongues to the ground.

We were better than a week crossing the Baker Valley and another yet picking our way through the Blue Mountains. All that time the hot dry days and chill nights sapped our strength. Summer was fast fading, and dread of facing snow in the Cascades loomed ever closer.

"I'd welcome snow just now," Marty told me. "You can melt it into water, can't you?"

"You don't know the kind of snow that'll come," Tim warned. "Better hurry your wagons. I lost two brothers to a blizzard, and I wouldn't welcome another."

We faced another trial as well. Other companies rolled past us. Their stock seemed to have fared better along the way, and their spirits soared a bit knowing they might have shared our plight. Often three or four wagons would roll by in advance of the others.

"Trains break up in this country," Shea explained. "Not much fear o' Indian attack, and some seem eager to see trail's end."

I suppose many among our band also desired to set off alone, but each relied on the other's stock to traverse the more difficult slopes. Moreover, a new comradeship had been born since the arrival of our Nez Perce benefactors. Weary as we were at day's end, there was always a bit of singing or tale swapping. Shea and I were greeted with a new belonging when we shared an evening meal with this family or that.

When we reached Emigrant Hill, the final obstacle remaining of the Blue Mountains, I think we all sighed with relief. The stock had survived, and so had we. The long climb up the hill failed to deter our progress, and we camped that night at a small bubbling spring that for once refreshed us.

"We've come out of the wilderness," Mr. Payne declared as he lifted his Bible. "Here's Jordan awaiting us."

The company raised in one great cheer, and as Payne read of Moses's triumph, we adopted the words for our own.

Emigrant Springs did seem to provide a sort of deliverance. Tall pines provided firewood, and abundant game, especially grouse and deer, were at hand. We hunted half a day and rested the remainder. Shea fumed a bit at the wasted day, but when we collected toward sundown to feast and dance and sing, I judged we would make up the lost miles in the days to come.

"A man's spirit needs feeding just like his belly," I remarked. "You taught me that yourself, Tom. These folks have had it hard."

"Hard?" he asked. "Snows find us short o' the Willamette, they'll think this easy."

I frowned my agreement. But I knew, too, that the respite from the trail was necessary.

From Emigrant Springs the main trail diverged. Three different paths took trains westward. One headed to the Columbia and across to Ft. Walla Walla. The Whitman's mission had been up that way until the Cayuse wiped them out. Another trail sought the south bank of the Columbia and followed it to The Dalles. The final and best route cut across country past the Umatilla River through the flatlands until reaching the John Day and Deschutes rivers and joining the Columbia at The Dalles.

"Saves days, maybe a week," Shea told Captain Martinson. "It's a fair trail most o' the way, though there are rocks and gulches. Not much water, though. Pitiful dry this time o' year."

"Drier than what we've just come through?" Mrs. Warner asked.

"Sometimes you can't find a drop o' water from the Umatilla to the John Day," Shea replied. "Near as bad as Meeks's cut-off, 'cept not near so long."

"We're short of time," the captain reminded everyone. "I don't see where there's much choice."

The others sadly nodded, and next morning we swung north and then due west.

I knew that road for the hardships it provided, but I'd passed that way in a wet year and in winter. Even though we filled every barrel and flask, pot and kettle before leaving the sandy Umatilla, we soon felt the scourge of thirst.

"Got to be springs somewhere in this country!" the captain exclaimed after three days of rolling through barren country using buffalo chips for our fires and watching the water levels in our barrels drop lower and lower. Soon water was reserved only for the animals and the children. Men and women labored the long hot days with only a cup meted out morning and night. Later even that ration was omitted. Fevers struck, and sick children cried out in the night. Their screams haunted my dreams.

"Won't last forever," Shea said as we encouraged the train onward. Horses began to falter. Unlike the mules and oxen who had grown acccustomed to the trail's hardships, the spotted ponies came from a country of bounty. I anxiously watched as Shadow seemed to lose his spirit. I reluctantly tied him behind the Martinson wagon and walked beside the captain near the vanguard of the train.

The trail provided hazards, too. Ravines often ate away at the trail, making detours necessary. Whenever we encountered a stand of trees, the wind would inevitably uproot one at the very spot our trail crossed. An hour's labor with an ax exhausted even the strongest man among us, and I watched in dismay as the sun blistered my flesh and left my tongue swelling inside my parched mouth.

I think if we had been a single day longer reaching the John Day River, we might all have perished. As it was, the horses sniffed the river well in advance of our sighting, and they drove forward with renewed zest. I sniffed the moisture myself soon thereafter, and my weary feet took wing. Shadow broke his tether and galloped alongside. When we reached the banks of the river, we rushed forward as one, jumping into the shallows and near drowning ourselves in the effort to drink the river dry.

A hundred yards away ferrymen shook their heads and went about the work of transporting another company to the far shore. I supposed the sight of a hundred crazed emigrants tossing clothes in the air and screaming in celebration was an ordinary occurrence. The more modest among us made their way upstream before disrobing. Children raced along the bank naked as the day they were born, and some of the men weren't a bit more bashful. I myself sank into the sandy bottom and eased out of my dusty clothes. The Frey boys splashed over and did the same. For most, civilization had been left behind months ago, and even their mother's scolding could not hold back the urge to free themselves of dust and thirst.

I washed myself and my clothes, then hung them in the lower branches of a willow while I swam races with Tim and some of the older boys across the river and back. By early afternoon a brisk wind blew down from the north, and a chill began to gnaw at my bare back.

"Summer's gone," Tim observed, frowning as he gazed at the darkening sky.

"Yes," I agreed. "But we're almost there."

"Where's there, though?" he asked. "You've got a sister on the Willamette, but we've got nobody."

"Your mama sews and cooks," I told him. "She'll find work easy enough. And there are lots of farms needing extra help."

"Not in winter," he told me.

"Winter doesn't last forever. I'll likely pass the months sleeping in a barn myself. Probably room for others there."

He sighed, then mustered a grin. For myself, I couldn't believe anyone who had weathered a blizzard and crossed the Blue Mountains could worry about anything ever again!

We found the ferrymen reasonable and availed ourselves of their services that same evening. We camped on the John Day's west bank, then rolled west again the next morning.

For the first time since leaving Ft. Boise we encountered settlers. Small towns and logging camps popped up here and there, and the people welcomed us with fresh loaves of bread, baskets of fruit, and what scraps of clothing could be spared. Stores replenished our supplies, though their prices seemed high to me. And when we arrived at The Dalles and first viewed the mighty Columbia, the townfolk turned out a brass band to announce our arrival. A real preacher led us in prayer, and some of us even spent the night under a roof, the guests of farmers or merchants.

Nick and Tommy Hull met their uncle there while Hunter and Hyacinth Normile were taken in by an innkeeper till their relations could arrive to greet them. The Conways, Dixons, and Sadlers left us as well, for The Dalles was a town of growing opportunity, and each family met a need.

Walter Cochrane's brother arrived the day we were to leave, so the Cochranes and Brunings left us as well. I couldn't help staring at the eleven remaining wagons, most of them cut down to two-wheeled carts, and recall what an impressive train we had been at Scott's Bluff.

"Not feelin' sad, are you?" Shea asked as I climbed atop Shadow.

"Some," I confessed. "The rest'll be leaving soon, and we'll be on our own again."

"Thought sure you'd welcome that, Darby. Me, I've choked on enough traildust for a bit."

"Sure, but you get to know folks on a train. They get to be a family of sorts."

"Shouldn't take 'em so to heart," he advised. "They got their own path to take, and we got another."

"Can't help myself, Tom"

"Well, it'll pass, this kind o' sadness. Got to think they're the lucky ones, those who've already met trail's end. The rest o' us've got some tough ground yet to cover."

"Yeah," I said, nodding. "Cascades haven't moved."

"And we didn't have too much luck on the Barlow Road headin' east," he reminded me. "There's need o' keepin' a watchful eye on the trail ahead."

"And behind," I added, gazing nervously at a pair of idlers giving us a bit too long a look. "I'll warn the captain."

"Already did," Shea told me. "Now, what do you say we get this train movin'?"

"Seems best," I told him, and he waved the others onward.

Chapter 19

At one time emigrants had to abandon their wagons or carts at The Dalles and travel downriver on rafts or flatboats. Some even bartered for Indian canoes. It was a perilous route, and sometimes half a company would perish when the Columbia upset their craft and left them to flounder in midstream. A man named Barlow put an end to that ordeal by hacking a trail through the Cascades to Oregon City.

Barlow's toll road skirted the shoulders of massive Mt. Hood, and seeing the white mountain rise out of the mist reminded me how close we were to trail's end.

"Only a couple of weeks now," I told the others.

I saw in their eyes how long that seemed. But Mt. Hood beckoned to them, too. Marietta called it a beacon of hope, and indeed it seemed to be just that.

"There's hard travelin' yet to come," Shea warned, but the Barlow road crossed numerous small streams and later ran beside a pair of rivers. The forests provided bountiful firewood, and the hunting was excellent. After our recent privation, we welcomed it with open arms.

We had, in a sense, returned to civilization. We soon passed lumber camps and fruit growers. Often we camped near a farmhouse or loggers' settlement. Most of the residents had come up the same trail themselves, and memories of hardships made them generous. We never wanted for anything they possessed, and often they shared their own high spirits.

"This country provides all a man needs," one grower proclaimed. "My children have grown tall and strong on the bounty of this place, and I'm sure it will bring you all the same good fortune."

Such talk couldn't help but lift our chins.

As with any new country, dangers lurked there as well. Shea and I kept the watches vigilant. Two winters before we'd learned the hard way that road agents infested Barlow's road.

"It's to be expected," Shea explained to Captain Martinson. "There's little law here, and a hundred places to hide. No man travels this trail without money to pay his passage, and other goods besides. Wherever there's money, men will come to take it away."

The captain nodded his understanding. Still, when the raiders did come, no one was prepared. Uriah Anderson and his boys had the watch, but they were watching the road. The bandits came from the south, through the trees, and they stealthily crept up behind our guards and caught them by surprise. The thieves might have stolen every horse and all our money to boot had not Miller Frey spotted them while answering nature's call. Miller roused his brothers, and Tim fetched Shea and me.

"How many?" Shea asked wearily as I rubbed the sleep from my eyes and scrambled into my clothes.

"Miller saw three," Tim said, "but there's sure to be more. A couple of 'em appear to be gatherin' the horses."

"Get the cap'n," Shea told Tim. "Darby, come along," the grizzled scout added as he tied his pistol belt around his waist and grabbed a pair of rifles. I tucked my own pistol in my belt and cradled a rifle in my hands. I had little desire to use either, but I was a boy no longer. Duty required I shoulder arms, and if it called on me to shoot, I would.

It was odd how quickly events turned on the raiders. Captain Martinson roused the men one by one, and Shea soon had them encircling the bandits. In no time we had a rifle tracking each one of the scoundrels. Finally Captain Martinson called out, and the raiders froze.

"Best hold up there, boys!" the captain suggested. "We've got guns on your backs, and we'll shoot if there's need. Drop your weapons and stand to."

"The devil we will," the outlaw leader replied. "Sayin' it don't make it so. Boys, let's scatter!"

The first two to attempt flight met with a shower of buckshot, though, and they fell to the ground, their faces and shoulders peppered with lead.

"Lord, Johnny, he's tellin' the truth," one called from the right flank. "Got us trapped proper."

"Give you the count of ten to decide!" Martinson shouted. "What's it to be?"

Two of the raiders dropped their rifles, but another pair climbed atop horses and galloped away. The leader tried to do the same, but a rifle ball struck his horse, and the animal fell, writhing as its lungs exploded.

The other three raced to join their leader, and the four of them holed up in a rocky hollow not far from where the Andersons had maintained the night watch.

"Well?" Shea asked, joining Captain Martinson as the captain surveyed the field.

"I don't know," the captain answered. Shea muttered to himself, but I couldn't see how anybody could know what to do. You couldn't see five feet ahead of you, and except for an occasional powder flash from the rocks to keep us away, the raiders simply disappeared.

The remainder of the company gathered around the captain. Meanwhile Ollie Zachary located the Andersons and untied them while Mr. Bragg brought in the two captives.

"You all right?" Captain Martinson asked Mr. Anderson.

Mallie spoke for them all when he nodded, then turned angrily away.

"The horses are still here," Mr. Schroeder then announced. "We've suffered no loss. What do we do with the four in the rocks?"

"Shea?" Captain Martinson asked.

"Two got away already," Shea reminded us. "Let these four run, too, and we're sure to have another visit. Might not be so lucky next time."

"Can't just rush down there and take 'em, either," Mercy Zachary argued. "My man's no soldier. I won't see him killed, not this close to our new home."

The other women voiced like sentiments.

"Well, I've got a score to settle with 'em," Uriah Anderson said, taking Odell Zachary's shotgun.

"Me, too," Mallie added, grabbing a musket.

Captain Martinson nodded grimly. Shea waved for the women to return to camp, and most of the men went along. The captain then inched his way closer to the rocks, and the Andersons took station on his left. Shea and I followed, as did a handful of others. Mr. Sutherland had been keeping watch on the rocks, and he announced the raiders still there.

"So, how do we go about it?" Anderson asked.

"Best to wait 'em out," Shea declared. "Come dawn, they may give it up. If not, well, we stand a better chance o' not shootin' each other in the daytime."

The others seemed in agreement. Except for the Andersons, nobody appeared eager to press things. I myself followed Tom Shea to a nearby boulder and huddled at his side.

"Seems like we been here before," he whispered.

"We have," I said, recalling our duel with road agents not ten miles from that very spot. "I guess we should've been keeping our eyes out for 'em."

"Oh, they went about it clever enough. Don't figure

they'd hit us if we had somebody watchin' the flanks."

"Miz Zachary's right, you know," I told him. "This isn't our line. Somebody could get killed."

"Figure to let 'em go, do you?"

"Two are dead. That ought to convince 'em to stay clear."

"If you let these go, what do you do with the next ones to come?"

I frowned and recalled dueling the renegades on the Snake. There'd been little choice then, and there was none now. I sighed as I shifted my weight. Then the rocks seemed to explode.

"Down, boy," Shea shouted, pushing my head to the earth as bullets whined off the boulder. Shotguns exploded, and then the world itself seemed to erupt. Pistols and rifles barked, spitting fiery flashes to and from the rocks. A voice cried out in pain. Another cursed. Mallie Anderson screamed his father's name. Then a shadowy figure appeared from the dark, and I raised my pistol.

"Don't," a stranger said with pleading eyes as he fumbled with his own gun. I hesitated a second. Then he turned his gun toward Shea, and I fired.

I don't know when the shooting stopped. It seemed to go on for hours. In the end we found but three bodies. The fourth likely escaped, or perhaps he wandered, bleeding, into the pines and fell there. It didn't matter. Mallie had a ball through his left foot, and another grazed Captain Martinson's right elbow. No one had much taste for fighting afterward.

Shea found me sitting beside the dead raider at sunrise. I couldn't forget his frightened eyes. They stared skyward now, and I couldn't manage to reach over and close them.

"Time we broke camp, son," Shea whispered as he turned the corpse over. "I'll throw some dirt over him. Why don't you see to the horses?"

"I killed him, Tom, I said, shaking as he helped me rise. "I killed another man. It's three now."

216

"This one merited his end, Darby. Others, too. It's hard country up here sometimes, and to survive you got to be hard, too."

"Maybe I'm not hard enough."

"Never found you lackin' yet," he told me. "Now run on and see the horses get saddled. We got some miles to cross today."

I did as he instructed, though my legs wobbled, and my stomach could hold down no food. I rode that morning with a light head, and my face was pale as death.

"Maybe you ought to ride in the wagon with Papa," Marty suggested. "Get some sleep. You don't look too good, Darby."

"Do, Darby," Marietta pleaded.

I shook my head and nudged Shadow into a faster trot. How could they understand I dreaded sleep most of all? A thousand phantoms lurked about, eager to haunt my dreams.

We made camp that night at Rock Creek, and I walked off into the trees in hopes of finding some peace. None came. Finally I wandered back to camp and huddled beside Tim Frey and his brothers around a warming fire. The wind was blowing fiercely, and I shivered from the cold.

"Can't take it so much to heart, Darby," Mrs. Frey said as she threw a blanket over my shoulders. "My man was a soldier, and trained to kill the enemy, but his letters told how he felt. You had no choice, son. You know that in your heart. Don't grieve so for a man who isn't worth it."

"I've been a long time on my own," I said, fighting back a flood of tears. "I never figured it'd work out this way. We'd have adventures, Tom and me, but I didn't dream it'd mean killing anybody. Mama'd frown on it heavy. She wanted me to be a teacher, and she set such store by books and music. Look how I've turned out!"

"Pretty fair, I'd say," Mrs. Frey declared. "Lord knows we'd all of us be dead if you hadn't found Tim in the snow.

I know you feel all the gentleness has been stomped out of you, son, but you wouldn't feel that way if a lot of it wasn't still there. I buried two boys in the mountains, and I think about 'em every day. But you've got to think of the living."

"Who?" I asked. "In a week or so you'll all scatter to new homes, and me, I'll just ride on."

"Thought we were goin' to winter in your sister's barn," Tim said, gripping my arm firmly. "Don't think you'll shed us all so easy as that."

"How 'bout blowin' us a tune, Darby?" Miller asked. "Haven't heard 'Sweet Betsy from Pike' in weeks."

"Doesn't seem fitting to play a mouth organ with death's shadow so near," I replied.

"Best do some serious playin'," Mrs. Frey advised. "Chase that shadow back down the trail!"

"Yeah," Little Michael said, sitting beside me near the fire. "Play, will you, Darby? It's cold, and we need a song to warm us up."

"Go on," Tim said, slapping my back. Miller added his encouragement, and I drew out the mouth organ and pressed the cold brass against my lips. I swallowed hard and blew a few notes. A song didn't want to come, so the boys struck up a chorus of "Sweet Betsy" on their own. The melody warmed me, and I soon joined in. I played rather better as the song continued, and others joined in from all over the camp. At first I thought it just the singing warmed me, but as assorted hands reached out and touched my shoulders or patted my back, I began to understand it was the sense of belonging that chased off the cold.

I played close to an hour. Then my lips began to turn purple, and I put the mouth organ away. Mrs. Frey set a pot of stew on the fire, and Tim led his brothers off to search for firewood. The Whitsells huddled over the fire, and I set off to locate Shea.

Marietta cut me off at the edge of camp.

"He's gone off ahead," she explained. "Said for you to stay

218

in the camp and keep an eye out for trouble."

"Did he?" I asked. Didn't sound like Tom to leave me behind while he took the lead alone.

"Actually I asked if he could spare you," she admitted. "Papa's still abed with his arm, you know, and Marty's little help. I thought you could build up our fire some. Later on you might share a story. Mr. Shea says you killed a bear up here once."

"Seems that's what I mostly do hereabouts," I grumbled. "Kill things."

"I'll hear no self-pity from you, Darby Prescott!" she barked. "My papa might've lost an arm, and you're feeling sorry for the man who likely shot him! Come on. It's help I need, not a lot of mumbled nonsense."

I don't think there was another person on this earth who could raise my dander like Marietta Martinson. I stomped off after her, my color rising every step. Then when we reached her wagon, I found Marty had a roaring fire going. Mrs. Martinson handed me a hot biscuit dipped in honey, and the captain welcomed me to dinner.

"You haven't eaten with us in quite a while," Mrs. Martinson remarked as she filled bowls with rabbit stew. "We've missed you, Darby. I'm pleased you could come."

I glanced at Etta's scheming face and knew I'd been snared as surely as the rabbit in that kettle. Just then it felt good, though, and I accepted my fate with a rare smile.

Later, after helping scrub the plates clean and stoke up the fire a bit, I set off with Marietta toward the creek. Each of us carried a water bucket, but there was more to our walk than a simple chore.

"Papa says we'll be in Oregon City soon," she whispered as she dipped her bucket in the shallow stream.

"Soon," I agreed. "Come a fair ways now. Not much trail left."

"What'll it be like?" she asked. "When it's over, I mean."

"Oh, it's pretty country there, Etta. Bluest river you ever

219

did see. Tall mountains crowned with snow like white lace collars. Farms spread out here and there, with little towns in-between. There are fruit trees, and fields of wheat and corn in summer so golden you'd think you were walking the streets of Paradise. Skies are blue with fluffy white clouds. Rains come regular so you never thirst for water."

"I don't mean the Willamette," she complained. "I mean what will you do?"

"Got a lot of trail left before we get there."

"You're avoiding my question."

"Yes, I am," I said as I filled my bucket.

"Tell me, Darby. Don't you think I have a right to know?"

"I figure it's my business," I grumbled.

"I thought maybe after all these miles, you could share it with me. We're not strangers, you know."

"Yes, we are," I told her. "You don't know me. Shoot, I don't know who I am myself. I do know pretty soon you'll have a new home to build and a world of work facing you."

"And what will you have, Darby?"

"Another trail to ride."

"Doesn't have to be that way. I spoke to Papa. He said you're welcome to stay with us."

"As what? A brother? You've got one of them. And I can't see your papa allowing it could be more."

I reached down and plucked a stone from the ground. I tossed it hard into the water, and it skipped three times before bounding onto the far bank.

"Darby?" she called.

I handed her my bucket and sat down at the edge of the water. She sighed and touched my shoulder with her soft fingers. I slid over to my left, and she turned slowly and returned to her camp.

I stayed an hour at the creek, listening to the birds sing in the treetops and the frogs croak at the setting sun. Then I set off to find Shadow. Shea wouldn't be so far ahead that I couldn't find him.

The two of us camped a mile in advance of the train those next five days. Shea told others it was to keep an eye out for trouble, but I knew better. The time was fast approaching when we would be alone, and it was a weaning of sorts.

We reached Barlow's tollgate on the far slopes of Mt. Hood early that next morning, and Captain Martinson turned over a fair portion of our precious greenbacks to pay the passage. We also bought what supplies couldn't await our arrival in Oregon City. Then we continued.

"Half a week left now," Shea told me as we rode.

"Seems we've been on this trail forever," I observed. "Be good to have the job done and the folks safely settled on the Willamette."

"Looks like we've beat the snows, too."

"We've made good time since The Dalles. Kind of wish it was going a little slower. Be lonely when they're all gone."

"Yes," Shea confessed. "Trail's end is a mixed blessin'. But we'll have adventures ahead of us aplenty. Yes, sir, Darby. Adventures aplenty!"

I nodded my agreement, but it didn't warm me much.

Chapter 20

I guess I was about the only person in the company not to feel a surge of enthusiasm as we edged ever closer to Oregon City. Our trail-weary companions took to singing and laughing even while carrying out the most irksome of chores. Women took time to clip their hair and wash their clothes. Children who hadn't known a pair of shoes or a comb for weeks suddenly found themselves walking in patched trousers, with their toes jammed into leather shoes more often than not a size too small. Haircuts were the order of the day, and I even took a razor to my scraggly cheeks.

"Seems like we're going to Sunday services," I remarked to Shea.

"Nobody likes to look shabby when appearin' for a visit," Shea told me. "These folks're arrivin' in a new home, and they wouldn't want others thinkin' they were a band o' urchins escaped the St. Louis waterfront."

I only shook my head in an amused fashion. No one in Oregon was ignorant of the trials and tribulations encountered en route. Such pretense was wasted. But soon I began to realize it wasn't for the Oregonians that women sewed lace on their daughters' collars or patched a son's sleeve. It was to recapture that pride and self-respect that had slipped away on the road west.

I spent those final days on the trail riding through the company, and I shared meals with one family or another, silently bidding them farewell and good fortune listening to their plans for the future.

"And what will you do, Darby?" Mrs. McIntosh asked.

"Visit my sister awhile," I answered between bites of berry pie. "After that, most likely head into the mountains, make my way east to guide another train west."

"I can't imagine anyone wishing to undertake this journey a second time," Mrs. McIntosh said, shaking her head. "Surely a young man like yourself must have other possibilities."

"Maybe so," I admitted. "But not better ones. Just now you recall only the hardships, but in time you'll think back to the grand sights, to the friendships forged, and you'll know this crossing's been an adventure you'll remember all your life."

Two days out of Oregon City Tom Shea drew me aside.

"Tomorrow's our final night with the company," he reminded me. "Figured we'd join in the dancin' and such. Tonight, though, I got the urge to camp up in the mountains."

"Alone?"

"Oh, I wouldn't mind a little company. Know a scout who'd join me?"

"Sure," I agreed. "We might find a deer or two for the feasting while we're up there."

And so when the wagons formed their circle just shy of the Clackamas River, Shea and I rode off into the wilderness nearby. We spread out our blankets beside a bubbling spring and toward twilight shot a pair of deer who came there to drink.

"We came through here before, just after Papa died," I recalled as I started skinning the animals.

"Was th'other side o' the river," Shea pointed out as he

223

lent a hand.

"Maybe, but it's more or less the same. That was just after harvest, too. 'Bout this same time of year. We rode east then, but we didn't even get to Ft. Boise before the snows caught us. Guess there's not much point in trying to beat winter this time around."

"No," he muttered. "Never get to the Tetons 'fore first snow. Got any notions yourself on how to pass the winter?"

"No, not much." I pulled the hide from the first deer, and Shea began butchering the meat. I set the skin aside and started on the second animal. We silently worked close to ten minutes. Then Shea spoke.

"You'll be welcome at your sister's, I'll wager," he told me.

"Likely," I admitted as I pulled the second skin free. "We could ride into the Cascades, though, maybe hire out to supply meat to the lumber camps. It'd be fair work."

"Winter's hard on men out in the open."

"We could build a cabin. There's time for that."

"Darby, I was thinkin' you might choose a bit more settled life."

"Oh? Think maybe I ought to put up a regular house, buy some pigs and chickens, make a real farmer out of myself?"

"Know a fellow raises horses north o' here. He'd surely take to the idea o' pairing some o' his mares with that spotted stallion o' yours. You get along with horses just fine. Be a good line o' work."

"I've got a line," I reminded him. "I'm a scout."

"Don't think much o' that as a life, son. And life in the high country's not the same. Shoot, the Barlow road's got road agents, and woodcutters'll soon have the Cascades tame as a dairy cow. You've got your growth now. Time you thought o' settlin' yourself, makin' a home."

"Home?"

"Home can be a fine thing."

"But you've never taken to one."

"Well, it's more t'other way 'round, Darby. Home never took to me. I tried it, though, with the Crows. Maybe if she'd been a white woman, and it'd been in civilized country, it would've took better. Too close to Sioux country for a man to expect a long life."

"I don't suppose you'd have much inclination to raise horses, though, would you?" I asked as I began working the hides.

"No, I'd grow tiresome so far's company goes after a bit. Likely I'd head east come first thaw."

"I figured we were partners," I said, setting my knife aside and gazing at him with sullen eyes.

"More'n that, son," he told me. "Two years back, when we rode out together, I thought maybe you needed ole Tom Shea. You were young, and wasn't anybody else to show the way. Well, you've traveled the hard path now, Darby Prescott, and no guide can take you anywhere you can't get on your own."

"Maybe not," I admitted.

"You're finished with bein' a boy. The softness been worked out o' you, and the beard's comin' along all the time. You got to break your own trail now."

"We've ridden together a long time, but you still don't understand much, do you?" I asked. "Isn't out of need I went along, Tom Shea! Nor just out of wanting to learn from you. We make good partners, the two of us. So I always figured anyway."

"You been the best o' partners. But I thought maybe you might try a different road. That lil Martinson gal's set her cap in your direction. Could do worse there. She cooks fair, and there's good oak wood to her backbone."

"She'd have me turn farmer," I explained. "Wall me up and put a roof over my head. What self-respecting mountain man'd let that happen to himself?"

"Not much chance to get scalped inside a farmhouse," he told me, grinning as he began to pack the meat on a drying rack. "I don't know that everyone'd look at it as a poor bargain."

"Maybe not," I confessed. "But Darby Prescott would. And besides, her papa's pretty sour on the notion."

"He'd warm to it," Shea declared. "You got a habit o' bringin' folks around, Darby. Me, I first thought you a pesterin' sort o' Illinois pilgrim. Never knew you'd prove a fair hand with a horse, much less a buffalo hunter after my own heart."

"But now you've grown tired of my company, eh?"

"No such thing!" he barked. "Only thought you might find better fortunes elsewhere."

"Not possible," I assured him. "Isn't a better fate than riding the mountains with Tom Shea."

We'd ridden a lot of miles together, and I judged I'd seen every side to Tom Shea there was. I never before noted the kind of satisfied smile that filled his face just then, though. And I think for that one night he forgot about the long dead Crow wife and child, for he never once glanced at the missing fingers.

We took to our blankets rather early. The night was unusually chill, and the wind whined eerily through the pines. The sky overhead was choked with clouds, and there was no moon or stars to bid good night.

Shea snored away to my right. A battery of cannon wouldn't rouse him from such a slumber. For my own part, I tossed about anxiously before my eyes finally closed.

It didn't prove to be a peaceful night. To begin with, no soothing dreams came my way. Instead I rode Shadow out across the Baker Valley with Flies Over The Mountains at my side. We blazed our way across the snow-covered hills, hunting buffalo. I saw the great shaggy head of the white buffalo itself greeting me from a distant mountainside.

"Take courage, my son," its voice seemed to call. "Another trial comes your way."

Then I saw a pale white horse gallop by. It was Snow, and I greeted his familiar gait with a wild heart. But as I jumped down from Shadow's back and ran to greet Snow with open arms, the white horse turned into an enormous horned monster. I awoke with a start and found myself shivering from head to toe.

"Lord, it was just a dream," I said, trying to convince myself. I might have managed it had not Shadow suddenly screamed from the nearby trees. The ground seemed to shake, and a great, lumbering shape broke through the pines.

"Heaven help me," I muttered as I watched the phantom rip apart the light framework of my stretching rack and leap upon the venison beyond. I frantically pulled on my trousers and grabbed my rifle. As I fought to fix the cap in place and ram down a charge, my eyes began to focus. The moon suddenly emerged from the clouds, and in the dim light I saw the familiar silver-edged coat of a grizzly bear.

"No!" I shouted as I rammed back the hammer and prepared to fire. "This is my camp. Go elsewhere for your food."

Bears aren't much for taking challenges, and this one looked to have taken on enough fat to get him through the winter already. He should have rumbled off into the trees, but some grizzlies have bad tempers, and this one turned instead and started toward me. I pressed the trigger, and my rifle sent a ball slicing into the bear's belly.

"Darby?" Shea called as he shook himself into consciousness.

"Here," I said, fumbling with my pistol as the wounded bear halted, then hurried past us down the mountainside.

"What was that?" he asked.

"Grizzly," I explained. "I hit him fair. Won't be back here,

I'd guess, but he could be a problem elsewhere."

"The camp?" he asked as I threw a blanket around my shoulders, stuffed my pistol in my belt, and reloaded my rifle.

"Headed that way," I told him. "I'll have a look."

"Wait up," he urged.

"No time," I said, hurrying down the slope.

The train was encamped a mile or so below us next to the Barlow road. With the wind blowing into my face, I reckoned my shot might not have even been heard. The thought of a wounded grizzly, and a mean one to boot, rampaging through a sleeping camp full of women and children brought horrific images to my mind. I dared not run, what with a loaded rifle in my hands and little more than indistinct shapes ahead of me in the pale moonlight. Still I moved with great urgency.

I heard the bear long before I saw it again. It ripped through a tangle of scrub cedars, then hit the back of a wagon with such force that I heard wood splinter. Cries of alarm split the air, followed by the shrieks of startled children. The bear bellowed and grunted its reply, and I heard the calming voice of Mrs. Frey.

"Hold still, dears," she instructed. "Move slowly around behind me now." The bear roared angrily, and a shotgun blasted Mrs. Frey's answer.

By the time I reached the camp, the entire company had assembled around the Whitsell wagon. Two planks were torn from the side, and the canvas cover was shredded and strewn here and there. Mrs. Whitsell cradled baby Seth in her arms, and Mrs. Frey guarded Miller and Michael like a nesting hen protecting her egg.

"Was a grizzly," Tim declared when I stared at a bloody splotch of earth.

"Don't think I hit it," Mrs. Frey explained. "Sent him packin', though."

"I shot it up on the ridge," I told her. "Anybody hurt!"

"Thank God, no," Captain Martinson said.

"It's sure to come back, though," Mr. Bragg said, frowning. "Wounded animals are the worst kind of bad luck. Better double the guard."

The captain nodded.

"Be better to go after it," Tim declared, taking his mother's shotgun. "Darby?"

Shea arrived then and argued against it.

"We're almost to the Willamette," Mrs. Frey argued. "Tim, we'll be twenty miles from here tomorrow, and that bear . . ."

"Will be somebody else's trouble?" I asked. "I shot it. My job to finish, eh, Tom?"

"Isn't right to leave an animal in pain," Shea admitted. "Still . . ."

He never finished. One of the mules screamed out and bucked wildly as the bear staggered among the stock.

"Let's go," I said, and I headed out to where the horses were tethered. Oxen groaned, and mules whined in terror as the bear flayed away with its claws. Shea was off to the left a bit, his rifle probing the darkness with its angry barrel. Tim and I were five or six yards closer to the animals.

"Darby, look out!" Shea shouted as the bear suddenly sniffed out our approach and turned to deal with the danger.

"Lord, help us!" Tim cried, dropping to one knee and firing off both barrels of the shotgun. The blast illuminated the night, but the powder smoke that followed blinded us all. The bear was too far away for the shot to do any real damage, but the lead eating away at its vitals raised a furious growl as it leaped toward us.

I raised my rifle and prepared to fire, but the bear moved like lightning. It was on us before I could think, and it flung the rifle aside and slashed my left arm at the same instant. I howled in pain and rolled away only moments before a second slap of the paw narrowly missed my head.

Shea shouted something, but I didn't understand. I drew the pistol from my belt and pointed the barrel at the mass of jagged teeth looming over me. The grizzly seemed to halt a moment as if to welcome the end of its torment. I rammed back the Colt's hammer and fired, did so again and again until I emptied all five chambers that carried a ball. The projectiles sliced an ear, struck the bear's nose, clipped its chin. But it roared its contempt and prepared to fall upon me with renewed vigor. Shea fired then, and the bear managed a final, rather woeful grunt before slumping onto one shoulder and breathing out its life.

"Darby Prescott, you fool boy!" Shea shouted as he reached my side. He shook me by the shoulders and tried to lift me to my feet. My fingers touched something warm and sticky. Then I realized it was blood flowing from my arm. My legs began to wobble, and I would have fallen had not Shea caught me.

"Fool boy," Shea growled as he and Tim helped me to the closest wagon. "Got yourself sliced up good. Can't make a livin' out o' killin' grizzlies, you know!"

"Didn't kill this one," I muttered.

"Got him started toward his rest," Shea told me. He began to laugh a bit as he flung aside my blanket and tore away what remained of my shirt. "I'd guess you'll have another set o' scars to show them Nez Perce friends. It's bleedin' fierce, but the cuts don't 'pear to be deep. Bind you up, throw you atop Shadow, and you'll be good enough tomorrow to blow that mouth organ."

"He better be," Marietta cried, kneeling beside me. Her mother laid a basin of warm water beside my elbow, and between them they began washing the wound.

"You're in good hands," Tim said, grinning at me.

"Think I'll see about skinnin' a bear. I know a certain scout who looks in need of a winter coat."

"Make it big," Shea warned. "He's growin' these days."

"He will so long as bears don't slice too much of him," Mrs. Martinson declared. "Now keep still, Darby, and I'll see this mess bandaged."

I turned myself over to their care, and I passed what was left of the night in the bed of the captain's wagon. Morning found me a tinge feverish, and Marietta insisted I stay where I was.

"Sure," Marty said, grinning at me from the rim of the wagon. "Can't expect a man to kill bears and ride a horse the same day."

"I didn't kill this one," I insisted.

"More likely than not, you did," Marietta countered. "One good sniff of your sour hide did more harm than Shea's rifle."

"You complaining?" I asked. "Then give me leave to find Shadow. He likes me well enough."

"Got a better solution," she said, setting a bucket of water beside me. "A good scrubbing."

"Well, it's a fair notion, I'll admit, but you're sure not going to do it, Etta Martinson. I'm not so sick I can't wash myself."

"And I thought it would be such fun."

"You want fun," I told her, "go chase the little ones around a fire. And leave me to look after myself."

She dipped a rag in the bucket and grinned. Then she flung the wet rag at my face and scrambled out of the wagon.

"See what happens when you upset a sensitive woman?" Captain Martinson asked as he loaded a trunk in the wagon.

"That what I did?" I asked. "Guess I better learn not to do it anymore."

231

"You learn that trick, you'll be well ahead of the rest of us," he told me. "Far, far ahead."

I wrung out the rag and washed the dust and grit from my face.

"Guess some mysteries are supposed to stay that way," I suggested. "Keeps up the interest, so to speak."

He laughed heartily, then shook my good right hand.

"You'll survive this frontier life, Darby Prescott," he told me. "Anyone who can laugh at misfortune and philosophize about women is certain to do fine."

Chapter 21

It seemed a trifle unfair that I should have been wounded so close to trail's end. In all my life I'd not been pampered with the zeal now demonstrated. By noon my arm felt as good as new, and my head cleared of fever even before that. But Marietta and her mother insisted I remain in the wagon. Moreover, they mopped my brow, fed and watered me continually, and even read me stories from a book of adventures.

Half of me could have stayed in that wagon forever. The other half was more than relieved when Shea arrived to spring me from the snare.

"Better?" he asked.

"Wasn't much more'n a good scratch," I declared, scrambling out of the wagon before Marietta had a chance to block the way. "I'll be just fine once I limber it up some."

"You leave it be a couple of days!" Mrs. Martinson barked. "Wouldn't do to get the bleeding started up again. Besides, you two have done your job. We're almost there."

And in truth, we were. That night, sitting around a huge campfire eating venison steaks and sharing recollections of the trail, I could gaze down at the lights glowing from farmhouses along the Willamett. We would make Oregon City before midday, and those who had started west as pilgrims would become settlers.

It was hard not to feel a certain sense of pride when listening to the people talk of the farms or shops they would own. Those dreams had been forged by the trials of the trail, and paid for with blood. Some of it had been my own.

It was a ritual of sorts that on the final eve spent on the trail the company gathered to dance and sing and give thanks for the Lord's protection. The Martinson company, what remained of it, did so in grand style. Even the littlest children, those at least who could walk, danced around to the music of our makeshift band. The ladies donned their finest garb, and several of the men wore cravats and fine, woolen coats. I had little of anything better than my buckskins, and if the trousers were too short, no one seemed to mind much.

"How else should Darby Prescott be remembered?" Bart Sawyer asked. "Made you a reminder of sorts. Hope you'll keep it and remember us all."

He handed me a block of carved pine. A grizzly bear was etched into one side, and a slender boy atop a white horse was on the other. I admired it, then shook Bart's hand and stuffed the carving in my pocket.

"Didn't get your coat finished," Tim Frey said, resting his right hand on my shoulder. "Shea helped with the skinnin' some, but I'll need Ma's advice to do a proper job of it. Ma says we'll make a try at town livin'. Guess you'll have to come visit us in a few weeks and get it then. You'll be around, won't you?"

"Most likely," I said, gripping his hand. "Seems like we've come a long way since that night in the snow."

"We have," he said, grinning. "Got my life, and my family, to thank you for."

"No, I'd guess somebody else was behind it all, Tim. Me, I just sleep light. Sometimes gets me a new friend. Other times I run across grizzlies."

He laughed at my jest, but he wouldn't let go of my hand

until I promised to make a visit.

I passed among the others, expressing my hopes for their success, shaking hands with the men, getting hugs from the ladies, and swapping memories with everyone. Mallie Anderson and I remembered the Howell boys. Randy and Ray McIntosh talked me out of a good skinning knife. Last of all I arrived at the Martinson camp.

"Guess we'll have to come up with our own tales from here on out," Marty said, forcing a sad grin onto his face. "Don't suppose you need another partner, do you?"

"Figure you'll have lots to do on that farm your pa's sure to buy," I told him.

"That's what I'm afraid of. Still, Mama'd skin me if she knew I was thinking of leaving."

"Skin us both," I added, laughing.

I moved along to Mrs. Martinson next. She gripped my shoulders, then gave me a hug that close to took the wind out of me.

"Thanks for all your tending," I told her. "And all the suppers, too."

"Was only my very great pleasure, Darby," she replied. "You know you're welcome at any table I set."

I grinned my thanks and then shook the captain's offered hand.

"Darby, I had my doubts you'd prove up to the job, but I never once had cause to regret signing you and Shea on. You've weathered every storm, and you led us through more troubles than I can properly recall."

"It's a scout's job," I answered.

"We had a scout before. You two were more. Family almost."

"It's how it is on the trail," I explained. "And no matter where you go afterward, you're always part related to those you came west with."

"We'll meet again one day, I hope."

"The world's a circle, so say the Crows. All paths are

bound to cross."

I did my best to dodge Marietta, but she was lying in ambush. She said nothing, just grabbed my hand and dragged me to the campfire. We joined the handfull still dancing, and for a time we lost ourselves in the music. Her fingers seemed oddly cold, and her whole body seemed to tremble everytime I took her hand. Finally, when the musicians called it quits, we walked past the last wagons and gazed down at the faint pinpricks of light that spelled civilization.

"So tomorrow's the end?" she whispered.

"Be in Oregon City by noon," I replied. "That's as far as we take you. You'll be busy then. Best we say our good-byes tonight."

"Seems like there ought to be more said than good-bye."

"It's as good a word as another, Etta."

"But I've got so much more I want to . . ."

"Won't make it easier," I whispered. "Besides, I know it all. It's been fine talking to you along the way, knowing there was somebody who cared if I caught an arrow or got clawed by a bear. Now the wind's blowing us separate ways. No point to questioning why. Best thing is to ride out the storm and get on with what life throws our way."

"It could be different."

"Could be," I confessed. "Won't. Good-bye, Etta. I'll be thinking of you sometimes."

Her eyes welled up with tears, and she reached out as I backed away. Her fingers touched my chest, and I paused. But she'd want and need more than I could offer, so I turned and walked on to where Shea and I had made our camp.

Next morning we hitched teams to wagons and headed out early. I don't think anyone ate breakfast. A fervor of anticipation afflicted the entire company.

As we turned up the market road to Oregon City, the first of many farm families welcomed us. Children brought baskets of food, and their parents offered advice as to where best to purchase supplies and which sections of land appeared best suited to wheat or corn.

A little shy of noon we appeared in Oregon City. It wasn't much of a town yet, but a minister invited us into his church for a thanksgiving prayer, and the land agent came down afterward to help everyone who wanted land to select an appropriate parcel.

Any new train offered customers for the shops, neighbors to the isolated, new friends and schoolmates for the children, and most of all news from the east. In no time at all, half the town descended upon us, offering congratulations and extending what aid was available.

"Guess you'll be riding on now," Captain Martinson said as he doled out the promised banknotes for Shea to split between us. "Wish there was enough put by to pay a bonus, as you've surely earned it."

"We've had it already," I said, nodding to the others.

"Been a fair ride, cap'n," Shea added. "Good luck to you."

"And to you," Captain Martinson added as we mounted our horses and rode south.

It wasn't far to the farm Papa had bought along the Willamette. It was a verdant stretch of plain surmounted by low hills. There was wood aplenty, and a precious orchard planted in memory of my mother. I found the place easily, for I'd lived there two long years. I then led the way up to the house. My sister Mary sat on the porch, nursing a baby, and when we approached, she cried out in alarm.

"Honey, it's Tom Shea," her husband Mitch shouted as he set aside a shotgun and trotted out to greet us. "And this other fellow's like to be your brother."

"Darby?" she cried in disbelief as I tossed aside my hat and jumped down from the saddle.

I rushed to her like a parched man rushing to water. She passed her small, human bundle to Mitch, then wrapped both arms around my waist and clutched me as if she

237

couldn't otherwise be certain I wasn't a mirage.

"I'd given up on you coming back," she said, turning me over to Mitch.

"Little earlier, you could've helped with the harvest," Mitch said, pointing to the overflowing corncribs beside the barn.

"Knew that," I told them, winking at the baby. "When did you ever know me to hurry along to work."

Mary laughed, then introduced me to the newest member of the family, my nephew Matthew.

"Figure to run this farm proper, we'll need a full dozen," Mitch said, "so I thought we'd name 'em after the Apostles."

I took the baby in my arms and held it a moment, but the infant set to wailing right away, and I passed him back to his mother. At the same time the front door opened, and a sleepy-eyed girl of three stepped out onto the porch.

"Bessy?" I asked, amazed any child could have grown so much in two years.

"You've changed some yourself," Mary reminded me. "Well, you better go introduce yourself. She scarce remembers she has an uncle."

I rushed forward to do that very thing, and in minutes Bessy was atop my shoulders, gleefully recalling her Uncle Dabby and telling me all about her baby brother.

Shea had sat atop his horse the whole while, hardly flinching. I now insisted he join the reunion, and he did so somewhat reluctantly.

"Come for a visit or to stay a bit?" Mitch finally asked.

"You can't mean to ride off right away," Mary complained. "I've got a million questions, and there's so much news of the family."

"It's late into the season," I explained. "We thought perhaps to winter in the Rockies."

"Nonsense," Mitch argued. "You're staying right here. I want to put in a cellar, and I'll need your help. We've plenty of room. Now it's settled, isn't it?"

"Guess we could stay till spring, eh, Tom?" I asked.

He smiled as little Bessy touched his bearded cheek with her tiny hand. Then he nodded.

"Have to excuse us if we take to the hills once in a while, though," I explained. "We've not been under a roof in a long time."

"We get another winter like the last one, you'll be glad of that roof," Mary declared. "Now, what first? Are you hungry? Would you like to wash?"

"I'm hungry," Shea answered. "Darby, well, it seems to me maybe he's got someone to settle with back in Oregon City."

"Oh?" I asked.

"Lil gal with a face long as winter in the Rockies. Don't think you did much of a job sayin' your good-byes."

"I told her," I objected.

"What? How you were a wayfarer? How you'd head to the mountains in the mornin'? Seems to me you might be a good deal closer."

"A girl, Darby?" Mary asked.

"Might be better if she thought me buried in snowdrifts," I told their questioning eyes.

"Nonsense!" Mary barked. "Look at your hands. She must be special to give you the shakes like that. Ride into town and tell her, little brother. That horse looks like a runner. Test him!"

I didn't quite know how to respond. Part of me resented their instructions. But I thought of the long months ahead, and I couldn't help welcoming Etta into what was sure to be a bleak winter otherwise.

"Got a biscuit to keep me from starving?" I asked as I helped Bessy down from my shoulders.

"I'll fry you up a pork chop and some cornbread," Mary announced, heading for the kitchen.

I had a little supper before starting for Oregon City. I feared the Martinsons might have finished their business and headed on to some isolated stretch of prairie. But their wagon remained as before, idly stopped outside the land commissioner's office. I left Shadow tied to a hitching post and started up the street. Marietta stepped out from behind the wagon when I was still twenty feet away.

She walked toward me slowly, but my pace was somewhat brisker. We met silently, and I conducted her from the street without saying a word.

"I saw my sister," I told her. "Looks like Shea and I will be staying nearby."

"Staying?" she asked.

"Till springtime."

"Then we'll see each other some?" she asked.

"If you like. And if your papa agrees. Winter can be a hard time hereabouts. Maybe I can ride out and help you raise your cabin."

"You said till spring. What then, Darby?"

"I ride west with Tom Shea into the Rockies," I explained. "You see, Etta, there are mountains to climb there, and rivers to cross. More companies to bring west."

"But you don't have to . . ."

"Somebody has to. Somebody who knows the way. And for me, well, it's a good sort of life. Hard, and lonely, too, sometimes. But there's a special satisfaction getting folks across the mountains. Shea knows that, and so do I."

She smiled, nodded, and clutched my hand. And I knew winter would not be so cold as before.